INTEGRATED ENGLISH
LANGUAGE ARTS

Currents in Literature

British Volume

Harold Levine • Norman Levine
Robert T. Levine

AMSCO

Amsco School Publications, Inc.
315 Hudson Street/New York, N.Y. 10013

Contributing Writer: Mary L. Dennis

Reviewers
Krista Chianchiano, English Teacher, Indian Hills High School, Oakland, NJ
Rachel Matthews, Social Studies Teacher, Passages Academy, New York, NY
Erin M. Stowell, English Teacher, Huntington Beach High School, Huntington Beach, CA
Howard Withrow, Reading Teacher, Ida S. Baker High School, Cape Coral, FL
Melissa White, Instructional Specialist Secondary Reading and English Language Arts,
    Montgomery County Public Schools, MD

Cover Design and Photo: Wanda Kossak
Text Design: A Good Thing, Inc.
Composition: Publishing Synthesis, Ltd.
Illustrations: Anthony D'Adamo

Please visit our Web site at: *www.amscopub.com*

When ordering this book, please specify:
either **R 060 W** *or* CURRENTS IN LITERATURE, BRITISH VOLUME.
ISBN: 978-1-56765-145-4
NYC Item 56765-145-3

Printed in the United States of America
1 2 3 4 5 6 7 8 9 10   11 10 09 08 07 06

To the Student

Most famous writers say that while they were growing up they read the work of many different authors, and that they continue to be insatiable readers. Reading good literature as young people provided them with examples they could follow as authors, and gave them inspiration and motivation to write their own stories, poems, articles, and plays.

With this book, you can do the same. In each unit, you'll find four carefully chosen selections by British Isles authors. Each one is linked to its own unit theme: "Epiphanies," "Relationships," "Other Places, Other Times," or "Acts of Love and Kindness."

Along with each selection, you'll find a strategy to help you become a better reader. Using these methods will lead you to deeper understandings of literature and of life as you think about the unit themes and your own experiences.

With a bit of effort, you will soon find yourself becoming a better writer. You'll build a more powerful vocabulary and learn to correct common mistakes. You'll feel the pride and satisfaction of writing an essay, story, or poem that represents you at your best.

In addition, you will enjoy the work of sixteen different authors who all have something interesting for you to think about, write about, and discuss. They are the inspiration for everything this book has to teach you.

Enjoy your journey into the fascinating world of language!

The Authors

Contents

Introduction

What Is British Literature?

British Literature used to be more commonly referred to as "English Literature," but that was a confusing label—it sounded like it meant anything written in the English language, when it was really referring to literature *from* England. Now, the term British Literature is more often used, and it usually implies British *Isles* Literature–in other words, it doesn't just include literature from one nation, England, but from the entire British Isles—England, Scotland, Wales, Ireland, Northern Ireland, Channel Islands, Gibraltar, the Isle of Man, and St. Helena.

Our book uses this broader definition of British Literature, so that you can enjoy an assortment of regional Irish and British authors. In addition, we include writers from a variety of time periods. We don't limit our focus to the older authors like William Shakespeare and Jane Austen, whom you're likely already reading in school. Instead, we supplement your studies with some newer names on the British literary scene. In this volume you'll still find classic writers like Charles Dickens and William Wordsworth, whose works are valuable and timeless, but you'll also meet some contemporary writers, such as Edna O'Brien and Kazuo Ishiguro, whose works are influential on *both* sides of the Atlantic.

Note when you're reading the selections that some of the spellings are a bit different from what you're used to. For example, some *-or* words are spelled *-our* (color/colour, labor/labour). In addition, many British writers use single quotes for dialogue instead of double quotes (for example, instead of *He said, "Hello!"* they write *He said, 'Hello!'*). We left the originals because we wanted to stay true to the original works and to give readers a taste of British spelling and punctuation. Enjoy your exploration of the British Isles!

Our Voyage Through the British Isles

This volume consists of four units, each with its own theme. We have organized the book in this way to help you make connections among the readings. Comparing and contrasting certain authors' styles and ideas will enhance your critical thinking skills and thus help you in all of your academic endeavors; in addition, looking at common themes or ideas in literature can help you relate it to your own life, which will make the reading experience more meaningful for you.

The theme of Unit One is "Epiphanies," or realizations. The unit opens with "The Clever One," a short story by Irish author Maeve Brennan, about a time she learned something surprising about her sister. How does this affect her view of her? Then you'll read an excerpt from *A House Unlocked* (2001), a memoir by Penelope Lively, in which she describes her grandmother's unusual house in England, and tells of the realization she comes to there about the struggles of others. The next reading is from the well-known Irish author James Joyce's novel *A Portrait of the Artist as a Young Man* (1916), and tells of the teenage protagonist Stephen who has an epiphany about his future. Should he do what is expected of him, or follow his heart's desire? Next, we go even further back in time with a selection from poet William Wordsworth, who wrote during the English Romantic period (1770–1850). His piece, "The Solitary Reaper," describes a narrator's powerful vision of beauty.

Unit Two is titled "Relationships." We begin with a look at one's relationship with oneself. You'll read "Chasing the Evanescent Glow," an article published in 2005 by Irish journalist Nuala O'Faolain, who asks, can we be happy when we are alone? Then, you'll read an excerpt from *The Bay of Angels* (2001), a novel by English writer Anita Brookner about a seventeen-year-old girl's relationship with her mother, who is getting married. Next is a selection from contemporary writer Kazuo Ishiguro, whose widely read novel *The Remains of the Day* explores relationships among people of different ranks and classes. Finally, in Edna O'Brien's *August Is a Wicked Month* (1965), you'll be drawn into the life of a woman who struggles with a painful home situation involving her husband and young son.

In Unit Three, "Other Places, Other Times," you'll be taken on both real and imaginary journeys. The first piece is a nonfiction excerpt from *The Aran Islands,* written in the 1880s by Irish author J. M. Synge, about his research on a group of islands where he is surprised to find a way of life that is quite different from his own. Then we'll move to a description of a very different kind of island: Irish writer Jonathan Swift, in *Gulliver's Travels* (1726), tells a fantastical story about a man who is shipwrecked in a strange land. The next selection is also about a journey, but this time it is a trip into the future. English novelist H. G. Wells, in *The Time Machine* (1894), tells of a Victorian inventor who propels himself into year 802,701. Finally, the unit wraps up with a leap back to the eighteenth century. In the selection from Daniel Defoe's 1719 novel *Robinson Crusoe,* we learn about an eighteen-year-old's desire to go on a dangerous journey at sea—how does he try to convince his parents to let him? Though the piece was written almost three centuries ago, you might see similarities between the way he attempts to get what he wants and the way people still do so today.

The theme of Unit Four is "Acts of Love and Kindness." British writer Beryl Markham, in *West With the Night* (1942), tells of a moving childhood experience with a horse in Kenya. The famous nineteenth-century British author Charles Dickens, in *The Old Curiosity Shop* (1841), describes a strange encounter with a little girl who is lost on the street. Contemporary writer Beryl Bainbridge, in the fictional *Every Man for Himself* (1996), describes the interactions among people on board the *Titanic* as it is sinking. Finally, we end with a poem by British Romantic poet Sarah Kilham Biller (1837). "To Anna" describes a narrator's wishes for a young Anna on her birthday. How are her wishes to Anna similar to what a parent or friend might wish for you?

During your journey through the British Isles, you'll witness specific moments of epiphany, you'll be taken into deep emotional relationships, you'll travel to imaginary lands and into the future, and you'll get to glimpse into the minds of people who are trying to do the right thing. The literature in this volume may have been written across the Atlantic, but the concepts are universal and timeless.

UNIT ONE

Epiphanies

Chapter One

Prereading Guide

Words to know and ideas to consider before you jump into the reading.

A. Essential Vocabulary

Word	Meaning	Typical Use
aghast (*adj*) uh-GAST	suddenly horrified or frightened; stunned	Environmentalists were *aghast* when they saw how many trees had been cut down in the wildlife refuge.
defiance (*n*) dih-FY-unce	opposition to a contrasting force, authority, or person; resistance	Efforts to bring democracy to the region were met with *defiance* by the insurgents.
duplicity (*n*) doo-PLISS-uh-tee	deliberate dishonesty; deceptiveness	His *duplicity* caught up with him once his friends began comparing his stories.
eloquence (*n*) EL-o-qwence	skill in speaking; fluency	Danielle's *eloquence* assured her a spot on the debate team.
grimace (*n*) GRIM-us	a contorted facial expression showing disapproval or pain; a scowl	Jane's smile turned into a *grimace* when it started to rain on her picnic.
loom (*v*) LOOM	1. to seem about to happen, usually related to a bad situation; to impend 2. to come into view	The possibility of failing math *loomed* large in Matt's mind. Large oaks *loomed* along the roadside ahead of us.
notion (*n*) NO-shun	an impulsive idea; a whim	On Saturday, Kim got a *notion* to take the train to Philadelphia to see her cousin.
precarious (*adj*) pre-KARE-ee-us	subject to sudden change; uncertain	Scott's condition has improved somewhat, but it is still *precarious.*
raucous (*adj*) RAW-kus	loud and disorderly; boisterous	The crows' caws were *raucous* as they swarmed the bird feeder.
solemn (*adj*) SAHL-um	deeply serious and important; formal	Einstein was a deep thinker with a *solemn* expression.

B. Vocabulary Practice

Exercise 1.1   Sentence Completion

Using your new vocabulary knowledge, choose the best way to complete the following sentences. Circle the letter of your answer.

1. I was aghast when I realized _____.
   A. my shoes did not match
   B. I had gotten straight A's

2. Lighten up and enjoy life! You're always so _____.
   A. eloquent
   B. solemn

3. The prediction of _____ loomed over our picnic.
   A. sunny weather
   B. afternoon rains

4. Kerri could tell by Justin's grimace that he _____ the meal she had cooked him.
   A. liked
   B. could hardly eat

5. Emma had a notion to _____.
   A. do homework
   B. move to Europe

6. She had deceived us all along. We could hardly believe her _____.
   A. compliance
   B. duplicity

7. "I _____ do what you want," said Aimee defiantly.
   A. won't ever
   B. will be glad to

8. The climber clung to the mountainside, waiting for help. His position was _____.
   A. defiant
   B. precarious

9. "Give me liberty or give me death!" is an example of Patrick Henry's _____.
   A. duplicity
   B. eloquence

10. The day _____, students at our school tend to be quite raucous.
    A. before vacation
    B. of a big test

Exercise 1.2 Using Fewer Words

Replace the italicized words with a single word from the following list. The first one has been done for you.

raucous	defiance	precarious	aghast	duplicity
grimaced	eloquence	notion	loomed	solemn

1. Last weekend I had a(an) *impulsive idea* to ride my bike 20 miles.

   1.   notion

2. Don't assume that you'll always be first-chair violin; that position is *subject to sudden change.*

   2._____

3. His *skill in speaking* was admirable, but he still lost the election.

   3._____

4. I was *suddenly horrified* when I realized the horrible thing she had done.

   4._____

5. The little boy *contorted his facial expression* when the doctor said his knee would need stitches.

   5._____

6. We were having a(an) *deeply important and serious* conversation until you came along and made us laugh!

   6._____

7. You show too much *opposition to authority* to be a good candidate for military service.

   7._____

8. Those *loud and disorderly* students in the hall are making it difficult for me to concentrate.

   8._____

9. The house that everyone said was haunted *came into view* at the corner of Cherry and Maple.

   9._____

10. The *deliberate dishonesty* of much advertising is well-known.

    10._____

Exercise 1.3 Synonyms and Antonyms

Fill in the blanks in column A with the required synonyms or antonyms, selecting them from column B. (Remember: A *synonym* is a word similar in meaning to another word. *Autumn* and *fall* are synonyms. An *antonym* is a word opposite in meaning to another word. *Beginning* and *ending* are antonyms.)

	A	B
_____	1. synonym for *stunned*	grimace
_____	2. antonym for *compliance*	solemn
_____	3. synonym for *whim*	eloquence
_____	4. antonym for *sincerity*	notion
_____	5. synonym for *fluency*	aghast
_____	6. antonym for *stable*	defiance
_____	7. synonym for *scowl*	loom
_____	8. antonym for *harmonious*	precarious
_____	9. synonym for *impend*	duplicity
_____	10. antonym for *casual*	raucous

C. Journal Freewrite

Before you begin the reading on the next page, take out a journal or sheet of paper and spend some time responding to the following prompt.

TIP: Don't worry about grammar and spelling; just write what comes to mind. The purpose of freewriting is to explore ideas, not to produce a polished work.

> Think of someone to whom you are very close, such as a good friend or sibling. One day, you learn something about the person that completely changes the way you think about him or her. How would you feel about that kind of epiphany (realization)? What would it take to shock you?

The Clever One

by Maeve Brennan

About the Author
Maeve Brennan (1917–1993) wrote collections of short stories, many about middle-class life in Ireland, where she grew up and attended convent school. She moved to New York City in 1934 and worked at *Harper's Bazaar* as a copywriter. Later, she became a regular contributor to *The New Yorker*, where most of her stories were first published. Brennan's stories often depict characters who show understanding of common human weaknesses. This story, from her collection *The Springs of Affection*, gives the reader insight into one character's clever coping devices.

NOT long ago, I was staying in Washington, D.C., with my younger sister, Deirdre, who is married and has four young children. It was spring. We sat in her large, pleasant living room, with the trees all fresh and green outside on Garfield Street, and the shrubs bursting into bloom—white, pink, blue, yellow—in her garden, where the children were giving themselves wholeheartedly to some <u>raucous</u> game, and we began to speak, as we often do, of the time when we two were small together. There is less than two years between us. Our childhood was spent in Dublin, most of it in a small house in Ranelagh.

"The first time I remember seeing you," I said, "was before we went to live in Ranelagh. It was when we were living in the house on Belgrave Road. You must have been about eighteen months old, I suppose. Someone was holding you in their arms, and you snatched Emer's cap off her head and threw it in the fire, and she cried. It was a new woolen cap she had." Emer is our older sister.

"I don't remember that," Derry said, but she looked pleased at the thought of the burning cap. "I don't remember Belgrave Road at all."

"The next time I have a clear memory of you," I continued, "you must have been about three. We were living in Ranelagh. I went into the front bedroom and found you wandering around in your skin, crying for someone to dress you, and I dressed you."

"I don't remember *that*," Derry said.

"Well, do you remember when you were six or seven and almost got St. Vitus's dance? You kept shaking and dropping things all over the house."

"Oh, I remember that, all right," Derry said, smiling.

All the time we were talking, she was hemming a pink cotton dress for her older daughter. I looked at her hands, so steady and sure with the needle, and I thought of how we had all feared she would lose the use of them.

"You were never able to help with the washing up," I said, "for fear you'd break all the cups and saucers. When you weren't dropping things, you lay on the bed with your eyes wide open, not able to wake up. You looked awful. You gave Mother a terrible fright. She got the woman from next door in to look at you."

"I *remember* all that," Derry said impatiently.

"But you were asleep," I said.

"I was no more asleep than you are now," she said. "And I was no nearer getting St. Vitus's dance than you are now, either," she added, this time with a touch of <u>defiance</u>.

I stared, or glared, at her. "What do you mean?" I cried.

She looked me straight in the eye, but the color began to rise in her face.

"Do you mean to tell me you were putting it all on?" I cried, sounding almost as thunderstruck as I felt. Derry's delicate health had <u>loomed</u> as importantly in my childhood as the Catholic Church and the fight for Irish freedom. The first word I ever remember hearing about Derry was that she had been underweight when she was born and that her health was <u>precarious</u>. My mother always dressed us exactly alike, and people used to call us Mrs. Brennan's twins, but I was the large, hardy twin and she was the thin, pale one, always with me, and always silent, while I talked endlessly. Remembering how strongly all this had shaped our childhood, and the way it had determined everything between us and around us, I naturally was <u>aghast</u> to hear her now, more than twenty years later, calmly tearing it all away. I decided that she was joking.

"You're joking, aren't you?" I said.

"I am not," she said.

"But why did you do it?" I asked.

"Well, for one thing, I always got out of doing the washing up," she said. "And I was always too delicate to go to school much, if you remember."

"All those washing ups I did," I said. "And do you mean to say you never told anyone at all about it?"

She gave me an exasperated[1] look. "That would have been pretty silly, wouldn't it? The whole point was that no one knew."

"And you've kept it a secret all these years," I said.

"To tell you the truth, I hadn't thought about it for years, till you brought it up just now. Of course, I really did have colds sometimes, and I did have those terrible chilblains[2] in the wintertime." She began to laugh, and so did I, but not very heartily.

Just then, two of her children began a battle under the windows, and she ran out to investigate them, leaving me to think about her <u>duplicity</u> all those years ago, when she was so small and frail it would have taken a strange-minded person to accuse her of the least offense, let alone of keeping the house in an uproar over her health for years on end. I was more admiring than anything else, because I hadn't really minded doing the washing up alone, since I always received high praise from my mother for doing it, but I was stunned

---

[1] irritated and impatient
[2] painful sores on the hands, ears, or feet caused by cold, damp weather

to think that Derry had been capable, so young, of thinking up and carrying through such a black and complicated plot, and of not speaking about it to anyone—not even to me.

It was then I remembered that this was not the first time she had set me back.

The first time it happened, she was not more than seven and I was almost nine. In those years, as I say, I was larger than she was, and I won't say I bullied her, but I did boss her around. All her life, I bossed her unmercifully until the moment of which I am about to speak, and I suppose that even after that things did not really change very much between us. I remember I had a favorite game called "sitting on Derry." I used to make her lie flat on the floor while I sat on her stomach and stared into her face, <u>grimacing</u> in a manner that we both considered terrifying. It was a simple game, but I suppose she must sometimes have grown weary of it.

I felt superior to her and protective toward her because she was so tiny, and because she hated school and never did well in her lessons, and because she got ugly, painful chilblains in the cold weather and I never did, and most of all because she was shy. As a matter of fact, I never gave her a chance to say a word. People were always told that I had the brains in the family. "Derry has the beauty," they used to say, "but Maeve has all the brains." I believed every word of this. I used to look at Derry and think <u>solemnly</u> about my brains and about how I never had any trouble in school and always got good marks. In games, I always hammered myself into the lead, while Derry played off by herself somewhere, and I was always first to enter myself in singing competitions, although I had no voice, and in reciting contests, although I had no <u>eloquence</u>. I had even made up my mind to become an actress, but I had not spoken to anyone at school or in the family about my ambition, for fear of being laughed at.

However, one day Derry and I were sitting together in the back garden of our house in Ranelagh. It must have been summertime, because we were sitting on the grass and there were forget-me-nots and London pride in bloom in my mother's flower beds. We had a bead box on the grass between us, and we were stringing necklaces and enjoying my conversation.

"When I grow up," I said to Derry, "I'm going to be a famous actress. I'll act in the Abbey Theatre, and I'll be in the pictures, and I'll go around to all the schools and teach all the teachers how to recite."

I was about to continue, because I never expected her to have anything to say, but she spoke up, without raising her head from her necklace. "Don't go getting any <u>notions</u> into your head," she said clearly.

I was astounded. Where had little Derry picked up such a remark? I had never said it, and I was not sure I had ever even heard it. Who had said it to her? I was astounded, and I was silent. I had nothing to say. For the first time, it had occurred to me that little Derry had *brains*. More brains than I had, maybe, even?

Understanding the Reading

Complete the next three exercises and see how well you understood "The Clever One."

Exercise 1.4   Multiple-Choice Questions

Answer the following questions about the reading. Circle the letter of your answer.

TIP: Don't try to answer the questions from memory; go back to the text as often as necessary.

1. After Derry revealed that she had only pretended to be ill, the narrator Maeve
   A. was extremely angry and left immediately.
   B. ran outside to resolve a quarrel between her children.
   C. was at first shocked but then admiring of Derry's cleverness.
   D. called her older sister to discuss the matter with her.

2. When Derry and Maeve were children, Maeve was
   A. an unmerciful bully to her sister.
   B. the outgoing one who succeeded at most things.
   C. the shy one who did poorly in school.
   D. the clever one who had everyone fooled.

3. From the context of the story, you can determine that St. Vitus's dance is a disease that
   A. is incurable.
   B. affects the nerves.
   C. affects the brain.
   D. causes shaky hands.

4. Derry's attitude when revealing her lie can best be described as
   A. defiant.
   B. loving.
   C. impatient.
   D. generous.

5. When Derry said, "Don't get any notions," Maeve realized that Derry
   A. was quoting someone without knowing what the words meant.
   B. would be an actress when she grew up.
   C. did not have St. Vitus's dance.
   D. might be smarter than she seemed.

Exercise 1.5   Short-Answer Questions

Respond to the following questions in one to two complete sentences. Go back to the text, as you did on the multiple choice.

6. How does Derry feel about the fact that she deceived her sister? What clues in the story helped you determine this?

_____

_____

_____

7. Describe the attitude Maeve had toward Derry when they were younger.

_____

_____

_____

8. Why did Maeve never expect Derry to have anything to say?

_____

_____

_____

9. What does Maeve realize about her sister's intelligence, and why is this realization significant?

_____

_____

_____

Exercise 1.6   Extending Your Thinking

Respond to the following question in three to four complete sentences. Use details from the text in your answer.

10. Imagine you were going to write an additional scene to the story. Predict how the narrator's epiphanies about her sister might continue to affect their adult relationship.

_____

_____

_____

_____

_____

Reading Strategy Lesson
Identifying Author's Purpose and Point of View

Author's Purpose

Every kind of writing has a purpose. Advertisements try to sell something. Comics are intended to make you laugh. Mysteries entertain you by keeping you on the edge of your seat. Newspapers, magazines, textbooks, and other nonfiction materials provide information. The following table shows the most common purposes for writing and gives examples of the genres (types of writing) that are most often used to accomplish each purpose.

Purpose	Genres Most Often Used
To inform: to provide the reader with facts	textbooks, newspaper and magazine articles, nonfiction books about various topics, encyclopedias, dictionaries, informational Web sites, biographies
To persuade: to sell the reader an idea or product	advertisements, blogs and Web sites devoted to a particular group's view
To instruct: to explain a process	how-to books and articles; directions on a product that tell how to install it, use it, or fix it; on-screen instructions on your computer
To entertain: to keep readers interested and absorbed in the story or article	novels, dramas, humorous articles, poetry, autobiographies
To give an opinion: to express what the author believes about an issue or idea	newspaper editorials and columns, blogs and opinion-based Web sites

Keep in mind that purposes may overlap. Authors often have more than one purpose for writing. For example, historical novels and autobiographies are entertaining but also supply the reader with factual information. Persuasive pieces may include opinions.

Your job is to determine the author's **main purpose**. You can do this by paying close attention to the author's word choices and to the details he or she emphasizes. For example, **informative** writing includes facts that answer questions like "Who?" "When?" "Where?" "Why?" "What?" and "How?" **Persuasive** pieces try to convince you to change your mind about something by telling you why what you believe is wrong or by presenting a particular view about an issue. As with persuasive writing, the author who is giving an **opinion** may be trying to sway your belief. On the other hand, an author may just be saying, "Here's what I think, and here's why I think it."

Writers **entertain** you in many ways. The primary purpose of literary fiction and serious drama is to say something important about life. Humorous fiction and drama make you laugh, while mystery and suspense stories keep you thinking and wondering as you try to figure out what will happen next.

You have probably read lots of **instructive** writing without really thinking about it. If you have ever assembled a bike or computer desk, you likely needed the instructions. Games always include an instruction book, and video game cheats help you get ahead. Automobiles, televisions, electronic devices, and even less-complicated items like coffeemakers and toasters include instructions. If writing tells you how to do something, it is probably instructive.

To determine an author's purpose as you read, imagine that the author is talking directly to you. Ask yourself, "What is this author trying to do? Entertain me? Convince me of something? Tell me how to do something? Or is the author just providing facts or offering an opinion?" Your answers will help you decide the author's purpose.

If a reading includes background information, be sure to read it. It may state the author's purpose or at least give you more clues.

Exercise 1.7   Practice the Reading Strategy

Read the following excerpts and state the author's *main* purpose. Explain what details you used to determine your answer.

1. "Joseph Addison was born on the first of May, 1672, at Milston, of which his father, Lancelot Addison, was then rector, near Ambrosbury in Wiltshire, and appearing weak and unlikely to live, he was christened the same day. After the usual domestic education, which, from the character of his father, may be reasonably supposed to have given him strong impressions of piety, he was committed to the care of Mr. Naish at Ambrosbury, and afterwards of Mr. Taylor at Salisbury." (Samuel Johnson, *Life of Addison*)

The author's main purpose was to: _____

Explanation: _____

_____

2. The First Continental Congress met in Philadelphia on September 5, 1774. All of the colonies sent representatives except Georgia. This congress continued in session until October 26, 1774. By then it had passed resolutions calling for a boycott against British trade.

The author's main purpose was to: _____

Explanation: _____

_____

3. "I scarcely know where to begin, though I sometimes face-tiously place the cause of it all to Charley Furuseth's credit. He kept a summer cottage in Mill Valley, under the shadow of Mount Tamalpais, and never occupied it except when he loafed through the winter months and read Nietzsche and Schopen-hauer to rest his brain." (Jack London, "The Sea-Wolf")

The author's main purpose was to: _____

Explanation: _____

_____

4. First, click on the "Accessories" file under "All Programs" and select "System Tools." From there, go to "Disk Cleanup." Disk Cleanup will calculate how much space you can free on your hard disk if you elect to remove certain files. Usually, these files are unnecessary and can be safely deleted, but you may want to click on "View Files" for more information.

The author's main purpose was to: _____

Explanation: _____

_____

5. "No pain, no gain," is no longer how most physical trainers think, unless they happen to be drill instructors. Indeed, it has been found that walking briskly is just as effective as run-ning, and that the gentle art of yoga can not only strengthen and stretch muscles but bring peace of mind and relaxation as well.

The author's main purpose was to: _____

Explanation: _____

_____

Exercise 1.8   Apply the Reading Strategy to "The Clever One"

Look back at "The Clever One" on page 7. Think about Maeve Brennan's purpose. Reread the author sidebar and consider her word choices and details in the story. What do you think her pur-pose was in writing "The Clever One"?

_____

_____

_____

_____

_____

Author's Point of View

When you read fiction and some other types of writing, it is impor-tant to identify the author's point of view, or the vantage point from which he or she sees the story. Authors usually choose one point of view and stick to it. The three most common points of view are:

- **First person:** The narrator is a character in the story and refers to herself or himself using the pronoun *I*.

    I ran after the bus as fast as I could, but it was pulling away just as I got alongside. I screamed "Please stop!" and incredibly, the bus pulled over.

- **Omniscient third person:** The narrator knows what everyone in the story is thinking and feeling at all times. The characters are referred to by name, as "he" or "she," or by another identifier such as "the nurse" or "the bus driver."

    In a panic, Miranda yelled for the bus to stop. The bus driver heard her and pulled back to the curb. He had seen her running and for a minute thought she was his little sister. The nurse in the seat behind the driver moved her tote bag so Miranda could sit down. She wanted to get this bus moving again as soon as possible.

- **Limited third person:** The narrator knows how one character feels and thinks, and tells the story from that person's limited point of view.

    Something told Miranda she should simply get away from the man who had looked at her so strangely in the museum. She saw a bus stopped down the street, loading passengers, and she began running.

    "Please stop!" she screamed, panicked now by the thought that the man might be right behind her.

Why is it useful to know point of view? The story still gets told, right? Point of view matters because it affects how much you'll learn about the plot and the various characters. When you read a story with a first-person or limited third-person point of view, you'll get one character's perspective on a situation. When you read something with an omniscient point of view, on the other hand, you might get many characters' perspectives.

Nonfiction Points of View

When you read certain kinds of nonfiction, point of view means something a little different. Point of view is how the author sees an issue or idea, where he or she is "coming from." For example, if you read a newspaper column by a writer who works for a political organization, he or she may have a left- or right-wing viewpoint, and you are unlikely to get both sides of the issue. Similarly, a persuasive piece is usually written to convince you to adopt the point of view the author has on the subject.

Informational and instructional materials are *not* usually written from a person's point of view. The authors of your math textbook do not write, "I'm going to tell you my perspective on this problem." They just give you the factual information you need to solve it.

Autobiographies, however, are informational and are written in the first person. You're getting the person's own view on his or her life. Other books may also be written in the first person, with a limited subject. For example, you might see books like *Take Off the Pounds Without a Frown: I Did It and So Can You* and *The NASCAR Life, by Those Who Live It.*

Exercise 1.9 Practice the Reading Strategy

Identify the point of view of each of the following passages.

FP = first person   TPL = third person   TPO = third person
                            limited   omniscient

_____ 1. "My second mate was a round-cheeked, silent young man, grave beyond his years, I thought; but as our eyes happened to meet I detected a slight quiver on his lips. I looked down at once. It was not my part to encourage sneering on board my ship. It must be said, too, that I knew very little of my officers." (Joseph Conrad, "The Secret Sharer")

_____ 2. "He had only himself to please in his choice: his fortune was his own; for as to Frank, it was more than being tacitly brought up as his uncle's heir, it had become so avowed an adoption as to have him assume the name of Churchill on coming of age. It was most unlikely, therefore, that he should ever want his father's assistance. His father had no apprehension of it." (Jane Austen, *Emma*)

_____ 3. "This piece of rudeness was more than Alice could bear: she got up in great disgust, and walked off: the Dormouse fell asleep instantly, and neither of the others took the least notice of her going, though she looked back once or twice, half hoping that they would call after her: the last time she saw them, they were trying to put the Dormouse into the teapot." (Lewis Carroll, *Alice's Adventures in Wonderland*)

Exercise 1.10 Apply the Reading Strategy to "The Clever One"

Now see if you can determine Maeve Brennan's point of view. (Remember that "The Clever One" is nonfiction.) On the lines provided, answer the following questions in complete sentences: (a) What is Brennan's point of view? Explain how you determined this.

(b) How would the story be different if she had used another point of view?

_____

_____

_____

_____

_____

Writing Workshop
Thinking About Audience, Purpose, and Task

Audience

Professional writers like Maeve Brennan do not just pick up a pen or sit down at the computer and rattle off a novel, short story, or memoir. The same is true of authors who write articles, essays, and advertisements. Before they begin, they think and plan. One of the key prewriting considerations is audience—who will be reading your work?

Suppose you have invented a video game that teaches basic reading skills to children. You think about your **audience** before you decide how to write your advertising and where to place your ads. You can first narrow your audience by asking, "Who is going to buy my game?" The most likely purchasers are parents, grandparents, other caregivers, and teachers. So although your game is for children, you'll want your ads to appeal to a different audience. Since the children would not be able to read your ad anyway, you might write a second ad for them that will appear on TV shows aimed at children. Even though they may not be able to read, you can show pictures of children playing the game, learning to read, and having a great time.

When you write anything, one of your first questions to yourself should be, "Who is my audience?" Your writing should be tailored to that audience.

If you are writing in response to an assignment or to an essay prompt on a test, your audience may already be spelled out for you. For example, the question may say, "Write a letter to the editor of your local paper" or "Your teacher has asked you to write an essay about . . ." If no audience is specified in the question, assume you are writing for well-educated people who are aware of the topic, the best approaches to it, and the conventions of grammar.

Purpose

Once you have your audience in mind, you should clarify your purpose. Much of the writing you do in school has one of two purposes: to **explain** or to **persuade**. Expository writing explains something. Imagine that at the beginning of a new school year, your English teacher writes this topic on the board:

> I want to get to know you better. Name your three favorite books, plays, or short stories. *Explain* why you made these choices.

It should be obvious that your teacher will be the audience for this essay, but what is your purpose? Look at the italicized word in the prompt. Your purpose is to *explain*.

Let's look at another topic:

> Your best friend has taken up smoking, and you are concerned. Write your friend a one-page letter trying to *persuade* him or her to give up the habit.

Who is your audience? What is your purpose? In this example, your *best friend* is your audience, and your purpose is to *persuade*.

A third purpose of writing is to **entertain**. There are many forms of writing that entertain, but the ones you will most likely encounter in school are the fictional (made up) **short story** and the **personal narrative** (a true story about yourself). We'll look more closely at the personal narrative a little later.

Task

After you've determined your audience and purpose for a writing assignment, there is one more prewriting question to ask yourself: What is my task? A **task** is a job or an undertaking. Your task on an assignment might be to write

- an article for a newspaper
- a letter
- an advertisement
- a journal entry
- an essay

- an interview
- a handbook
- a conversation
- a newscast
- a personal narrative

Always look at the prompt to identify your **task**. Determine what you will write, and how you will write it. In the prompt we looked at earlier, which asked you to persuade a friend to give up smoking, **what** you were asked to write is a letter. **How** you will write it is in one full page, as a letter, using persuasive techniques.

Exercise 1.11 Practice the Writing Lesson

Read the following prompts. Identify the audience, purpose, and task for each.

1. Write a paragraph for your class describing something funny that happened to you or a friend.

Audience: _____

Purpose: _____

Task: Write what? _____

      Write how? _____

2. Some people are worried about the future of our environment. Write a letter to the president of the United States explaining what you think is wrong and what can be done to improve the situation.

Audience: _____

Purpose: _____

Task: Write what? _____

      Write how? _____

3. Think about a movie you have seen recently. Then write an article for the "Movie Reviews" section of your paper, persuading people to see the movie or skip it.

Audience: _____

Purpose: _____

Task: Write what? _____

      Write how? _____

The Writing Process

Now that we've examined some important prewriting considerations, let's review the rest of the writing process. You are likely familiar with the following steps:

Step 1: Prewriting

Prewriting, or planning your essay, is a key part of the process. You wouldn't start walking to a friend's house if you didn't know where you were going. You would probably call up and get some directions. You might even write them down and keep them with you in case you got lost.

Prewriting gives you the "directions" for your essay. Once you know your audience, purpose, and task, you'll know which direction you're going to go with your writing. You'll be able to start down the road to completion with confidence that you will arrive at your destination: an essay that carries out the assignment.

Step 2: Your First Draft

Don't be intimidated by the drafting stage. Your essay doesn't have to be perfect the first time. Just get your ideas on paper—you can polish it afterward. Professional writers never publish their first drafts. In fact, they have professional editors who help them decide

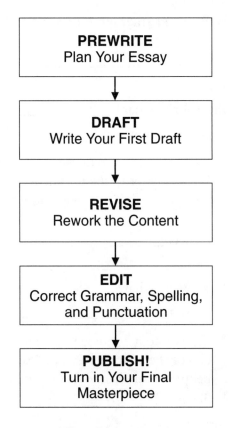

The Writing Process

where the content should be changed, and other editors who check their work for correct grammar, spelling, and punctuation. Their writing may go through a dozen drafts before it is ready to publish.

Steps 3 and 4: Revising and Editing

Your first draft may not be perfect, but you should be proud that you finished this important part of writing. Now you have something to work with. Use what you've learned about effective writing and the conventions of English to revise and edit your draft.

TIP: Remember to revise and edit; they are not the same thing. Revising means looking at the bigger picture, such as the content and flow of your essay. Editing involves the more fine-tuned work: tweaking your grammar, spelling, and punctuation.

Step 5: Publish!

Finally, you'll input your changes and produce a clean copy. You should feel a sense of accomplishment!

Exercise 1.12 Apply the Lesson to Create Your Own Narrative

You're ready to use what you've learned about the writing process to tackle a prompt on your own. You're going to write a **personal narrative**—a true story, most often told in the first person, about an experience you've had. First, carefully read the topic. Think about your **audience, purpose,** and **task.** Use the prewriting planner that follows to plan your personal narrative. Then take out a separate sheet of paper and begin drafting.

Topic:

> In "The Clever One," Maeve learns something unexpected about her sister Derry. Think about a time you learned something about a friend, relative, or acquaintance. Write a personal narrative about that moment. Include how you learned what you did, what your reaction was, and how it affected your relationship or your view of the person.

As you write, consider Maeve Brennan's style. She uses dialogue to bring the story to life. She also uses descriptive words to show what the characters are feeling. Like Brennan, show rather than tell your audience about the moment you choose.

Prewriting Planner: Personal Narrative

Audience: _____

Purpose: _____

Task: _____

Notes:

The person I will write about is: _____

The surprising thing I learned about him or her is: _____

_____

I learned this when: _____

How I reacted: _____

_____

How it affected my view of him or her: _____

_____

Getting Organized: Paragraph Suggestions

Introduction: Who is this person and how do I know him or her? (Set up the scene.)	Body paragraphs: What did I learn about him or her, and how? How did I react?	Conclusion: How did this knowledge affect me or affect our relationship? What did I learn from the experience?

Now you're ready to begin writing. Don't forget to revise and edit your draft. Share your completed narrative with your class, or give it to the person you admire.

Grammar Mini-Lesson
Subject-Verb Agreement

A common writing and speaking mistake is having subjects and verbs that do not agree. In this lesson, you'll see what exactly is meant by agreement and why it's important to clear communication.

> GRAMMAR REFRESHER: When you look at a sentence, it helps to think of the **subject** as the person(s) or thing(s) doing the action or in a state of being. The **verb** is the action or state of being.
>
>   Michelle was happy about the team's win.
>   SUBJECT VERB
>
>   The coaches were shouting with joy.
>   SUBJECT   VERB

What Is Agreement?

A **singular subject** must be with a **singular verb**. A **plural subject** must be with a **plural verb**.

Look at these examples from "The Clever One."

Emer is our older sister.
singular subject (*Emer*) + singular verb (*is*)

Derry and I were sitting together in the back garden.
plural subject (*Derry and I*) + plural verb (*were*)

Notice what happens if we change the subjects:

Emer and Derry are Maeve's sisters.
plural subject (*Emer and Derry*) + plural verb (*are*)

Derry was sitting in the back garden.
singular subject (*Derry*) + singular verb (*was*)

TIP: *Verbs ending in* s *are usually singular:* is, was, knows, has, does, eats, sleeps, *and so forth. This is easy to remember:* s *at the end is a* singular *verb.*

Agreement mistakes often occur because of uncertainty as to which word in the sentence is the subject. Usually, the subject comes before the verb. In the following cases, however, the subject appears after the verb:

* In a question:
   Are the boys home? (The subject is *boys*. The *boys* are home.)

* In a sentence beginning with *There is*, *There are*, *Here is*, or *Here are*:
   There is food on the table. (The subject is *food*, not *table*. *Food* is on the table.)
   Here are your friends. (The subject is *friends*, not *here*. Your *friends* are here.)

Be careful: An "of" phrase between a subject and its verb has no effect on agreement.

    A box *of cookies* is on the shelf.

If you aren't sure which verb to use, try reading the sentence without the "of" phrase.

    A <u>box</u> is on the shelf.

The singular subject *box* requires the singular verb *is*. It doesn't matter how many cookies are inside the box; we're talking about the box, one box (singular).

Exercise 1.13 Practice the Agreement Rules

In each sentence, there is a subject without a verb. If the subject is singular, select a singular verb for it. If it is plural, choose a plural verb. Write the correct verb in the space provided.

1. Here (is, are) _____ your stack of papers.

2. There (was, were) _____ four children playing outside.

3. (Where's, Where are) _____ the toys?

4. Maeve's relatives (was, were) _____ convinced that she was the smarter one.

5. A pack of loose-leaf paper (sells, sell) _____ for $1.29.

6. (There's, There are) _____ several benefits to being honest.

7. How much (have, has) _____ prices gone up?

8. A bunch of flowers (was, were) _____ growing in the garden.

9. (Doesn't, Don't) _____ they see the truth?

10. One of my binders (seems, seem) _____ to be missing.

Polish Your Spelling
Adding Suffixes to Form New Words

A **suffix** is a word part added to the end of a word to form a new word.

WORD		SUFFIX		NEW WORD
hope	+	ing	=	hoping
hope	+	ed	=	hoped
hope	+	less	=	hopeless
hope	+	ful	=	hopeful

Common Suffixes

SUFFIX	MEANING	SAMPLE WORD
able	able to be	observable (able to be observed)
ation	act of	observation (act of observing)
er	one who	observer (one who observes)
ly	in a _____ manner	observably (in an observable manner)
ed	ending of past participle	Yesterday I *observed* them.
ing	ending of present participle	Today I am *observing* them.

Adding Suffixes to Words

What happens to the *e* at the end of a word when we add a suffix? It usually depends on whether the suffix you are attaching begins with a vowel or a consonant.

- **If the suffix begins with a vowel, drop the *e*.**

  observe + able = observable
  Because -*able* begins with a vowel (*a*), we dropped the *e*.
  Exceptions: manageable, changeable, noticeable

- **If the suffix begins with a consonant, keep the *e*.**

  acute + ly = acutely
  Because -*ly* begins with a consonant (*l*), we kept the *e*.

TIP: Here's an easy way to remember the rule: The word vowel *has an* e *in it.* Consonant *does not. Drop the* e *at the end of a word only if the suffix begins with a vowel.*

Study these additional examples:

WORD		SUFFIX		NEW WORD
predict	+	able	=	predictable
perceive	+	able	=	perceivable
expire	+	ation	=	expiration
fix	+	ation	=	fixation
teach	+	er	=	teacher
believe	+	er	=	believer
bloat	+	ed	=	bloated
note	+	ed	=	noted
thank	+	ing	=	thanking
please	+	ing	=	pleasing

Exercise 1.14 Practice the Spelling Rules for Adding Suffixes

Add the suffix shown and write the new word on the line.

1. acute + ly = _____

2. moderate + ed = _____

3. limit + ation = _____

4. inquire + er = _____

5. target + ed = _____

6. alter + ation = _____

7. market + able = _____

8. believe + able = _____

9. trouble + ing = _____

10. satisfy + ing = _____

Chapter Two

Prereading Guide

Words to know and ideas to consider before you jump into the reading.

A. Essential Vocabulary

Word	Meaning	Typical Use
allocate (*v*) AL-o-kate	1. to set aside for a specific purpose; earmark; reserve 2. to assign or give out; designate	As soon as they *allocate* the funds, they'll start building the new stadium. One teacher was *allocated* to each group of 15 students on the field trip.
avant-garde (*adj*) ah-vahnt-GARD	experimental and original; out of the mainstream (especially in the arts or fashion)	Most people wore simple black dresses to the party, but Hannah showed up in a funky electric blue *avant-garde* outfit she designed herself.
benign (*adj*) be-NINE	1. kind and gentle; charitable 2. harmless	Because of her *benign* nature, people often took advantage of her. The tumor was nothing to worry about; it was *benign*.
chasm (*n*) KA-zum	1. a deep gorge or ravine in the earth's surface 2. a separation or break between two groups or people	Ausable *Chasm* is a popular tourist attraction in upstate New York. The *chasm* between some liberals and conservatives is at times very large.
engaging (*adj*) en-GAY-jing	charming and appealing in nature; fascinating	Zachary, handsome and *engaging*, was very popular with the girls.
excursion (*n*) ex-KUR-zhun	1. a brief trip or journey; an outing 2. a straying from what is normally done; deviation	With the long weekend coming up, we should plan an *excursion* to Midland. In an *excursion* from their usual evening of TV, Mom and Dad played cribbage.

Word	Meaning	Typical Use
genteel *(adj)* jen-TEEL	polite and well mannered; classy	She came from a very *genteel* family, and they were horrified by her choice of friends, who were unlike them.
histrionic *(adj)* hiss-tree-ON-ik	overly dramatic; theatrical; emotional	Her *histrionic* pleading was usually successful with her father, who gave her what she wanted.
legendary *(adj)* LEH-jen-dare-ee	widely known; famous (often for heroic deeds or for shocking behavior)	Spurrier's coaching was *legendary*, and teams who faced the Gators did not often expect to win.
protégé *(n)* PRO-tuh-zhay	a person guided by a more experienced person, often in a career; student	Pilar saw Andrew's potential, and he soon became her *protégé*.

B. Vocabulary Practice

Exercise 2.1   Sentence Completion

Using your new vocabulary knowledge, choose the best way to complete the following sentences. Circle the letter of your answer.

1. As an excursion from painting, Caitlin turned to
   _____.
   A. watercolor
   B. sculpture

2. Jeremiah, at six feet six inches, was _____ on the basketball court.
   A. legendary
   B. hindered

3. _____ people are usually courteous and well spoken.
   A. Genteel
   B. Gentle

4. They didn't allocate enough textbooks, so we have to
   _____.
   A. send some back
   B. share

5. His campaign speeches were so _____ that he easily won the election.
   A. engaging
   B. avant-garde

6. She's a good friend of mine. My _____ nature balances her histrionic one.
   A. illogical
   B. quiet

7. We were all _____ when the vet told us our cat's tumor was benign.
   A. happy and relieved
   B. sad and worried

8. The Grand Canyon is the largest _____ in America.
   A. excursion
   B. chasm

9. Marisol is helping Elizabeth with her college plans. Elizabeth is her _____.
   A. mentor
   B. protégé

10. Joyce's writing techniques were enormously _____ and avant-garde.
    A. experimental
    B. traditional

Exercise 2.2   Using Fewer Words

Replace the italicized words with a single word from the following list. The first one has been done for you.

excursion	legendary	genteel	allocated	engaging
avant-garde	chasm	protégé	benign	histrionic

1. At Thanksgiving, we'll make a(an) *short trip* to my aunt's house.

   1. _excursion_

2. Some people liked his speech to the student body, but I found it ridiculously *dramatic and theatrical.*

   2. _____

3. He has a very *charming and appealing* way about him.

   3. _____

4. If you want to succeed in a career, it's helpful to be a(an) *person who follows an older and more experienced person.*

   4. _____

5. "Aaron, stop chewing with your mouth open. You know that *polite and well-mannered* people like us don't do that!"

   5. _____

6. A sure way to create a(an) *separation between people* is to start a discussion on a controversial topic.

   6. _____

7. Mrs. May is a(an) *kind and gentle* elderly lady who had no idea she was being taken in by a scam.

7._____

8. I love how Bianca dresses. She's definitely *out of the mainstream.*

8._____

9. Only one tiny mailbox has been *set aside* for each apartment.

9._____

10. Although Paul Revere is *widely known* for his midnight ride, he was also a silversmith.

10._____

Exercise 2.3 Synonyms and Antonyms

Fill in the blanks in column A with the required synonyms or antonyms, selecting them from column B. (Remember: A *synonym* is a word similar in meaning to another word. *Autumn* and *fall* are synonyms. An *antonym* is a word opposite in meaning to another word. *Beginning* and *ending* are antonyms.)

	A	B
_____	1. synonym for *separation*	allocate
_____	2. antonym for *traditional*	protégé
_____	3. synonym for *outing*	avant-garde
_____	4. antonym for *unknown*	benign
_____	5. antonym for *malignant*	chasm
_____	6. synonym for *theatrical*	engaging
_____	7. synonym for *earmark*	excursion
_____	8. antonym for *repellent*	genteel
_____	9. antonym for *uncouth*	histrionic
_____	10. antonym for *mentor*	legendary

C. Journal Freewrite

Before you begin the reading on the next page, take out a journal or sheet of paper and spend some time responding to the following prompt.

TIP: Don't worry about grammar and spelling; just write what comes to mind. The purpose of freewriting is to explore ideas, not to produce a polished work.

Think of a time you met or heard about a group of people who live very differently from you. What surprised you about their lifestyle? What did you learn from hearing their story?

from A House Unlocked

by Penelope Lively

About the Author
Penelope Lively
(1933–) grew up in
Somerset, England, and
is the author of more
than forty books for
adults and children.
Most of her adult novels
are about how social
history, love, and per-
sonal recollections
affect our lives. This
excerpt is taken from *A
House Unlocked*, a mem-
oir about Golsoncott,
the home Lively's
grandparents bought in
1923. The family had to
sell the house 72 years
later. Although the
author was sad to lose a
place that had always
been part of her life, she
realized that she would
always have her "mem-
ory house."

MY grandmother was a fine needlewoman—both creative
and technically accomplished. Her preferred medium was
Winchester work—wool embroidery in a subtle and intricate
colour spectrum. But she made <u>excursions</u> into other forms
and one of her *chefs-d'œuvre*[1] was the sampler that she made
of Golsoncott[2] itself in 1946, which stood as a fire-screen in
the drawing room and is now the centrepiece of my study in
London.

It is formal and stylized, in the sampler tradition, with the
house at the top and beneath it significant elements of the
garden—lily pond with goldfish shimmering beneath the blue
stitched water, dovecot with white doves, sundial, mole and
molehill, frog, toad, dragonfly . . . Below that is the stable
block, horses peering from loose boxes, each named, and a
row of prancing dogs beneath—Sheltie and Waif and Merlin
and the famous Dingo, a real Australian dingo bought from
London Zoo by my aunt Rachel.

At the very bottom is a line of children. Not, as you might
think, grandchildren, but the wartime evacuees.

There were six of them—six children under five. Rachel
went to London shortly after the outbreak of war to work
for the Citizens' Advice Bureau based at Toynbee Hall in
Whitechapel (then part of the London Borough of Stepney,
itself now incorporated into Tower Hamlets) which served as
a relief centre for those bombed out or otherwise in need of
help as a result of the Blitz.[3] In the autumn of 1940 she
informed her mother that Golsoncott was now an official
war nursery and that six children would shortly be arriving,
along with the matron <u>allocated</u> for such groups of under-
fives evacuated without mothers. My grandmother took it on
the chin and set about reorganizing the house. The old nursery and night nursery were made over to the party, along
with the attic rooms that had formerly been servants' quar-
ters. The evacuees ate in the servants' sitting-room next to

---

[1]masterpieces
[2]the author's ancestral home
[3]an intense bombing campaign of London by German forces during
World War II

the kitchen. At night the children must have lain staring up at the night-nursery ceiling on which Margaret Tarrant fairies flew around a midnight blue sky spangled with stars. The children came from Stepney, a borough where around 200,000 people lived at an average density of twelve per dwelling. From there to Golsoncott. Confronted with this situation, I assume that they did the normal and natural thing—howled for their mothers and wet their beds. My grandmother, who didn't have to do the washing, took a kindly interest and gave them much the same treatment as grandchildren received when there were any to hand—they had the run of the garden and were summoned to the drawing-room after tea where she read to them from Beatrix Potter. She found the evacuees' Cockney accents distasteful and hoped to correct these. (By contrast, Somerset accents were considered entirely agreeable and to be respected—a neat instance of the perceived aesthetic[4] chasm between town and country.)

Perhaps today, somewhere, there is a person of about my own age whose memory bank includes a bizarre fragment in which he or she sits on a cushion in a vast room while a benign madwoman with peculiar diction reads aloud from diminutive[5] books. I'm not sure how long the evacuees stayed but they were certainly there for two or three years and were legendary figures by the time I returned to Golsoncott in the late forties. Naughty and engaging Georgie of the golden curls, who climbed the cedar of Lebanon, got stuck and had to be rescued by ladder. Pert little Maureen, who once scarpered off down to the village and was found hanging around outside the Valiant Soldier. After the war, leftover money from the Anglo-American Relief Organization, which had funded several such evacuee nurseries, was used to pay for summer holidays for former evacuees. Rachel used to oversee this operation and distribute joyous leggy adolescents around the area. The evacuee experience was notoriously[6] various—these must have been among the happier instances. One of Rachel's protégés, a girl called June, was still coming to Golsoncott for a summer stint in the late forties, by which time she was a histrionic adolescent in love with my aunt, spending her time hanging around outside Rachel's studio and the stables in the hope of a passing word. One lad originally billeted[7] on a local farm continued to holiday in the area as the father of his own family and eventually set up as a butcher in Minehead.

Rachel acted as unofficial billeting officer in 1940, exploiting her network of local acquaintances, touring the area on horseback to target farms and cottages and allocate Toynbee Hall children. It is the role seized on by Basil Seal in Evelyn Waugh's *Put Out More Flags*, foisting the fearful Connolly family upon carefully selected genteel victims, the more frail and addicted to gracious living, the

---

[4]related to beauty and good taste
[5]extremely small
[6]famously
[7]lodged

better. Basil's motivation is pecuniary[8] and gleefully malicious. In Rachel's case her war work fired her social conscience. But west Somerset was not to know that and she may well have caused a certain consternation, trotting briskly into farmyards, smiling sweetly and talking not of the next meet but of numbers of bedrooms and sanitary facilities.

Rachel was one of the many for whom sudden exposure to the realities of pre-war urban poverty changed an entire perception of their society. She was in her thirties and had lived all her life in the country, her time divided between riding and hunting and her career as a talented wood engraver and <u>avant-garde</u> painter and sculptor. London was simply a place you visited for social or cultural reasons. For her, as for most middle-class people, the teeming tracts[9] of the East End were nothing but names on a map, Stepney, Bow, East Ham, Poplar. They were invisible and inconceivable. Then came 1940. Rachel saw—many saw—and their perception of society would never be quite the same again. The circumstances in which hundreds of thousands of children were growing up—the malnutrition, the absence of home hygiene—shocked even those who should have known. Neville Chamberlain[10] wrote to his wife: 'I never knew that such conditions existed, and I feel ashamed of having been so ignorant of my neighbours.'

---

[8]relating to money
[9]overcrowded, run-down areas
[10]British prime minister, 1937–1940

Understanding the Reading

Complete the next three exercises and see how well you understood the excerpt from *A House Unlocked*.

Exercise 2.4 Multiple-Choice Questions

Answer the following questions about the reading. Circle the letter of your answer.

TIP: Don't try to answer the questions from memory; go back to the text as often as necessary.

1. The author's main reason for describing the sampler in the first two paragraphs was most likely to
   A. praise her grandmother's needlework.
   B. give background information on Golsoncott.
   C. lead into the story about the children on the sampler.
   D. tell about the various dogs at Golsoncott.

2. The most important thing about Aunt Rachel in this story is that she
   A. changed her attitude toward the poor.
   B. told her mother what to do.
   C. was extremely well liked by the children.
   D. was a painter and sculptor.

3. The "benign madwoman with peculiar diction" who reads to the children is
   A. Aunt Rachel.
   B. the matron who looks after the children.
   C. the author.
   D. the author's grandmother.

4. This story shows the sharp contrast between
   A. Aunt Rachel and the author's grandmother.
   B. the lives of the urban poor and the lives of prosperous country people.
   C. conditions in Europe before and after World War II.
   D. Georgie and Maureen.

5. The author's main purpose for writing this memoir was most likely to
   A. entertain readers with a story about children from Stepney.
   B. honor her aunt by telling what she did for the children.
   C. point out that people in government are indifferent to poverty.
   D. point out that she came from a wealthy family.

Exercise 2.5 Short-Answer Questions

Respond to the following questions in one to two complete sentences. Go back to the text, as you did on the multiple choice.

6. Why do you think the children would have "lain staring up at the night-nursery ceiling" (paragraph 4)?

   _____

   _____

   _____

7. Using specific examples, describe how the grandmother treated the children.

   _____

   _____

   _____

8. What was the borough like from which the children came?

   _____

   _____

   _____

9. Why do you think the author compares Rachel to Basil Seal in *Put Out More Flags*?

_____

_____

_____

Exercise 2.6   Extending Your Thinking

Respond to the following question in three to four complete sentences. Use details from the text in your answer.

10. This unit is titled "Epiphanies." What was Rachel's epiphany, or revealing discovery, about society in 1940?

_____

_____

_____

_____

_____

_____

Reading Strategy Lesson
Using Context Clues

Context literally means "with text." It is the text that surrounds a word and helps to make its meaning clear, even if you've never seen the word before.

If you encounter a word you do not know, check for a footnote where the word may be defined. If no definition is given, you can use context clue strategies to determine what the word means. Here are four main ways to use context clues.

1. Look for clues in the phrases and sentences surrounding the unknown word.

Read the following example from *A House Unlocked*. From the text before and after *dovecot*, what can you determine about the meaning of the word?

> It is formal and stylized, in the sampler tradition, with the house at the top and beneath it significant elements of the garden—lily pond with goldfish shimmering beneath the blue stitched water, *dovecot* with white doves, sundial, mole and molehill, frog, toad, dragonfly . . .

From the text before the word, you know that a "dovecot with white doves" is a significant element of the garden. The other elements, with the exception of the sundial, are all creatures that live in the garden. The goldfish live in the pond, and the mole lives in the molehill. The phrase "dovecot with white doves" implies that the doves live in the dovecot, so it is probably a type of birdhouse. Look back at the paragraph in the reading (paragraph 2) and you'll see that this idea is further enforced by the horses in the stable, mentioned in the next sentence. If you check your educated guess with a dictionary, you'll find that a *dovecot* is "a small building used to house tame pigeons or doves," or something close to this.

2. See if the word is defined by synonyms or restatements.
The following sentence tells you exactly what *Winchester work* is by restating it.

> Her preferred medium was *Winchester work*—wool embroidery in a subtle and intricate colour spectrum.

Winchester work is defined as "embroidery in a subtle and intricate colour spectrum."

3. Check whether you're given examples that lead to the meaning.
Can you figure out what a *Blitz* is, from the examples in this passage?

> Rachel went to London shortly after the outbreak of war to work for the Citizens' Advice Bureau based at Toynbee Hall in Whitechapel . . . which served as a relief centre for those bombed out or otherwise in need of help as a result of the *Blitz*.

The author tells us that people in London were "bombed out or otherwise in need of help." These are examples of what the *Blitz* caused. If you were unfamiliar with the word, you could assume that bombs falling on London would cause people to lose their homes as well as cause them other problems—so the *Blitz* was a bombing campaign during the war.

4. Look for word-within-a-word clues.
What clues in the word *inconceivable* help you determine its meaning, so you can better understand these sentences?

> For her, as for most middle-class people, the teeming tracts of the East End were nothing but names on a map, Stepney, Bow, East Ham, Poplar. They were invisible and *inconceivable*.

There are three parts to the word *inconceivable*. If you know that *conceive* means "imagine," then *conceivable* must mean "able to be imagined." Adding the prefix *in-* makes the word the reverse of "able to be imagined." In other words, most middle-class people were not able to imagine the conditions in the East End.

HINT: No matter which method you use, always reread the sentence, replacing the word in question with the definition you've decided upon. It should still make sense.

When you encounter a word you don't know in a reading selection, look for the most obvious context clues first.

1. The **phrases and sentences around the word** may make its meaning clear.
2. You may find that it is **restated**, a way of defining the word in the text.
3. There may be an **example** that helps you figure out what the word means.
4. Finally, you may be able to use **word-within-a-word** clues to determine word meanings.

With context clues, you'll be able to arrive at definitions for many words without having to look them up in a dictionary.

Exercise 2.7 Practice the Reading Strategy

Look back at the reading and use your context-clue skills to determine the meaning of each *italicized* word. Then circle the letter of the correct answer.

1. "At the very bottom is a line of children. Not, as you might think, grandchildren, but the wartime *evacuees*" (par. 3).
   A. guests of the estate
   B. nursery-school students
   C. people moved from a dangerous place
   D. grandchildren

2. "At night the children must have lain staring up at the night-nursery ceiling on which *Margaret Tarrant* fairies flew around a midnight blue sky spangled with stars" (par. 4). *Margaret Tarrant* was most likely
   A. a friend of grandmother's.
   B. a fairy similar to Tinker Bell in *Peter Pan*.
   C. a well-known person in their old neighborhood.
   D. an artist popular at the time of the story.

3. "She found the evacuees' Cockney accents *distasteful* and hoped to correct these" (par. 4).
   A. bad tasting
   B. unpleasant
   C. false
   D. humorous

4. "Pert little Maureen, who once *scarpered* off down to the village and was found hanging around outside the Valiant Soldier" (par. 5).
   A. escaped
   B. skipped
   C. ran away
   D. cantered

5. "It is the role seized on by Basil Seal in Evelyn Waugh's *Put Out More Flags, foisting* the fearful Connolly family upon carefully selected genteel victims, the more frail and addicted to gracious living, the better" (par. 6).
   A. forcing
   B. depositing
   C. introducing
   D. offering

Exercise 2.8   Apply the Reading Strategy

Go back to the reading and find the words listed here. Using context clues, write a brief definition for each.

1. matron (par. 4) _____
2. pert (par. 5) _____
3. stint (par. 5) _____
4. exploiting (par. 6) _____
5. malicious (par. 6) _____

Writing Workshop
The Power of Description

When Penelope Lively writes about Golsoncott, she uses specific adjectives and descriptive phrases to help us picture the children. She talks about "*naughty* and *engaging* Georgie of the *golden* curls." She uses the adjectives *pert* and *little* to describe Maureen.

Without such language, we would not get as clear and vivid an image of the children and the action in the house.

Using Descriptive Words

Including description in your writing is a good way to keep your reader's attention and to give your writing muscle. Which sentence in each pair is more effective?

   A. Computers are great, but sometimes they can make you mad.
   B. Technology can be everything from enlightening to enraging.

C. He lived in a small room in New York.

D. The room where he lived in New York faced Washington Square and was long and narrow like a hallway.

E. She was a splendid-looking girl with wonderfully glossy brown waves of hair that cascaded down her slim, strong back.

F. She was very pretty and had shiny brown hair.

You probably found B, D, and E the most powerful of these six sentences. How can you write similar sentences? The answer is to start with whatever you have and revise it to make it more interesting and exciting. Here is a sample first paragraph to a personal narrative. Read it and consider how it can be revised.

A Person I Learned About

My dance instructor has really inspired me. She overcame a lot to be where she is today. She is really strong. She also gives me really good tips on my dancing. She really motivates me.

What problems do you see in this paragraph? _____

_____

_____

Did you notice that the title is not very interesting? How many times is the word *really* used? This writer tried to tell the reader a lot about her dance instructor but uses repetitive sentence structures—every sentence but one begins with *She*. In addition, the writer uses vague, unspecific language, so the reader is not inspired to keep reading.

Now read this version and examine how it is different.

Dancing Against the Odds

On my first day of dance class, I was immediately turned off by the instructor, Elena. She was petite, with soft blond hair and delicate features, but when she opened her mouth to give us instructions, she suddenly morphed into an army sergeant. She pushed us and pushed us, barking away the entire hour. *Isn't dancing supposed to be fun?* I was frustrated and tired. Then, at the end of class, Elena sat us down and made a frightening announcement.

What do we learn about the dance instructor that we didn't know from the original paragraph? We know specific details about her, such as her name. We are also beginning to see what she looks like. She is petite and has delicate features, but has a loud, forceful tone. Now we know how the narrator met the instructor, and we're curious to keep reading to find out what she learns about her.

Let's look at how we'd continue this story. Instead of listing more traits about Elena or mentioning them outright, we'll *show* the reader some of those traits by *describing* more action:

> "Class," Elena began, her voice less harsh but still condescending, "I know that today was tough. But I've danced on Broadway, and I know that you don't become successful there or anywhere without sweat and perseverance. This spring, on the last day of class, we're going to have a recital at the convention center downtown. Thousands of people will be there. You're going to have to work very hard to be ready."
>
> I gulped. I like to dance, but I signed up for the class just for fun. I certainly didn't want to do it professionally. Having to perform in front of that many people would make me extremely nervous. It didn't seem fair of Elena to rope us into something so big.
>
> When I got home, I pulled my mom aside and told her I wanted to quit dance lessons. "Why?" she prodded, sounding annoyed. "I'm paying a lot for this." I explained how I thought Elena was too harsh, insensitive, and arrogant. She had probably never been shy. My mom gave me a funny look. What is it? "Things didn't come easy for Elena," Mom said. "She didn't tell you what she went through two years ago?"

These paragraphs show us more about the narrator—for example, that she is dancing only for fun and that she gets stage fright. We are also beginning to learn that there is more to Elena than meets the eye. The writer uses dialogue to bring the characters to life and involve us in the story, rather than just tell us what happened.

Exercise 2.9   Practice the Writing Lesson

On a separate sheet of paper, write one to two additional body paragraphs for this story, as well as a conclusion. Jot down some notes for your paragraphs before you begin writing them. What does the narrator learn about Elena's past? How will it affect her decision to stay in the class and the performance, and how might it affect her life or influence her outlook in general? Look at the narrative planner you used in Chapter One (page 21) and review the suggestions given for the paragraphs of a narrative.

Exercise 2.10 Apply the Lesson to Your Own Writing

Reread your own personal narrative that you wrote for Chapter One. Think about how you can apply what you've learned in this section to give your narrative a more powerful effect. Use the following checklist as you revise your narrative. Write your final draft on separate paper.

☐ Did I introduce my friend, relative, or acquaintance, and give the reader enough details to make the person come alive?

☐ Did I show how I learned something new about the person and how it affected me (during that moment as well as in the future)?

☐ Did I include dialogue?

☐ Did I sum up my feelings in my last paragraph?

☐ Did I avoid repetition and use powerful, descriptive words?

Grammar Mini-Lesson

Participles and Participial Phrases

When you describe a *speeding car*, what part of speech is *speeding*? You're using *speeding* to describe a noun, the car, so *speeding* must be an adjective, right? But isn't *to speed* an action, which would make *speeding* a verb? In fact, both thoughts are correct. *Speeding* is a verb form acting as an adjective, which we call a participle.

What Are Participles and How Do We Form Them?

A **participle** is a **verb form acting as an adjective** and modifying or describing a noun or pronoun. As you'll see, participles help show relationships between ideas in a sentence, add details and information, and help to create sentence variety.

1. Present participles
Present participles (like *singing* or *trotting*) are formed by adding *-ing* to the base word (*sing, trot*), doubling the final consonant if necessary. Examine the following examples.

> The *speeding* car skidded as it turned the corner.
> (*Speeding* describes *car*.)

> The *howling* wind stirred up leaves in the yard.
> (*Howling* describes *wind*.)

Note: Although all present participles end in *-ing*, not all words ending in *-ing* are present participles. Remember, participles function *only* as adjectives.

> *Writing* is my favorite part of English class.

> *Writing* is the subject of this sentence, so it's a noun—a thing—not an adjective. It's another verbal form, called a gerund, which you'll learn about in the next chapter.

2. Past participles
Past participles are usually formed by adding *-ed*.

> The *frightened* toddler ran from the scary clown.
> (*Frightened* describes *toddler*.)

> There were no seats left in the *crowded* room.
> (*Crowded* describes *room*.)

However, some past participles end in *-en, -d, -t,* or *-n.*

The *frozen* pond was still not safe for skating.
(*Frozen* describes *pond.*)

All there was to eat was *burnt* toast.
(*Burnt* describes *toast.*)

Be careful: There are many words that end in *-ed, -en, -d, -t,* or *-n* that are not participles. You must look at the word's function in the sentence to determine this.

The hurricane *destroyed* the house.
(*Destroyed* is a verb: The hurricane did what?)

The house was *beyond* repair.
(*Beyond* is an adverb modifying *repair.*)

Common Irregular Past Participles

beaten	begun	bitten	bought
brought	caught	chosen	eaten
fallen	forgotten	found	hung
led	lost	made	meant
read	risen	seen	shone
spoken	stolen	stood	struck
taken	taught	thought	thrown
told	wept	worn	written

Exercise 2.11 Practice Using Present and Past Participles

On the blank line, write the correct past or present participle of the given verb.

Example: <u>Arriving</u> at the theater early, we easily found a parking spot. (arrive)

1. _____ by his teacher's comments, he finished writing his story. (encourage)

2. _____ to art at an early age, David loved to sketch. (introduce)

3. _____ late, we knew we would miss the first quarter of the game. (leave)

4. The children, _____ after a long day, fell asleep quickly. (exhaust)

5. The sun was barely _____, and Josh was already out for a run. (rise)

What Are Participial Phrases and Why Are They Useful?

A **participial phrase** consists of a participle plus any words modified (described) by or related to it. The whole phrase acts as an adjective—it describes a noun or pronoun.

The sentences in the exercise you just completed contain participial phrases. Can you figure out what they are? Let's look at the one that was done for you:

Arriving at the theater early, we easily found a parking spot.

- *Arriving at the theater early* is the participial phrase. (*Arriving* is the participle and *at the theater early* tells us more about it—where and when we were arriving.)

- The whole phrase functions as an adjective, describing the pronoun *we* (what *we* were doing when we easily found a spot). Without the participial phrase, the sentence would just read: *We easily found a parking spot.* The reader wouldn't know how or why. Adding participial phrases will help your readers understand exactly what's going on in the situation you're describing.

Placement of a Participial Phrase

Place the participial phrase as close as possible to the noun or pronoun it describes, and be sure the noun is clearly stated; otherwise, your sentence could be confusing. Read the following sentence and see if you can figure out what's wrong with it.

Completely forgetting his homework, Eduardo's father is very annoyed.

It sounds as if Eduardo's father is the one who has forgotten his homework. To make the meaning clear, put the participial phrase closer to the noun *Eduardo*, since he's the one the participial phrase is describing (he's the one who forgot his homework). See the difference:

Eduardo, *completely forgetting his homework*, annoyed his father.

A participial phrase in the wrong place is called a "dangling participle."

Dangling: *Spending money like crazy*, her clothes were gorgeous.

Her *clothes* were not spending money. *She* was. How would you correct this?

Revised: *Spending money like crazy*, she bought gorgeous clothes.

See if you can tell what is wrong with these and then fix them:

1. Driving home in rush-hour traffic, a light was out at a major intersection.

   Revised: _____

2. Running up the stairs, her foot slipped and fell.

   Revised: _____

Punctuating Participial Phrases

Set off a participial phrase with commas when it

- comes at the beginning of a sentence
  Wondering which way to turn next, the puzzled driver stopped to consult his map.

- comes at the end of the sentence and is separated from the noun or pronoun it modifies
  The puzzled driver stopped to consult his map, *wondering which way to turn next.*

- is in the interior (middle) of the sentence, but the sentence would still be complete without it
  The puzzled driver, *wondering which way to turn next,* stopped to consult his map.

Do not set off a participial phrase in the middle of the sentence if it is essential to the sentence's meaning:
  Drivers *wondering which way to turn* are traffic menaces.

"Drivers are traffic menaces" is a complete sentence, but it needs the participial phrase to qualify exactly which kinds of drivers you mean. Not *all* drivers are traffic menaces.

Exercise 2.12 Practice Punctuating Participial Phrases

Insert commas where necessary.

1. The front porch with its sharply slanting floor was not inviting.

2. Spending the summer at camp Marcus had made lots of new friends.

3. Alexis gave up on reading interrupted constantly by phone calls.

4. The old desk holding piles of newspapers sat in the corner.

5. Children leaving home for the first time are usually nervous.

6. Touched by the movie's ending even Ben could not hold back tears.

7. Stretching out on a sofa near the fire Trevor fell asleep.

8. Amanda seeing us by the window waved happily and joined us.

9. Buses delayed by heavy traffic usually run behind schedule.

10. Convinced that I am dependable my friend loaned me money.

Polish Your Spelling
Writing Base Words Correctly

When you become skillful at spotting base words, you can greatly increase your vocabulary. In addition, when you are comfortable adding and removing prefixes and suffixes to and from base words, you can expand your writing skills.

- It is often possible to change a derivative (a word formed from a base) back into the base word by simply dropping the prefix and/or suffix.

Examples:

WORD	PREFIX/SUFFIX		BASE
discontent	– dis	=	content
developed	– ed	=	develop
unbuttoned	– un . . . ed	=	button

- Sometimes you need to restore a letter to the base—such as an *e* that was dropped when the suffix was added.

Examples:

WORD	SUFFIX	RESTORED LETTER		BASE
blazing	– ing	+ e	=	blaze
imaginable	– able	+ e	=	imagine

- If a final consonant was doubled when the prefix was added, you will need to "undouble" it, that is, drop one of the consonants.

Examples:

WORD	SUFFIX	CONSONANT		BASE
committed	– ed	– t	=	commit
baggy	– y	– g	=	bag

- If a final *y* was changed to *i* when the suffix was added, change it back to *y*.

Examples:

WORD	SUFFIX	I BACK TO Y		BASE
hurried	– ed	hurri – i + y	=	hurry
happiness	– ness	happi – i + y	=	happy

Exercise 2.13 Practice Spelling Base Words

Write the base of each word on the blank line.

1. dangling _____

2. bigger _____

3. foggy _____

4. pompous _____

5. unhappiness _____

6. advertisement _____

7. unreliable _____

8. listener _____

9. frayed _____

10. indescribable _____

11. recommence _____

12. visitor _____

13. compelled _____

14. weariness _____

15. wrinkled _____

16. ghastliness _____

17. marvelously _____

18. unflinchingly _____

19. achiever _____

20. accompanied _____

Chapter Three

Prereading Guide
Words to know and ideas to consider before you jump into the reading.

A. Essential Vocabulary

Word	Meaning	Typical Use
breakwater (*n*) BRAKE-wah-tur	a seawall meant to keep a beach from washing away; jetty	Fishing from the *breakwater* seemed like a good idea until she fell in.
brood (*v*) BROOD	to worry anxiously; fret; mope	Ryan is quiet again today; he's still *brooding*.
delve (*v*) DELV	1. to probe further into something, as for more information 2. to dig with a spade or shovel; excavate	I don't know who the twenty-fourth president was, but I can *delve* into it. My younger sister loves to *delve* into the sand with her little shovel.
envoy (*n*) EN-voi	a person sent on an errand or mission on another's behalf; a messenger	As soon as we learn what went wrong, we'll send an *envoy* to let you know.
plaintive (*adj*) PLANE-tiv	sad or mournful; sorrowful	"Do you think I could go with you?" she asked in a *plaintive* tone of voice.
profound (*adj*) pro-FOWND	1. of great depth; far-reaching 2. intense; important	The bottom of the ocean is almost too *profound* to imagine. Changing to a different school had a *profound* effect on him.
repose (*v*) re-POZE	1. to rest quietly; to sleep 2. (*n*) rest or sleep	After walking a mile, we decided it was time to *repose*. We took our *repose* at a fountain in the park.
rivulet (*n*) RIV-yoo-let	a small stream or creek; a brook	Drought had reduced the wide river to a mere *rivulet*.
squalor (*n*) SKWAH-lor	a dirty and shameful condition; filth	After the flood, they were forced to live in *squalor*.
subterfuge (*n*) SUB-tur-fyooj	deliberate misrepresentation and deception; trickery	The ad saying you could buy a car for $99 was complete *subterfuge*.

B. Vocabulary Practice

Exercise 3.1   Sentence Completion

Using your new vocabulary knowledge, choose the best way to complete the following sentences. Circle the letter of your answer.

1. The breakwater kept the _____ from coming ashore.
   A. rainstorms
   B. waves

2. She always spoke so plaintively that she usually _____.
   A. was ignored
   B. got her way

3. Let's delve into our homework problems; I want to _____.
   A. get them started
   B. put them off

4. We looked around and decided the best place to repose was on _____.
   A. a bench in the shade
   B. the roller coaster

5. My horse shies at _____; he won't cross even a tiny rivulet.
   A. highways
   B. water

6. _____ have profoundly affected our entire society.
   A. Ballpoint pens
   B. Computers

7. He's a profound thinker, and that's why he often seems to be _____.
   A. shallow
   B. brooding

8. Despite _____, the family continued to live in squalor.
   A. winning the lottery
   B. crushing poverty

9. _____ in the past were afraid to deliver messages that the recipient wouldn't like because of the practice of "shooting the messenger."
   A. Rulers
   B. Envoys

10. If a pop-up ad says you've won a laptop, it is probably a _____.
    A. lucky break
    B. subterfuge

Exercise 3.2 Using Fewer Words

Replace the italicized words with a single word from the following list. The first one has been done for you.

breakwater   delve   rivulet   squalor   subterfuge

profound   envoy   reposing   plaintive   brooding

1. The *seawall meant to contain the waves* needs repair.   1. <u>breakwater</u>

2. A(an) *person sent on an errand or mission* often plays an important role.   2._____

3. *Deliberate misrepresentation* is sometimes, but not always, considered a crime.   3._____

4. We need to *probe further* into why our company is losing money.   4._____

5. The little boy's cries were *sad and sorrowful*, but we assured him we would find his mother.   5._____

6. If your landlord refuses to fix things, you may have no choice about living in *a dirty and shameful condition*.   6._____

7. The Grand Canyon is a *deep and far-reaching* chasm.   7._____

8. *Worrying anxiously* about it isn't going to make you feel any better.   8._____

9. You cross a(an) *small stream* and then you come to our street.   9._____

10. Exhausted by our long drive, we looked forward to *resting quietly*.   10._____

Exercise 3.3 Synonyms and Antonyms

Fill in the blanks in column A with the required synonyms or antonyms, selecting them from column B. (Remember: A *synonym* is a word similar in meaning to another word. *Autumn* and *fall* are synonyms. An *antonym* is a word opposite in meaning to another word. *Beginning* and *ending* are antonyms.)

	A	B
_____	1. synonym for *messenger*	breakwater
_____	2. synonym for *fret*	delve
_____	3. synonym for *sleep*	rivulet
_____	4. antonym for *openness*	brood
_____	5. synonym for *jetty*	squalor

_____	6. antonym for *cleanliness*	subterfuge
_____	7. synonym for *excavate*	envoy
_____	8. antonym for *insignificant*	plaintive
_____	9. synonym for *brook*	repose
_____	10. antonym for *elated*	profound

C. Journal Freewrite

Before you begin the reading on the next page, take out a journal or sheet of paper and spend some time responding to one of the following prompts.

TIP: Don't worry about grammar and spelling; just write what comes to mind. The purpose of freewriting is to explore ideas, not to produce a polished work.

Imagine this scenario: Since you were small, you've known what would be expected of you when you got older: for example, learn a trade, work in a relative's business, or become a doctor. However, that is not *your* dream. Would you do what was expected, or would you try and pursue your own passion? Explain.

OR

Have you ever gone for a walk and noticed something or someone that struck you as being particularly beautiful or unique? Describe the moment and why it had an effect on you.

from A Portrait of the Artist as a Young Man

by James Joyce

About the Author

James Joyce (1882–1941) is an Irish author who had a monumental influence on contemporary literature. He devoted his life to perfecting his literary style, noted for its experimental use of language and unorthodox literary methods. Because his writing was so avant-garde, he had difficulty getting published and often had financial problems. A number of grants from patrons who believed in him allowed him to continue writing. This excerpt is from *A Portrait of the Artist as a Young Man*, which Joyce based on his own life. His other major works include *Dubliners*, *Ulysses*, and *Finnegans Wake*.

Reader's Tip: In this excerpt, we meet a teenage Stephen Dedalus as he realizes he must leave the school where he has been studying for the priesthood and follow his true calling—to be an artist. Joyce uses a stream-of-consciousness technique, giving us Stephen's rambling thoughts so we can understand his true feelings.

He looked northward towards Howth. The sea had fallen below the line of seawrack[1] on the shallow side of the <u>breakwater</u> and already the tide was running out fast along the foreshore. Already one long oval bank of sand lay warm and dry amid the wavelets. Here and there warm isles of sand gleamed above the shallow tide and about the isles and around the long bank and amid the shallow currents of the beach were lightclad gayclad figures, wading and <u>delving</u>.

In a few moments he was barefoot, his stockings folded in his pockets and his canvas shoes dangling by their knotted laces over his shoulders: and, picking a pointed salt-eaten stick out of the jetsam[2] among the rocks, he clambered down the slope of the breakwater.

There was a long <u>rivulet</u> in the strand: and, as he waded slowly up its course, he wondered at the endless drift of seaweed. Emerald and black and russet and olive, it moved beneath the current, swaying and turning. The water of the rivulet was dark with endless drift and mirrored the highdrifting clouds. The clouds were drifting above him silently and silently the seatangle was drifting below him and the grey warm air was still: and a new wild life was singing in his veins.

Where was his boyhood now? Where was the soul that had hung back from her destiny, to <u>brood</u> alone upon the shame of her wounds and in her house of <u>squalor</u> and <u>subterfuge</u> to queen it[3] in faded cerements[4] and in wreaths that withered at the touch? Or where was he?

---

[1]seaweed lying on the beach
[2]things thrown off boats and ships that float up onto the land
[3]slang for "to act superior and bossy," i.e., like a queen
[4]shrouds or wrappings for the dead

He was alone. He was unheeded, happy and near to the wild heart of life. He was alone and young and wilful and wildhearted, alone amid a waste of wild air and brackish[5] waters and the seaharvest of shells and tangle and veiled grey sunlight and gayclad lightclad figures, of children and girls and voices childish and girlish in the air.

A girl stood before him in midstream, alone and still, gazing out to sea. She seemed like one whom magic had changed into the likeness of a strange and beautiful seabird. Her long slender bare legs were delicate as a crane's and pure save where an emerald trail of seaweed had fashioned itself as a sign upon the flesh. Her thighs, fuller and soft-hued as ivory, were bared almost to the hips where the white fringes of her drawers were like feathering of soft white down. Her slateblue skirts were kilted[6] boldly about her waist and dovetailed[7] behind her. Her bosom was as a bird's soft and slight, slight and soft as the breast of some darkplumaged dove. But her long fair hair was girlish: and girlish, and touched with the wonder of mortal beauty, her face.

She was alone and still, gazing out to sea; and when she felt his presence and the worship of his eyes her eyes turned to him in quiet sufferance[8] of his gaze, without shame or wantonness.[9] Long, long she suffered his gaze and then quietly withdrew her eyes from his and bent them towards the stream, gently stirring the water with her foot hither and thither. The first faint noise of gently moving water broke the silence, low and faint and whispering, faint as the bells of sleep; hither and thither, hither and thither; and a faint flame trembled on her cheek.

—Heavenly God! cried Stephen's soul, in an outburst of profane[10] joy.

He turned away from her suddenly and set off across the strand. His cheeks were aflame; his body was aglow; his limbs were trembling. On and on and on and on he strode, far out over the sands, singing wildly to the sea, crying to greet the advent[11] of the life that had cried to him.

Her image had passed into his soul for ever and no word had broken the holy silence of his ecstasy. Her eyes had called him and his soul had leaped at the call. To live, to err, to fall, to triumph, to recreate life out of life! A wild angel had appeared to him, the angel of mortal youth and beauty, an <u>envoy</u> from the fair courts of life, to throw open before him in an instant of ecstasy the gates of all the ways of error and glory. On and on and on and on!

---

[5]slightly salty and often bad smelling
[6]tucked up
[7]Although this is a real word, meaning "to fit together," Joyce has used it in an unusual way to add to his comparison of the girl with a dove. Just picture a bird's tail, and you can picture how her skirts looked.
[8]tolerance
[9]lewdness; obscenity
[10]irreverent; since Stephen was studying for the priesthood, he felt this expression was like a curse, although it might be seen as praise for life
[11]arrival of something that has been expected

Understanding the Reading

Complete the next three exercises and see how well you understood the excerpt from *A Portrait of the Artist as a Young Man.*

Exercise 3.4 Multiple-Choice Questions

Answer the following questions about the reading. Circle the letter of your answer.

TIP: Don't try to answer the questions from memory; go back to the text as often as necessary.

1. This story takes place
   A. on a beach.
   B. by a river.
   C. by a stream.
   D. in the town of Howth.

2. Stephen (the "he" in this story) was "near to the wild heart of life" because he
   A. knew there were lots of fish and marine mammals in the sea.
   B. loved hearing the children's voices.
   C. was out in the world, watching real people living their lives.
   D. had finally learned how to swim.

3. In paragraph 6, Joyce compares the girl to
   A. a white cloud in the blue sky.
   B. an ordinary seagull.
   C. the children calling on the beach.
   D. a seabird and a dove.

4. The beautiful girl on the beach is unforgettable because
   A. she was so bold and flirtatious.
   B. she awakened Stephen to what life could be like.
   C. they had a fascinating conversation.
   D. she was embarrassed by Stephen's attention.

Exercise 3.5 Short-Answer Questions

Respond to the following questions in one to two complete sentences. Go back to the text, as you did on the multiple choice.

5. How does the girl react to the boy's gaze? Be specific.

   _____

   _____

   _____

6. In writing, you're often told not to repeat words, yet Joyce uses repetition quite a bit. Think about why that could be. (Why might he repeat *drift* in the third paragraph, for example?) What effect does the repetition create?

_____

_____

_____

7. What colors does Joyce use in describing the girl? What might these colors represent?

_____

_____

_____

Exercise 3.6 Extending Your Thinking

Respond to the following question in three to four complete sentences. Use details from the text in your answer.

8. What role does the girl play in Stephen's epiphany? What do you think she helps him to realize, and how?

_____

_____

_____

_____

_____

_____

The Solitary Reaper

by William Wordsworth

About the Author
William Wordsworth (1770–1850) was a major poet of the English Romantic Period. His definition of poetry as "emotion recollected in tranquility" shocked the literary world, which at the time considered intellectual subjects and proper form (rhyme and meter) the only true components of poetry. Wordsworth helped shape a new kind of poetry, which emphasizes the senses, the imagination, and the beauty of the natural world. "The Solitary Reaper" is a well-known example of Wordsworth's theories at work.

Behold her, single in the field,
Yon[1] solitary Highland lass,[2]
Reaping and singing by herself;
Stop here, or gently pass!
Alone she cuts and binds the grain,
And sings a melancholy strain;
Oh, listen! for the vale profound
Is overflowing with the sound.

No nightingale did ever chant
So sweetly to reposing bands
Of travelers in some shady haunt
Among Arabian sands:
A voice so thrilling ne'er was heard
In springtime from the cuckoo-bird,
Breaking the silence of the seas
Among the farthest Hebrides.[3]

Will no one tell me what she sings?
Perhaps the plaintive numbers flow
For old, unhappy, far-off things,
And battles long ago:
Or is it some more humble lay,
Familiar matter of to-day,
Some natural sorrow, loss, or pain,
That has been and may be again?

Whate'er the theme, the maiden sang
As if her song could have no ending;
I saw her singing at her work,
And o'er the sickle bending.
I listened motionless and still;
And, as I mounted up the hill,
The music in my heart I bore
Long after it was heard no more.

---

[1]that distant
[2]young woman
[3]about 500 mostly uninhabited islands off the northwest coast of Scotland

Understanding the Reading

Complete the next three exercises and see how well you understood "The Solitary Reaper."

Exercise 3.7 Multiple-Choice Questions

Answer the following questions about the reading. Circle the letter of your answer.

TIP: Don't try to answer the questions from memory; go back to the text as often as necessary.

1. The "solitary Highland lass" (line 2) is singing
   A. while planting flowers.
   B. while harvesting grain.
   C. in Arabia.
   D. on one of the islands in the Hebrides.

2. The speaker in the poem is curious to know
   A. the girl's name.
   B. where the girl lives.
   C. why no one is helping her with such a heavy task.
   D. why her song sounds so sorrowful.

3. The comparisons the poet makes in stanza 2 show that
   A. the girl had an extraordinary voice.
   B. the girl must have recently had a bad experience.
   C. the poet decided to stop and listen.
   D. the girl's voice was loud enough to fill the entire valley.

4. The poem expresses the idea that
   A. singing while you work makes the time go by faster.
   B. if you are sad, singing can make you feel better.
   C. certain experiences are striking enough to be unforgettable.
   D. farm laborers should not have to work by themselves.

Exercise 3.8 Short-Answer Questions

Respond to the following questions in one to two complete sentences. Go back to the text, as you did on the multiple choice.

5. Describe one of the creatures to which Wordsworth compares the singer. What does this comparison show?

   _____

   _____

   _____

6. According to the speaker, why might the singer be sad?

   _____

   _____

   _____

7. Describe the form of the poem in your own words. How is it structured, where are the rhymes, and how does it flow?

_____

_____

_____

Exercise 3.9 Extending Your Thinking

Respond to the following question in three to four complete sentences. Use details from the text in your answer.

8. Why is this moment a significant event in the speaker's life?

_____

_____

_____

_____

_____

_____

Reading Strategy Lesson
Paraphrasing for Better Comprehension

Throughout your school career, you may be asked to tackle difficult texts like the Joyce excerpt and Wordsworth poem. Paraphrasing is a technique that will help you understand such high-level passages.

What Is Paraphrasing?

When you paraphrase a text, you restate its meaning in different words. When you write a research paper, you know that you are not supposed to copy your research material word-for-word. (If you did, it would be **plagiarism**—stealing someone else's words and passing them off as your own—which has serious consequences.) Instead, you know to restate the material in your own words, or put it in quotation marks.

The same process works for reading difficult material. As you read, you restate the material in language that is easier for you to understand. You may need to paraphrase each sentence or line before you go on to the next. You can even use a "talk to the author" technique to help you keep on task.

On the following page, we'll look at the first paragraph of *A Portrait of the Artist as a Young Man*.

Joyce Writes:	You Think and Paraphrase:
He looked northward towards Howth. The sea had fallen below the line of sea-wrack on the shallow side of the breakwater and already the tide was running out fast along the foreshore.	*OK, he's standing on the beach, and the tide is going out.*
Already one long oval bank of sand lay warm and dry amid the wavelets. Here and there warm isles of sand gleamed above the shallow tide and about the isles and around the long bank and amid the shallow currents of the beach were light-clad gayclad figures, wading and delving.	*He can see some places where the sand is sticking up above the water like small islands. There are people on the beach, dressed in light, bright-colored clothing. They are wading and digging.*

Now here is a stanza from "The Solitary Reaper" and a way you might paraphrase it.

Wordsworth Writes:	You Think and Paraphrase:
No nightingale did ever chant So sweetly to reposing bands Of travelers in some shady haunt Among Arabian sands: A voice so thrilling ne'er was heard In springtime from the cuckoo-bird, Breaking the silence of the seas Among the farthest Hebrides.	*Travelers in the desert who found a shady place to rest and heard a nightingale singing would not have been so impressed. Even a cuckoo-bird singing way out in the Hebrides Islands could not make such a wonderful sound. The girl sang more sweetly than a bird.*

Exercise 3.10 Practice the Reading Strategy with *A Portrait of the Artist as a Young Man*

Here is another paragraph from the Joyce selection, broken down into individual sentences. In the column on the right, paraphrase Joyce's words.

Joyce Writes:	You Think and Paraphrase:
Her image had passed into his soul for ever and no word had broken the holy silence of his ecstasy.	
Her eyes had called him and his soul had leaped at the call.	
To live, to err, to fall, to triumph, to recreate life out of life!	

A wild angel had appeared to him, the
angel of mortal youth and beauty, an
envoy from the fair courts of life, to throw
open before him in an instant of ecstasy
the gates of all the ways of error and glory.

On and on and on and on!

Exercise 3.11 Practice the Reading Strategy with "The Solitary Reaper"

Following is a stanza from "The Solitary Reaper." In the column on the right, paraphrase what Wordsworth is saying. You don't need to rephrase each line. Just write a sentence or two summarizing what this stanza is saying.

Wordsworth Writes: **You Think and Paraphrase:**

Whate'er the theme, the maiden sang
As if her song could have no ending;
I saw her singing at her work,
And o'er the sickle bending.
I listened motionless and still;
And, as I mounted up the hill,
The music in my heart I bore
Long after it was heard no more.

Writing Workshop
The Compare/Contrast Essay

What do the two readings in this chapter have in common? Think about the authors' descriptions.

- Each one describes an attractive young woman.

- Each author compares the girl to a bird to describe her beauty.

Reread this paragraph from *A Portrait of the Artist as a Young Man*, paying close attention to Joyce's portrayal of the girl.

> A girl stood before him in midstream, alone and still, gazing out to sea. She *seemed like one whom magic had changed into the likeness of a strange and beautiful seabird*. Her long slender bare *legs were delicate as a crane's* and pure save where an emerald trail of seaweed had fashioned itself as a sign upon the

flesh. Her thighs, *fuller and soft-hued as ivory*, were bared almost to the hips where the *white fringes of her drawers were like feathering of soft white down*. Her slateblue skirts were kilted boldly about her waist and *dovetailed behind her*. Her *bosom was as a bird's soft and slight, slight and soft as the breast of some darkplumaged dove*. **But her long fair hair was girlish: and girlish, and touched with the wonder of mortal beauty, her face.**

In the italicized phrases, Joyce compares the lovely girl and a bird. The final, boldfaced sentence shows a contrast with the former comparisons. Although the young woman reminded Stephen of a bird, her hair and face were "girlish." Joyce uses these comparisons to help his readers feel as if we are right there on the beach with Stephen, able to see the girl for ourselves.

Comparing and Contrasting in Your Writing

Comparing and contrasting is a useful way to develop an essay. You compare and contrast things all the time, even in your everyday life. For example:

- As you're getting ready for school, you choose between a T-shirt and a sweatshirt. You wore a T-shirt yesterday, and you were too cold. A sweatshirt will be warm enough—but will it be too warm?

- You're looking at the choices of breakfast cereal. You know those Chunky Chocolate Crispy Squares are loaded with sugar, but while the Organic Brown Ricey-Os would be healthier, they taste like Styrofoam packing pellets.

- Should you walk to school today, or see if you can ride with your friend? Walking has health advantages, and lately you've been thinking that your friend's driving might be hazardous to your health.

As you thought about what to wear, what to eat, and how to get to school, you **compared and contrasted**, and made a final decision. When you write a compare/contrast essay, you make a judgment about the things you are comparing. This judgment becomes your thesis statement.

For example, if you compare home cooking with fast food, your thesis statement might read:

> Home cooking is far preferable to fast food because it costs less, tastes better, and is better for you.

The body of your essay shows how you arrived at that conclusion. Your paragraphs might compare and contrast the two in terms of cost, taste, and health benefits.

Ways to Develop a Compare/Contrast Essay

1. Point by Point

When you use this method, you compare or contrast both subjects first on point one, then on point two, and then on point three. Here is a sample outline:

> **Thesis:** Home cooking is far preferable to fast food because it costs less, tastes better, and is better for you.
>
> **Point 1: Cost**
> A. home cooking
> B. fast food
>
> **Point 2: Taste**
> A. home cooking
> B. fast food
>
> **Point 3: Better for You**
> A. home cooking
> B. fast food

Let's examine a sample paragraph on point 3.

> If you can read, you can cook. This means you have control over the ingredients that are in your food. If you want a hamburger, you can purchase lean meat, season it the way you like it, and make sure it is thoroughly cooked. You can add a nice thick slice of tomato and a real piece of lettuce. You can even serve your burger on a healthy whole wheat bun. At a fast-food burger establishment, you can be pretty sure they are not using lean meat. If they were, their hamburgers would not be so greasy. You have no control over how long your hamburger is cooked or how long it sits around under a heat lamp. The lettuce and tomato you get there hardly qualify as vegetables. The tomato slice will probably be so thin and pale it's almost transparent, and the lettuce doesn't look anything like the leafy green stuff they show in their television ads. You can also forget the whole wheat bun.

When you use this method, you should always talk about the subjects *in the same order* in each paragraph. If you start out describing the cost advantages of home cooking in your first body paragraph, then you should start your second body paragraph by writing about home cooking's taste superiority. That is why the sample paragraph starts out talking about home cooking's health benefits.

2. Block Compare and Contrast

Here is a different way of organizing a compare/contrast essay. When you organize your essay using this method, your first body paragraph might discuss the three points regarding home cooking, and the second paragraph the same three points about fast food.

Thesis: Home cooking is far preferable to fast food because it costs less, tastes better, and is better for you.

A. Home Cooking
    1. Cost
    2. Taste
    3. Health benefits

B. Fast Food
    1. Cost
    2. Taste
    3. Health drawbacks

This method is a bit more difficult, because you will still need to connect the two subjects in both paragraphs. For example, in your first paragraph, even though you are talking *mostly* about home cooking, you might include these sentences:

> While fast food is inexpensive, it still costs less to purchase food at the supermarket and cook it at home.

> With so many convenient foods on the market, and so many fast and easy ways to cook them, you can probably put together a delicious meal in less time than it would take you to drive to the nearest burger joint.

Your second paragraph, which is *mostly* about fast food, might include these sentences:

> Fast-food restaurants have tried to create "healthy" menu items, but the calories and fat in their salads can be cut down considerably if you make the same salad at home.

> While it does take time to buy food at the supermarket, you can purchase enough for many meals with just one trip. When you eat fast food, you have to make a new trip every time.

Don't Chop It Up

Whichever organizational pattern you choose, you will need to make smooth transitions, so your reader can follow your argument. You want your essay to flow easily from one sentence to the next, and from one subject to the next. Here are transition words and phrases you can use.

COMPARE	CONTRAST
also	although
both	but
have in common	however
like	in contrast
in the same way	instead of
not only . . . but also	on the contrary
similarly	on the other hand
too	though
while	unlike

Exercise 3.12 Write Your Own Compare/Contrast Essay

Both Joyce and Wordsworth wrote about a moment in time. Write a four- to five-paragraph essay comparing and contrasting the two pieces. (Write at least five paragraphs if you use point-by-point comparison, and four longer paragraphs if you use the block comparison method.)

First, think of three ways the pieces are similar and/or different. Consider both structure and content. Then take out a sheet of paper and plan your essay, using one of the organizational methods you have learned. (Refer to the sample outlines on pages 61 and 62 as needed.) Finally, write your essay.

Grammar Mini-Lesson

Varying Your Sentence Structures with Gerunds

In the last chapter, you learned about participles—words that look like verbs but do not always function like them. Another kind of word that looks like a verb but has additional functions is called a **gerund**.

1. A **gerund** ends in *-ing* and has the characteristics of both a noun and a verb.

    Example: *Running* is good exercise.

    In this sentence, *Running* is a gerund with two functions:
    a. As a noun, *running* is the subject of the sentence and of the verb *is*.
    b. As a verb, *running* expresses action.

2. A **gerund phrase** contains a gerund.

    Example: *Running an office* is not easy.
    a. As a noun, the gerund phrase *Running an office* is the subject of the sentence and of the verb *is*.
    b. As a verb, the gerund *Running* takes the noun *office* as its object.

3. A gerund or gerund phrase functions in all the ways a noun does.

    *   As the **subject of a verb**: <u>Studying</u> *pays*.
                               SUBJ   V

    *   As the **object of a verb**: We *dreaded* <u>losing the game</u>.
                                 V   OBJ

    *   As the **object of a preposition**: Why did he insist *on* <u>doing that</u>?
                                 PREP   OBJ

- As a **predicate noun**: The hardest job *is* <u>getting started</u>.
  V   PRED. N

- As an **appositive**: The last step, <u>checking the answer</u>, is key.
  APPOSITIVE

How Gerunds Help Your Writing

Gerunds can provide you with several ways to vary your sentences, so they do not always sound the same.

1. You can use a gerund to replace an infinitive (*to* + verb).

    Instead of: <u>To err</u> is human. (infinitive)
    You could write: <u>Erring</u> is human. (gerund)

2. You can use a gerund phrase introduced by a preposition to replace a subordinate (dependent) clause.

    Instead of: You can save time <u>if you use the calculator</u>. (subordinate clause)
    You could write: You can save time <u>by using the calculator</u>. (preposition and gerund)

You could also rewrite this sentence by putting the last part of the sentence first. The gerund phrase becomes the subject of the sentence and of the verb *save*.

    You could write: <u>Using the calculator</u> will save you time. (gerund phrase)

3. You can use a gerund phrase introduced by a preposition in place of a participial phrase.

    Instead of: <u>Entering the house</u>, I heard voices. (participial phrase)
    You could write: On <u>entering the house</u>, I heard voices. (gerund phrase; preposition *on*)

Review

Let's review infinitives, participles, and gerunds (collectively known as verbals). The table on the next page compares their uses.

VERBALS		
Type of Verbal	**Use**	**Example**
Infinitive	Noun	*To forgive* is difficult. *To forgive* is the subject of the verb *is*.
Gerund	Noun	*Forgiving* is difficult. *Forgiving* is the subject of the verb *is*.
	Expressing action like a verb	*Forgiving* expresses action.
Participle	Adjective	*Forgiving* my sister for ruining my sweater, I suggested we go shopping together. *Forgiving* is an adjective modifying the pronoun *I*.

Exercise 3.13 Practice Rewriting Sentences with Gerunds

Replace each italicized expression with a gerund or gerund phrase. Add an introductory preposition to the phrase if necessary. Write the complete sentence on the line.

Example: *To know you* is a privilege.
    Knowing you is a privilege.

1. *To paint* the house is expensive.

2. Telephone us *when you arrive at the airport.*

3. *To see* is *to believe.*

4. *To be overconfident* is a mistake.

5. *If you delay*, you will miss the bus.

6. *When I went over her notes*, I found two errors.

7. *As I was leaving*, I forgot my watch.

8. We were relieved *when we found you at home.*

_____

9. *To wait longer* would be useful.

_____

10. *To meet you* was a pleasure.

_____

Polish Your Spelling
Troublesome Consonants

Sometimes it's hard to tell if a word has one or two consonants. Try inserting the missing letters:

Don't read my journal out loud; I'll be emba__a__ed!

Answer: Embarrassed has two r's *and two* s's. *I'll be* <u>embarrassed</u>!

The strategy: If a word has troublesome consonants, put it into a group with other words of similar difficulty and review the group until you have mastered it.

- **The 2 + 2 Group:** Every word in this group has a troublesome *doubled* consonant and, farther along in the word, another troublesome *doubled* consonant.

emba*rr*a*ss*	po*ss*e*ss*
a*ss*a*ss*inate	mi*ss*pe*ll*
a*cc*o*mm*odate	a*gg*re*ss*ion
Te*nn*e*ss*ee	a*cc*e*ss*
co*mm*i*tt*ee	a*ss*e*ss*ment

- **The 2 + 1 Group:** Every word in this group has a troublesome *doubled* consonant and, farther along in the word, a troublesome *single* consonant.

bu*ll*e*t*in	bu*ff*a*l*o
mo*cc*a*s*in	a*pp*e*t*ite
a*pp*a*r*el	a*cc*e*l*erate
o*cc*a*s*ion	va*cc*i*n*ate
a*cc*u*m*ulate	i*ll*i*t*erate

- **The 1 + 2 Group:** Every word in this group has a troublesome *single* consonant and, farther along in the word, a troublesome *doubled* consonant.

ne*c*e*ss*ary	ta*r*i*ff*
be*g*i*nn*ing	pa*r*a*ll*el
sa*t*e*ll*ite	to*m*o*rr*ow
re*b*e*ll*ion	Ca*r*i*bb*ean
re*c*o*mm*end	she*r*i*ff*

Exercise 3.14 Practice the Spelling Patterns for Consonants

Insert the missing letters. (*HINT: Up to four are missing from each word.*)

1. I ate little; my ap____tite was poor.
2. Use the front entrance; there is no ac____s from the rear.
3. Don't let rubbish ac____mulate.
4. Are you on the com____tee?
5. The sher____f arrived with his deputy.
6. What did she rec____mend?
7. If you started the fight, you are guilty of ag____sion.
8. We are approaching a town; do not ac____lerate.
9. Are the lines par____lel?
10. Come again tom____row.
11. No deposit is nec ____sary.
12. Put it on the bul____tin board.
13. Who tried to as____sinate the monarch?
14. It is beg____ning to snow.
15. A moc____sin slipped off my foot.
16. The motel cannot ac____odate so many people.
17. It's too warm to wear such bulky ap____rel.
18. The moon is a sat____lite.
19. Memphis is in Ten____see.
20. How did the reb____lion begin?

Unit One Review

A. Match each word with its definition.

DEFINITION	WORD
_____ 1. a contorted expression showing pain or fear	a. legendary
_____ 2. an impulsive idea	b. protégé
_____ 3. to worry anxiously	c. eloquence
_____ 4. a seawall to keep a beach from washing away	d. grimace
_____ 5. subject to sudden change	e. loom
_____ 6. widely known	f. notion
_____ 7. skill in speaking	g. precarious
_____ 8. someone guided by a more experienced person	h. delve
_____ 9. to come into view	i. breakwater
_____ 10. to probe further into something	j. brood

B. Match each word with its synonym.

SYNONYM	WORD
_____ 11. rest	a. allocate
_____ 12. filth	b. chasm
_____ 13. creek	c. excursion
_____ 14. messenger	d. aghast
_____ 15. appealing	e. repose
_____ 16. trickery	f. rivulet
_____ 17. designate	g. squalor
_____ 18. outing	h. subterfuge
_____ 19. stunned	i. envoy
_____ 20. ravine	j. engaging

C. Match each word with its antonym.

ANTONYM	WORD
_____ 21. orderly	a. avant-garde
_____ 22. jokingly	b. benign
_____ 23. superficial	c. genteel
_____ 24. joyful	d. duplicity
_____ 25. mainstream	e. raucous
_____ 26. harmful	f. histrionic
_____ 27. impolite	g. defiance
_____ 28. unemotional	h. solemnly
_____ 29. submission	i. plaintive
_____ 30. honesty	j. profound

Grammar Review

Each sentence or group of sentences may contain an error in an underlined word or phrase. Circle the letter of the error or, if there is no error, mark D.

1. I <u>had just began</u> my homework when my annoying little
        A

   brother <u>barged into</u> the room <u>and tried</u> to distract me. <u>No error</u>
          B   C   D

2. José <u>has been struggling</u> in studio art, his least favorite subject,
               A

   <u>but you like drawing</u>, so <u>you has had</u> a much easier time in that
          B   C

   class. <u>No error</u>
         D

3. I confess that <u>I have ate</u> all of the cookies and <u>have drunk</u>
               A   B

   <u>all of the milk.</u> <u>No error</u>
        C   D

4. <u>She has sang</u> that song <u>before, but</u> I cannot remember <u>what it is</u>
      A   B   C

   <u>called or where</u> I first heard it. <u>No error</u>
        C   D

5. <u>He knew</u> <u>he had saw</u> that <u>before, but</u> he wasn't sure where.
      A   B   C

   <u>No error</u>
     D

6. Once <u>you've written down</u> your answer <u>and did the extra</u>

                A   B

    credit, please <u>turn in</u> your test booklet. <u>No error</u>

      B   C   D

7. I'm sorry <u>I broke</u> your pencil; I <u>didn't realize</u> it was <u>your lucky</u>

               A   B   C

    one. <u>No error</u>

    C   D

8. <u>I have brung</u> that issue up to them in the past, but <u>they've never</u>

      A   B

    <u>seemed</u> willing to <u>discuss it</u>. <u>No error</u>

     B   C   D

9. <u>Did you see</u> <u>what I just seen</u>? <u>Have you ever seen</u> anything that

        A   B   C

    completely ridiculous? <u>No error</u>

                     D

10. I am impressed <u>that she ran the mile</u> in less than seven minutes.

                     A

    <u>Has she ever did</u> that before? The other members of the team

         B

    <u>are not</u> that fast! <u>No error</u>

     C   D

Spelling Review

1. Adding Suffixes

Add the suffix shown and write the new word correctly on the line.

1. profound + ly   _____

2. conceive + ed   _____

3. eliminate + ation   _____

4. observe + er   _____

5. inquire + ing   _____

6. imagine + ation   _____

7. discern + ible   _____

8. conceive + able   _____

9. trouble + ed   _____

10. modify + ing   _____

2. Identifying Base Words

Write the base of each word on the line.

1. remarkable _____
2. disappearance _____
3. unopened _____
4. planning _____
5. permitted _____
6. classy _____
7. improperly _____
8. flattened _____
9. hottest _____
10. inescapable _____

3. Spelling Words with Troublesome Consonants

Insert the missing letters in the space provided.

1. A birthday is a happy oc____sion.
2. We have no more; this is all we pos____s.
3. Is there a protective tar____f on imports?
4. I never saw a buf____lo herd.
5. Have you ever been to the Car____bean?
6. Imagine our embar____sment!
7. Reservations are unnec____sary.
8. The as____sment on the house was raised $500.
9. It is expensive to vac____nate a whole population.
10. The as____sination plot was discovered in time.

Writing Review

Choose one of the following topics. On a separate sheet of paper, plan and draft your essay. Then revise and edit your draft, and write your final copy. Be sure to identify your audience, purpose, and task before you begin planning.

> Write an essay comparing and contrasting the epiphanies experienced by Aunt Rachel in *A House Unlocked* and by Maeve Brennan in "The Clever One."
>
> OR
>
> Think about an epiphany you have experienced—a realization that changed your life or the way you look at life. Write a personal narrative describing your experience. Include descriptive details to help paint the scene for your readers.

Unit One Extension Activities

 SPEAK/LISTEN

Stage a Surprising Moment

In "The Clever One," Maeve Brennan tells how she learned something surprising about her sister. Working in a group of three or four, create a story about a time someone learned something unexpected about a close friend or relative. Instead of writing it as a narrative, however, write it as a short three- to five-minute play, and heighten the drama of the scene. (You can make it either humorous or serious.) Don't forget to include stage directions. Act it out for the class.

EXPLORE

Emotions in Poetry

In his *Preface to Lyrical Ballads*, a collection of verse written with Samuel Taylor Coleridge, Wordsworth defined poetry as "emotion recollected in tranquility." Find and read another one of Wordsworth's poems (available on many poetry and Wordsworth-specific Web sites). Then, thinking about both "The Solitary Reaper" and the new one you chose, try to determine what Wordsworth might have meant by that definition of poetry. Compare your answer with a partner's.

WRITE

Stream of Consciousness

Try writing a description using *stream of consciousness*, the technique James Joyce uses in *A Portrait of an Artist as a Young Man*. Close your eyes and picture yourself somewhere with a lot of action. It might be a park, a busy street, or your school's hallways at class change time. As images come to you, write them down and tie them together as if they are rambling thoughts. Write at least three full paragraphs this way, describing the scene.

CONNECT

Literature and Social Awareness

In *A House Unlocked*, Penelope Lively describes how she became aware of the poor conditions for children in other parts of England. How is child poverty still a problem in the world? With a partner, go online to World Bank Poverty Net (or another database that shows poverty statistics, such as the U.S. Census Bureau, UNICEF, or the UN's NetAid site). Choose a region and research poverty in that area. In your notes, complete the following tasks: 1. Give an overview of the problem (include statistics). 2. What poverty reduction strategies are in place? 3. Do you think these strategies are sufficient? Why or why not? Share your findings with the class.

UNIT TWO

Relationships

Chapter Four

Prereading Guide

Words to know and ideas to consider before you jump into the reading.

A. Essential Vocabulary

Word	Meaning	Typical Use
abstracted (*adj*) ab-STRAK-ted	removed, distracted	I told him the address, but I could tell he was *abstracted* and didn't hear me.
austerity (*n*) aw-STAIR-uh-tee	lack of luxury; simplicity; sternness	I'm on a program of extreme *austerity* to save money for college.
fortuitous (*adj*) for-TOO-i-tuss	happening in an unplanned but positive way; fortunate	The *fortuitous* combination of chocolate and cookie dough resulted in the creation of Toll House cookies.
impeccable (*adj*) im-PECK-uh-bul	in line with the highest standards; faultless	Her German is *impeccable*; she sounds like a native-born speaker.
implore (*v*) im-PLOR	to ask desperately or earnestly of someone to take an action; beseech	At least five times a day, Casey's mother *implores* her to turn down her music.
nuptial (*adj*) NUP-shul	1. relating to a marriage or wedding 2. (*n*) a wedding or marriage (usually plural)	The *nuptial* day was drawing closer. Exactly what day will the blessed *nuptials* take place?
recalcitrant (*adj*) re-CAL-si-trunt	stubborn and uncontrollable; problematic	The child was *recalcitrant* and kept throwing his toys, despite several warnings from his mother.
requisite (*adj*) REK-wi-zit	1. required and essential; indispensable 2. (*n*) something that is essential or required	She was wearing the *requisite* school uniform. Do you have all the *requisites* to get into that college?
rigorous (*adj*) RIG-ur-us	unyieldingly strict; rigid	We learn a lot because our teacher has *rigorous* standards.
summon (*v*) SUM-un	to call up or muster; to gather	Zoë *summoned* her nerve and asked him to the dance.

B. Vocabulary Practice

Exercise 4.1   Sentence Completion

Using your new vocabulary knowledge, choose the best way to complete the following sentences. Circle the letter of your answer.

1. On the day of the concert, the choir members were all wearing the _____ white shirt and black pants.
   A. nuptial
   B. requisite

2. No matter how often Mr. Shaw implores them, some students _____.
   A. sit quietly and listen
   B. will not pay attention

3. Jenna had to summon all her courage to _____.
   A. climb the rock wall
   B. play the video game

4. Although Kirsten is from _____, she speaks impeccable English.
   A. another country
   B. England

5. The angry property owners enforced the noise-nuisance rules _____.
   A. leniently
   B. rigorously

6. I _____ I did well on that test; I was abstracted.
   A. think
   B. don't think

7. On their nuptial day, they became _____.
   A. man and wife
   B. graduates

8. Spending all your money on clothes _____ a sign of austerity.
   A. is not
   B. is

9. It was _____ that we needed a new car when Mrs. Rubin was selling hers for a great price.
   A. unfortunate
   B. fortuitous

10. My little brother is recalcitrant; Mom is frustrated with his lack of _____.
    A. skills
    B. manners

Exercise 4.2 Using Fewer Words

Replace the italicized words with a single word from the following list. The first one has been done for you.

rigorous   requisite   impeccably   implore   summon

abstracted   recalcitrance   nuptial   austere   fortuitous

1. The army pulled back long enough to *call up* more troops.

   1.___summon___

2. I told him three times, but he was *not paying attention.*

   2._____

3. The actual *wedding* ceremony is at the church.

   3._____

4. Tired of staying at places that were *lacking in luxury,* we checked into an ornate hotel on Fifth Avenue.

   4._____

5. "I see you're wearing the *required and essential* pearls with your classy black dress," my mother's friend told her jokingly.

   5._____

6. "It's true," she replied. "I am dressed *in line with the highest standards.*"

   6._____

7. "Please, Dad! I *desperately beg* you to let me go out with him!"

   7._____

8. Every morning before school, Joe goes to the gym for a workout that is *unyielding and strict.*

   8._____

9. It was *unplanned but had a positive outcome* that we met.

   9._____

10. His *unbending stubbornness* makes him hard to get along with.

   10._____

Exercise 4.3 Synonyms and Antonyms

Fill in the blanks in column A with the required synonyms or antonyms, selecting them from column B. (Remember: A *synonym* is a word similar in meaning to another word. *Autumn* and *fall* are synonyms. An *antonym* is a word opposite in meaning to another word. *Beginning* and *ending* are antonyms.)

	A	B
_____	1. synonym for *beg*	impeccable
_____	2. antonym for *attentive*	rigorous
_____	3. antonym for *lenient*	requisite
_____	4. antonym for *elaborate*	implore
_____	5. antonym for *unfortunate*	summon
_____	6. synonym for *gather up*	recalcitrant
_____	7. synonym for *marriage*	fortuitous
_____	8. antonym for *imperfect*	austere
_____	9. antonym for *controllable*	nuptials
_____	10. antonym for *unnecessary*	abstracted

C. Journal Freewrite

Before you begin the reading on the next page, take out a journal or sheet of paper and spend some time responding to one of the following prompts.

TIP: Don't worry about grammar and spelling; just write what comes to mind. The purpose of freewriting is to explore ideas, not to produce a polished work.

> Think of a time you did something on your own (for example, ate a meal by yourself or went to a mall alone), and everyone else seemed to be with friends. How did you feel? Does being alone have to mean being unhappy?
>
> OR
>
> Think about a time when someone very close to you (a friend, sibling, or parent) moved away or got married, affecting the amount of time you could spend with him or her. How did you adjust to the change?

Chasing the Evanescent Glow

by Nuala O'Faolain

About the Author
Nuala O'Faolain (1940–) grew up in her native Ireland with seven siblings. There, she wrote book reviews, a column for the *Irish Times*, and presentations for radio broadcasts. She also studied at Oxford University in England and lectured at University College in Dublin. In 1999, she came to the United States for a residency at Yaddo, an artists' colony. She has written several memoirs and a novel. In this article, O'Faolain shares her view of personal happiness.

When I think about happiness, it is not an image I see, though I know the ads that show perfectly matched children hugging their toys or an <u>impeccable</u> couple strolling on the beach at an exclusive resort or a silver-haired pair holding hands beside a golf cart. My happiness moves. Where I live in the west of Ireland, often in the evening a bar of golden light blazes along the horizon of the ocean. Then small clouds, ragged and wistful, drift across the radiance and obscure it and thicken, and that's how the dusk comes. There's nothing I can do to make the gold arrive, and of its nature it dissolves. After dusk departs, the dark is not just dark. It contains the memory of what it was. And that's what I think happiness is like—radiant like the last of the sun, but always in the process of disappearing.

In the afterglow I hurry across the grass to the shed to fill my basket with sods of turf[1] for the fire. The dog throws herself in front of me, quivering at the amazing possibility that we're going for a walk—not one dog molecule of skepticism kept back to protect herself with. She lives entirely in the present moment. But happiness is conscious of the before and after—it is the brimming water in the bowl of a fountain that the slightest disturbance will spill. On my way to sleep I'll remember with satisfaction how high the turf was piled. If a rain shower spinning in from the ocean rattles the window, I'll feel how warm I am, and safe. I'll count the abundance of food and fuel and folded linen within my sturdy walls, and even though I'm on my own and my body is lonely—in the ads happy people are never alone—there are times when satisfaction grows to a state that is like a dense calm. The minute dot that is myself will be in balance for a while with the great universe.

This happiness was born back when I was small. It's the payback for years of want. If I had always had enough, what would it mean to me to have enough now?

Some pattern of light and shade was laid down, once upon a time, in that place that is both heart and mind where

---

[1]squares of peat or other vegetable matter from the top surface of the ground

the state of happiness lurks, and the pattern comes with each person on the crooked path out of the past and is part of their unique being. And therefore what makes us happy can divide us from each other, though the myth insists that it unites us. One person has found completion in looking into the eyes of a partner across the head of their newborn child, but the partner wants to sing an aria[2] as perfectly as it can be sung. Another person, exhausted with pleasure, prolongs a tender and grateful kiss to a lover; the lover is restlessly waiting to be released to check the stock market. Even the classic happy experiences—the letter that says the job is yours, the first crocus piercing the snow, an enemy routed, a candidate elected, a horse storming home to win by a neck at 10–1—have something solitary at their core. The admen pretend that happiness is a package, the better to sell it. But there is no warm, shared bath out there. Happiness is not cozy. It gleams most vividly against a background of black.

Because nobody can <u>summon</u> it up, nobody can say that it will never come again. But nobody can stop it from disappearing either. From one second to the next my rich balance abandons me. Rain streams down the window. I look up at the ceiling, my eyes <u>imploring</u> the dark. Is being happy like a current that disturbs the seabed? I was floating, and then anxiety swam up from underneath, and discontent, and regret. The old voice started crying again, Why am I not loved?

The waiting for the next time begins.

My great-grandfather told how during the Great Famine,[3] when everyone around his part of the country was starving, a crow flew past with a potato in its beak, which meant it was a good potato, not diseased, and men, women and children set off after the crow, stumbling into ditches, falling, jostling each other to be the one to get the food if the bird dropped it. That's what the pursuit of happiness is like. This is one of life's mysteries there's no coming to terms with—that as long as we have breath we have no choice but to go running after happiness, our poor faces strained upward as if we cannot get enough of it, as if happy is what we were meant to be, as if without happiness we would starve.

As we would.

———

[2]a solo voice piece sung in an opera or other elaborate production
[3]In the 1840s, Ireland's staple national food crop, the potato, failed. At least one million people died of starvation or disease. Many Irish immigrated to the United States during that time.

Understanding the Reading

Complete the next three exercises and see how well you understood "Chasing the Evanescent Glow."

Exercise 4.4   Multiple-Choice Questions

Answer the following questions about the reading. Circle the letter of your answer.

TIP: Don't try to answer the questions from memory; go back to the text as often as necessary.

1. The difference between the author's happiness and her dog's happiness is that the
   A. dog is happy only while it's going for a walk.
   B. author is happy only when she watches sunsets.
   C. dog's happiness is now; the author's includes before and after.
   D. author is happy only when she is with other people.

2. When the author says that happiness "gleams most vividly against a background of black," she means that
   A. stars are prettiest when there is no moon to lighten the sky.
   B. happy moments are most appreciated by those who have also been sad.
   C. Irish people who experienced the Great Famine knew the meaning of happiness.
   D. nobody can stop happiness from disappearing.

3. The story about the Great Famine is included to make the point that
   A. people were so hungry they tried to steal food from birds.
   B. a candidate who wins an election is not guaranteed happiness.
   C. your horse may win this race, but it might lose the next.
   D. our desperate search for happiness is like the starving people's pursuit of the crow.

4. O'Faolain's main message is that
   A. people need other people to be happy.
   B. everyone's happiness is different, and we are always looking for it.
   C. as long as you have a comfortable house and food to eat, that should be enough.
   D. you shouldn't pay attention to advertising's depiction of happiness.

Exercise 4.5 Short-Answer Questions

Respond to the following questions in one to two complete sentences. Go back to the text, as you did on the multiple choice.

5. According to O'Faolain, why doesn't happiness unite people?

    _____

    _____

    _____

6. What does O'Faolain suggest when she compares happiness to water in a fountain (paragraph 2)?

    _____

    _____

    _____

7. What makes the author feel satisfied in life?

    _____

    _____

    _____

Exercise 4.6 Extending Your Thinking

Respond to the following question in three to four complete sentences. Use details from the text in your answer.

8. According to O'Faolain, to what extent is personal happiness in our control? Is there anything we can do to feel satisfied in life?

    _____

    _____

    _____

    _____

    _____

    _____

from The Bay of Angels

by Anita Brookner

About the Author

Anita Brookner (1928–) was an art historian and professor for many years before her first novel was published in 1981. The child of Polish-Jewish immigrants, Brookner has said she has always felt herself to be an outsider. Her novels usually feature characters who attempt to change their lives into what they expect they should be. She won England's most important literary prize, the Booker, and her work has been compared to that of Henry James, Jane Austen, and the Brontë sisters.

My mother was married at Chelsea Register Office in a ceremony that was <u>rigorously</u> secular.[1] This seemed to me entirely appropriate, for, despite the almost miraculous manner in which it had come about, this union did not have the appearance of one blessed by God. It looked, unfortunately, as if advantage had been taken by both parties, of wealth being exchanged for comeliness[2] as in some dire Mannerist allegory, Simon wept copiously,[3] which was something I had not anticipated; my mother, on the other hand, seemed composed, almost <u>abstracted</u>. Though there was undoubtedly love of a sort it was not the sort that made an appeal to one of my age, for although it satisfied the requirements of legend it made me aware of what all the stories left out, namely the facts of what happened next. The stories had ended on the highest possible note, whereas what they should have indicated was the life that followed. The <u>nuptial</u> arrangements made me slightly uneasy, as did the wedding itself. It was not that I objected to its sparseness: that was acceptable. Anything more elaborate would have been unwelcome. My contact with religion came mainly from services in the school chapel, and I instinctively rejected all the warnings, the penalties and restrictions, as well as the childlike petitions[4] for forgiveness and the equally childlike promises of rewards, always postponed. If I sometimes felt unconsoled, in a strange uncomfortable way, it was because not all changes are welcome; even in the midst of our good fortune I had a feeling of loss. I knew that I would never lose my mother, but I also knew that she would not be at home to greet me in the early evenings, and that I should have to rely on my own company for a good part of the time.

The physical emptiness of the flat[5] I had left that morning did not frighten me, nor did I dread going back to it, but I began to see it in a new light, was struck anew by the loneli-

---

[1]not pertaining to spiritual or holy things
[2]beauty
[3]profusely
[4]prayers
[5]apartment

ness my mother must have felt—a loneliness compounded by the silence of the street and the yawning creak of her bedroom door, when, tired of standing at the window, she would rest on her bed in the afternoons, for the sake of the relief she would feel when the interval for such matters was safely past, and she could make tea and prepare for my homecoming. Now she would have a different home and there would be a different kind of preparation. I was a little disturbed by this vision, for my mother's previous life had been so singular,[6] in all senses of the word, and so dedicated, that it had left its trace on my own conduct, and for a brief moment of sadness I wondered whether I should now be obliged to take my leave of a certain way of life which had hitherto seemed to me to be lacking in nothing.

The <u>austerity</u> of the wedding ceremony was emphasized, even thrown into relief, by the hilarity of the girls, and even of the boys,[7] whose acquaintance Simon was and who thus <u>fortuitously</u> provided the link between all the participants. The boys were hearty and extremely enthusiastic, having adopted a manner which probably served them on all social occasions, particularly those in which the protagonists were not too well known to them. The girls were, of course, splendidly turned out, but their hands brought out delicate handkerchiefs at the right moment, and all in all provided the scenic change that turned the whole thing into a rite of passage. The wedding breakfast took place in Onslow Square, where a hired butler and waiters moved suavely among the guests, obliging them all to be on their best behaviour. Simon and my mother were to spend the night at the Ritz in Paris, a convention already out of fashion, and to go on to Venice, where they would stay for a fortnight,[8] returning home by way of France. This would be my mother's first introduction to his house, some miles inland from Nice: it would be a politeness to show her what would be her future home, to greet the *gardienne*,[9] Mme Delgado, to give a few discreet instructions, and to keep the visit tactfully short. Two nights at the Negresco were to follow, and then they would be home.

In some strange way I did not altogether believe in this homecoming. The champagne at the reception had left me with a headache and when I returned to Edith Grove I was newly aware of absence. We were now physically separated by more than a few streets, and soon she—they—would be out of reach. 'My home will be yours too,' Simon had said, but this was difficult to believe. I could not find the <u>requisite</u> image by which this future could be called to mind. I was landlocked, had been abroad only on school trips, had valued the fellowship of my friends rather more than my surroundings, and was indeed vaguely frightened by the prospect of a new life, however desirable. My mother had come to the door with me and said, 'You've got all the telephone numbers? And the girls will look in on you to see that you are eating properly.'

---

[6]individual; existing apart
[7]in this story, grown adults are called "the girls" and "the boys" by Simon
[8]two weeks
[9]housekeeper

'I am seventeen,' I had reassured her. By this time we were both in tears.

'I know, darling, I know.'

'Anne, the car is waiting,' Simon had reminded her. 'No more tears, now. This is a new life starting for all of us.' A wallet of money found its way into my pocket.

'Goodbye, dears,' sang Millie. '*Bon voyage!* We'll take you home, Zoë. Unless you'd like to come back with us? Yes, that might be best.'

But no, I had said. I'd been invited out. This was untrue. I wanted to see how I would fare on my own, promising myself a hot bath, my dressing-gown, routine comforts. This would be my first experience of what might be a tremendous ordeal, as I knew it to be for others, neighbours of ours who turned out bravely for unnecessary errands, aware all the time of their return to an empty house. On this particular evening I was too tired to feel anything but gratitude for the quiet street, for the dark flat, even for the sound of a <u>recalcitrant</u> tap dripping in the kitchen. My mother had seemed to think that I needed comforting: perhaps I did. Even a happy ending cannot always banish a sense of longing.

Understanding the Reading

Complete the next three exercises and see how well you understood the excerpt from *The Bay of Angels*.

Exercise 4.7   Multiple-Choice Questions

Answer the following questions about the reading. Circle the letter of your answer.

TIP: Don't try to answer the questions from memory; go back to the text as often as necessary.

1. When Zoë says that the union between her mother and Simon looked "as if advantage had been taken by both parties, of wealth being exchanged for comeliness," she means that
   A. Simon gave Anne money to marry him.
   B. one is more wealthy, and one is attractive.
   C. one's wealth makes up for the other's unattractiveness.
   D. Anne and Simon signed an agreement regarding finances before the wedding.

2. As Zoë thinks about her mother's marriage, she realizes that the fairy-tale endings of stories she had seen and read are
   A. realistic only for younger couples.
   B. realistic only if the couple is married in a church.
   C. less important than what comes after the happy ending.
   D. just as realistic for her mother as for anyone.

3. From the way Simon treats Zoë, it seems he will most likely
   A. try hard to be like a father to her.
   B. give her money to stay out of his way.
   C. make her feel unwelcome at his home.
   D. be pleasant to her so he can be with her mother.

4. Although Zoë wants to stay at the flat alone while her mother is gone, on her first night she
   A. is terrified of every sound.
   B. is angry at her mother for leaving her.
   C. realizes what it is like for others who live alone.
   D. wishes she had gone to France with her mother and Simon.

Exercise 4.8   Short-Answer Questions

Respond to the following questions in one to two complete sentences. Go back to the text, as you did on the multiple choice.

5. When Simon tells Zoë that his home will be her home, why does she find that hard to believe?

   _____

   _____

   _____

6. What is the point of "unnecessary errands" (last paragraph)?

   _____

   _____

   _____

7. Overall, how does the narrator cope with change? Explain.

   _____

   _____

   _____

Exercise 4.9   Extending Your Thinking

Respond to the following question in three to four complete sentences. Use details from the text in your answer.

8. What might Brookner be saying about the link between happiness and relationships?

   _____

   _____

   _____

   _____

   _____

   _____

Reading Strategy Lesson
Determining the Main Idea and Details

Figuring out the main idea of a text—whether you're reading non-fiction, like "Chasing the Evanescent Glow," or fiction, like *The Bay of Angels*—will greatly aid your comprehension. Simply defined, the main idea is the most important point in a piece of literature, an article, or an essay. When you are trying to identify the main idea, keep asking yourself, "What is this mostly about?" In addition, use the following four strategies.

1. Look for a word or phrase that is repeated several times. In "Chasing the Evanescent Glow," for example, O'Faolain repeats the word *happiness* and also makes several references to darkness and light.

2. Look for important details and ideas. Try to distinguish them from the unimportant ones. To explain why she thinks happiness divides people, O'Faolain gives an example of a lover who is distracted by thoughts of the stock market.

3. Look for topic sentences of paragraphs. A topic sentence may come at the beginning, in the middle, or at the end of a paragraph, but it will tie together the ideas in that paragraph and give you clues to the main idea. O'Faolain introduces her topic in the first paragraph, when she states that her happiness "moves."

4. Look at the title. It is often—though not always—a clue to the main idea. For example, the title "Chasing the Evanescent Glow" gives you a clue that the article will be about the search for something bright and fleeting. As you read on, you'll discover what O'Faolain means by "glow"—happiness.

Exercise 4.10 Practice the Reading Strategy

Read each paragraph. Then list the main idea on the first line and at least two details on the lines below.

Fruits and Vegetables for Better Health

1. Fruits and vegetables should be key parts of your daily diet. Everyone needs five to nine daily servings of fruits and vegetables for the nutrients they contain and for general good health.

Main idea: _____

    Detail 1: _____

    Detail 2: _____

2. While nutrition and health may be reasons you eat certain fruits and vegetables, there are many other reasons why you choose the ones you do. Perhaps it is because of taste, or physical

characteristics such as crunchiness, juiciness, or bright colors. You may eat some fruits and vegetables because of fond memories—like watermelon or corn at cookouts, your mom's green bean casserole, or tomatoes your dad brought in from the backyard garden. Or you may simply like them because most are quick to prepare and easy to eat.

Main idea: _____

    Detail 1: _____

    Detail 2: _____

Let's look at the **title** of the article. In this case, it is a good clue to the main idea of the article. You can infer that the article is about eating fruits and vegetables to be healthier. But what if the title were simply "Fruits and Vegetables"? It might be about how to grow them, how to choose fresh ones, or how many nutrients they have. To be sure of the main idea of the article, you would have to continue reading.

Did you find the **topic sentence** in paragraph 1? It tells you the main idea of the paragraph. The topic sentence is the first sentence in the paragraph. The important details are underlined in the passage that follows. Even though this paragraph is brief, it contains a main idea and some important details. There are no unimportant details in this paragraph:

> *Fruits and vegetables should be key parts of your daily diet.* Everyone needs <u>five to nine daily servings</u> of fruits and vegetables for the <u>nutrients</u> they contain and for <u>general good health</u>.

How about paragraph 2? Did you find the main idea and details?

> While nutrition and health may be reasons you eat certain fruits and vegetables, there are *many other reasons why you choose the ones you do*. Perhaps it is because of <u>taste</u>, or <u>physical characteristics</u> such as crunchiness, juiciness, or bright colors. You may eat some fruits and vegetables because of <u>fond memories</u>—like watermelon or corn at cookouts, your mom's green bean casserole, or tomatoes your dad brought in from the backyard garden. Or you may simply like them because <u>most are quick to prepare and easy to eat</u>.

This paragraph is mostly about the reasons you prefer some fruits and vegetables to others. The most important details are underlined, but other details in the paragraph serve as examples. For instance, the author mentions crunchiness, juiciness, and bright colors as examples of physical characteristics of fruits and vegetables. Watermelon, corn, green bean casserole, and tomatoes are examples that help you understand what the author means by "fond memories." These are details, but they are not as important as the underlined ones. Look at the sample outline of this paragraph on the next page.

Paragraph 2: Many reasons for different choices
   A. taste
   B. physical characteristics
      1. crunchiness
      2. juiciness
      3. bright colors
   C. fond memories
      1. watermelon and corn at cookouts
      2. Mom's green bean casserole
      3. tomatoes Dad grew in the garden
   D. most are easy and quick to prepare

Exercise 4.11 Apply the Strategy to Complete an Outline

Continue reading the article that you started in Exercise 4.10. On the outline that follows, list main ideas next to the roman numerals, and details on lines A and B. Add the less important details on the numbered lines.

3. Fruits and vegetables give you many of the nutrients that you need: vitamins, minerals, dietary fiber, water, and healthful phytochemicals. Some are sources of vitamin A, while others are rich in vitamin C, folate, or potassium. Almost all fruits and vegetables are naturally low in fat and calories, and none have cholesterol. All of these healthful characteristics may protect you from getting chronic diseases, such as heart disease, stroke, and some types of cancer.

Main idea: _____

   A. Detail 1: _____
      1. _____
      2. _____

   B. Detail 2: _____
      1. _____
      2. _____

4. The most important thing is that you eat fruits and vegetables regularly. You don't have to like all varieties; you just need to find some that you really enjoy. If you're not a fan of the more common fruits like apples and bananas, try mangoes, papayas, pomegranates, or kiwis. Go to the grocery store and try some new varieties of vegetables as well. If you like spinach, experiment with other leafy greens such as kale and Swiss chard. With such a large selection of fruits and vegetables from which to choose, it should be easy to find some favorites. Then make sure to include them in your daily diet. Add fruits to your breakfast cereal, include fruits and vegetables with your lunch (many varieties, such as baby carrots and grape tomatoes, are very easy to take on the go), and

don't forget about them again at dinnertime. Getting into good habits now will pay off in the future.

Main idea: _____

    A. Detail 1: _____

        1. _____

        2. _____

    B. Detail 2: _____

        1. _____

        2. _____

Writing Workshop
Supporting Your Statements with Quotations

Suppose you have just been given this writing assignment:

> H. Jackson Brown Jr., author of *Life's Little Instruction Book*, said, "People take different roads seeking fulfillment and happiness. Just because they're not on your road doesn't mean they've gotten lost." Would Nuala O'Faolain agree with him? Write an essay explaining what her stance would most likely be. Support your statements with quotations from "Chasing the Evanescent Glow."

1. First you need to analyze the prompt. Since no **audience** is stated, you should assume you are writing the essay for a teacher or other well-educated person or group of people.

2. Next, you need to read the prompt to determine your **purpose**. It looks like you'll have to decide how Nuala O'Faolain would feel about Brown's statement, and then prove that you are correct. The prompt even tells you to *support your statements with details from "Chasing the Evanescent Glow."*

3. Exactly what, then, is your **task**? The answer to that also lies directly in the prompt: *Write an essay explaining what her* [Nuala O'Faolain's] *stance would most likely be.*

4. Suppose you determine that O'Faolain would agree with Brown's statement. Good. You've got your first sentence practically written for you:

> *Nuala O'Faolain would most likely agree with H. Jackson Brown's statement, "People take different roads seeking fulfillment and happiness. Just because they're not on your road doesn't mean they've gotten lost."*

5. Now that you've stated what you are going to prove, you need some **quotations** from the article to support your opinion. These quotations will serve as your **supporting details**.

Choosing the Best Quotations to Support Your Argument

As you look back at the article, you should do so with an eye for the most appropriate quotations to use. Let's look at the very first sentence:

> When I think about happiness, it is not an image I see, though I know the ads that show perfectly matched children hugging their toys or an impeccable couple strolling on the beach at an exclusive resort or a silver-haired pair holding hands beside a golf cart.

This is a useful quotation, because it shows that O'Faolain is aware of the depiction that happy people are "supposed to be" with other happy people. In fact, you can work this quotation into the next sentence of your introductory paragraph:

> *Nuala O'Faolain would most likely agree with H. Jackson Brown's statement, "People take different roads seeking fulfillment and happiness. Just because they're not on your road doesn't mean they've gotten lost." Like most of us, she has seen hundreds of advertisements that show people together: "perfectly matched children," "an impeccable couple," or a "silver-haired pair holding hands beside a golf cart." She says, however, that this is not what she sees when she thinks about happiness.*

Where do you go from here? You go back to the article, on a treasure hunt for more quotations you can use to enrich your essay. You've written what O'Faolain *doesn't* think happiness is, so it would be good to start explaining how she *does* define it. Useful details are right in the first paragraph:

> My happiness moves.
> And that's what I think happiness is like—radiant like the last of the sun, but always in the process of disappearing.

How can you work that into your essay? Here's an example of how you might end your first paragraph, make a transition, and begin your second paragraph:

> *Nuala O'Faolain would most likely agree with H. Jackson Brown's statement, "People take different roads seeking fulfillment and happiness. Just because they're not on your road doesn't mean they've gotten lost." Like most of us, she has seen hundreds of advertisements that show people together: "perfectly matched children," "an impeccable couple," or a "silver-haired pair holding hands beside a golf cart." She says, however, that this is not what she sees when she thinks about happiness. O'Faolain says that her happiness "moves."*
>
> *She compares happiness to the sun sinking below the horizon of the ocean. There is a bright, blazing moment when happiness is "radiant like the last of the sun," but it is "always in*

the process of disappearing." Happiness "moves" by appear-
ing and then disappearing. In other words, a person cannot
expect to always be happy, yet many people do expect just
that.

WRITER'S TIP:

Do not throw quotations into your writing without explaining
them. After you include a quotation, interpret it in your own
words and show how it helps you prove your point. Every
quotation you use should serve a purpose.

Exercise 4.12 Practice the Writing Lesson

Look back at the article to find more quotations you can use for
this essay. List them here. You don't need to write down every word
of a quotation. Paraphrase it and give yourself enough information
so that you can retrieve it later. You will be writing the remainder of
the essay in the next exercise.

Example: She is happy just to be warm and safe and have enough
food and fuel. (end of paragraph 2)

1. _____

_____

_____

2. _____

_____

_____

3. _____

_____

_____

4. _____

_____

_____

How to Cite Quotations as Details

When you include quotations from an article or another piece of
literature about which you are writing, you need to enclose the
author's actual words with quotation marks, as we did in this
sentence:

There is a bright, blazing moment when happiness is "radiant
like the last of the sun," but it is "always in the process of disappearing."

If you are paraphrasing the author's words or explaining what the author said, it isn't necessary to use quotation marks:

> She compares happiness to the sun sinking below the horizon of the ocean.

Exercise 4.13 Apply the Lesson to Your Own Writing

On a separate sheet of paper, write the rest of the essay. Use the quotations you gathered in the previous exercise. Be sure to tie together your thoughts in a concluding paragraph. Here is the beginning again:

> Nuala O'Faolain would most likely agree with H. Jackson Brown's statement, "People take different roads seeking fulfillment and happiness. Just because they're not on your road doesn't mean they've gotten lost." Like most of us, she has seen hundreds of advertisements that show people together: "perfectly matched children," "an impeccable couple," or a "silver-haired pair holding hands beside a golf cart." She says, however, that this is not what she sees when she thinks about happiness. O'Faolain says that her happiness "moves."
>
> She compares happiness to the sun sinking below the horizon of the ocean. There is a bright, blazing moment when happiness is "radiant like the last of the sun," but it is "always in the process of disappearing." Happiness "moves" by appearing and then disappearing. In other words, a person cannot expect to always be happy, yet many people do expect just that.

Grammar Mini-Lesson
Forming Complex Sentences

The Complex Sentence

I got the job. I passed the test. Simple sentences like these make sense, but they don't say much. Writing more complex sentences will help you provide readers with important details and information.

To form complex sentences, you first need to know the difference between groups of words known as independent and dependent clauses.

- An **independent clause** is a group of words that has a subject and a verb, and can stand alone as a sentence.

  Mike helped clean up.

  (independent; makes sense as a simple sentence by itself)

- A **dependent clause** is a group of words that has a subject and a verb, but cannot stand alone as a sentence (it is *dependent* on something else).

    after the guests left

    (doesn't make sense as its own sentence; needs to be linked to something else)

  To form a complex sentence, you join together an independent and dependent clause.

- A **complex sentence** consists of one independent clause and one or more dependent clauses.

    Mike helped clean up <u>after the guests left</u>.
    INDEP. CLAUSE   DEP. CLAUSE

Why Do We Use Complex Sentences?

Complex sentences help express relationships. In the example we examined, the dependent clause tells us exactly when the action in the independent clause occurred. It tells us *when* Mike helped clean up—*after* the guests left. If we kept the simple sentence without the dependent clause, we wouldn't know when or why the cleaning occurred. Adding dependent clauses and forming complex sentences will help you provide readers with important information.

How to Write a Dependent Clause

Dependent clauses usually begin with a key word such as

after	although	as	as if	because	before
if	since	so that	than	that	though
unless	until	when	where	which	whichever
while	who	whoever	whom	whomever	whose

    Mike helped clean up <u>**after the guests left**</u>.
    DEP. CLAUSE

    Dad took out the trash <u>**while Jordan raked the leaves**</u>.
    DEP. CLAUSE

  Here is another example of how and why you would add a dependent clause. First, read this simple sentence:

    The waiter brought us the check.

This sentence is boring; it doesn't tell us when or under what circumstances the event happened. Make it a more detailed, complex sentence by adding a dependent clause:

    after we asked for it five times

The new, complex sentence reads:

> The waiter brought us the check *after we asked for it five times*.

The dependent clause *after we asked for it five times* tells us more about *when* the waiter brought us the check. The complex sentence is more interesting and does a better job showing the relationship between events in the story; it even helps set the mood of the scene.

Compare the following ways O'Faolain could have expressed the same idea:

> A. Nobody can summon it up. Nobody can say that it will never come again.
> (two simple sentences)

> B. Because nobody can summon it up, nobody can say that it will never come again.
> (complex sentence)

Version A (two simple sentences) expresses two ideas but does not clearly show the relationship between them.

Version B adds *because* to the first simple sentence (making a dependent clause) and joins it to the second simple sentence (an independent clause), forming a complex sentence. The resulting complex sentence works better than the two separate ones because it shows the *cause-and-effect relationship* between the two ideas. It is *because* nobody can summon it (happiness) up that nobody can say it will never come again.

Here are some further examples of complex sentences from "Chasing the Evanescent Glow" and *The Bay of Angels*, broken down into clauses.

Complex Sentence	Independent Clause	Dependent Clause
In the afterglow I hurry across the grass to the shed to fill my basket with sods of turf.	I hurry across the grass to the shed to fill my basket with sods of turf	In the afterglow
I look up at the ceiling, my eyes imploring the dark.	I look up at the ceiling	my eyes imploring the dark
The nuptial arrangements made me slightly uneasy, as did the wedding itself.	The nuptial arrangements made me slightly uneasy	as did the wedding itself

Punctuating Complex Sentences

- A comma usually follows a dependent clause that introduces a sentence.

  <u>On this particular evening</u>, I was too tired to feel anything but gratitude.

- No comma is usually necessary if the dependent clause is at the *end* of a sentence:

  I sometimes felt unconsoled <u>because not all changes are welcome</u>.

Exercise 4.14 Practice Forming Complex Sentences

Combine each pair of sentences into a complex sentence. Do this by changing the italicized sentence into a dependent clause beginning with one of these words:

once	because	if	so	while
as if	before	so that	as soon as	until

Example: You went outside. *It stopped raining.*
  You went outside as soon as it stopped raining.

1. You turned pale. *You felt sick.*

   _____

   _____

2. I quit attending watercolor class. *I felt I had no talent.*

   _____

   _____

3. I loved the book. *I wanted to see the film.*

   _____

   _____

4. *You fill the birdfeeder.* The birds will find it.

   _____

   _____

5. Dad removed the hornets' nest. *No one will get stung.*

   _____

   _____

6. *You go out to the parking lot.* Get a friend to go with you.

   _____

   _____

7. *The fire alarm sounded.* We followed fire-drill procedures.

_____

_____

8. He read the menu again. *He waited for the server.*

_____

_____

9. *She insists on always getting her way.* She will lose some friends.

_____

_____

10. *We find a better method.* We must continue using the old one.

_____

_____

Polish Your Spelling
Adding -LY to Change Adjectives into Adverbs

1. **To change an adjective to an adverb, we usually add *-ly*.**

ADJECTIVE		SUFFIX		ADVERB
suave	+	ly	=	suavely
vague	+	ly	=	vaguely
equal	+	ly	=	equally

2. **Sometimes, adding *-ly* affects the word's spelling.**

   - If the adjective ends in a consonant plus *-le*, change the *-le* to *-ly*.

ADJECTIVE	ADVERB
impeccable	impeccably
idle	idly
ample	amply

   - If the adjective ends in *y* preceded by a consonant, change *y* to *i* before adding *-ly*.

ADJECTIVE		SUFFIX		ADVERB
hasty	+	ly	=	hastily
angry	+	ly	=	angrily

- If the adjective ends in *-ic*, add *al* before attaching *-ly*.

ADJECTIVE		SUFFIXES				ADVERB
drastic	+	al	+	ly	=	drastically
scientific	+	al	+	ly	=	scientifically

- Finally, note that the *e* is dropped in these three special exceptions:

ADJECTIVE	ADVERB
due	duly
true	truly
whole	wholly

Exercise 4.15 Adding -LY Correctly

Change each adjective into an adverb and write it on the line.

ADJECTIVE   ADVERB

1. acute + ly   _____

2. terrific + ly   _____

3. hearty + ly   _____

4. inquiring + ly   _____

5. delicate + ly   _____

6. scary + ly   _____

7. due + ly   _____

8. believeable + ly _____

9. satisfying + ly   _____

10. skillful + ly   _____

Chapter Five

Prereading Guide
Words to know and ideas to consider before you jump into the reading.

A. Essential Vocabulary

Word	Meaning	Typical Use
apportion (v) uh-POR-shun	to portion out; allocate; assign	We aren't going to *apportion* blame here; all of you are guilty.
bereft (*adj*) be-REFT	1. empty and lacking; deprived 2. grief-stricken	The dead oak was completely *bereft* of leaves. The *bereft* family gathered at the hospital.
blight (n) BLITE	1. a disease or defect that damages another 2. (v) to damage or cause to deteriorate	The pine bark beetles were a *blight* on the trees. His poor SAT grades *blighted* his otherwise outstanding record.
churlish (*adj*) CHUR-lish	1. impolite and surly; rude; arrogant 2. stingy and tightfisted	We found the waiter utterly *churlish* and so we *churlishly* did not leave him a tip.
competence (n) COM-puh-tence	sufficient capability; skill	Brad's *competence* as an actor is undeniable.
digress (v) die-GRESS	to wander from the main subject; to deviate; ramble	I *digress*—let me get back to what I was saying to begin with.
galling (*adj*) GAWL-ing	1. causing bitterness; troubling 2. (n) gall: impudence; nerve; inconsideration	Losing because of the ref's bad calls was *galling*. She had the *gall* to call me spoiled, but I worked for my money.
liaison (n) lee-AY-zon	1. a close relationship; connection; alliance 2. a link between two people or groups; a go-between	Their *liaison* goes back to middle school. His dad is a *liaison* between labor and management.
ravage (v) RAV-uj	1. to destroy violently or badly damage; ruin 2. (n) destructive or ruinous action; devastation	The victors *ravaged* the village and took everything of value. The *ravages* of the tornado were still evident a year later.
self-evident (*adj*) self-EV-i-dent	needing no proof; obvious	"We hold these truths to be *self-evident*."

B. Vocabulary Practice

Exercise 5.1   Sentence Completion

Using your new vocabulary knowledge, choose the best way to complete the following sentences. Circle the letter of your answer.

1. It's a _____ idea to make liaisons with influential people.
   A. bad
   B. good

2. With that _____ tone and expression, he seems quite churlish to me.
   A. arrogant
   B. solemn

3. I'm working at the hot dog stand this weekend, apportioning _____.
   A. sauerkraut
   B. music

4. The thunderstorms _____ our beach plans.
   A. galled
   B. blighted

5. He _____ when he tells stories; he digresses.
   A. stays on track
   B. goes off on tangents

6. _____ by the earthquake, the town was never the same again.
   A. Engaged
   B. Ravaged

7. After his best friend moved _____, Ethan was bereft.
   A. away
   B. next door

8. I find it galling that his brother _____.
   A. is so friendly
   B. called him such horrible names

9. Almost two feet of snow the night before made the school closings _____.
   A. self-evident
   B. doubtful

10. _____ the long jump and 50-yard dash showed Amanda's competence.
    A. Winning
    B. Losing

Exercise 5.2   Using Fewer Words

Replace the italicized words with a single word from the following list. The first one has been done for you.

apportion   bereft   blight   churlish   competence

digress   galling   liaisons   ravages   self-evident

1. The fact that I'm crazy about you should
   be *obvious and needing no proof*.

   1. _self-evident_

2. The inexpensive imported imitations are
   like a(an) *damaging disease* on the U.S.
   market.

   2._____

3. The United States has *close relationships*
   with NATO countries.

   3._____

4. Due to her *sufficient capability*, we're
   going to give her a raise.

   4._____

5. Feeling *empty and lacking* after her only
   child went off to college, she began tutoring
   high-school students.

   5._____

6. It is *causing bitterness* that you never seem
   to study but get better grades than me.

   6._____

7. You are way too *impolite and surly* to work
   here!

   7._____

8. When you *portion out* the tofu, you don't
   need to include me.

   8._____

9. If we can get Mr. Rhodes to *wander from
   the subject*, we might not have to take the
   test until next week.

   9._____

10. The *ruinous action* of arthritis did not keep
    the old man from enjoying golf.

   10._____

Exercise 5.3   Synonyms and Antonyms

Fill in the blanks in column A with the required synonyms or antonyms, selecting them from column B. (Remember: A *synonym* is a word similar in meaning to another word. *Autumn* and *fall* are synonyms. An *antonym* is a word opposite in meaning to another word. *Beginning* and *ending* are antonyms.)

	A	B
_____	1. synonym for *assign*	liaison
_____	2. antonym for *obscure*	churlish
_____	3. synonym for *grief-stricken*	apportion
_____	4. antonym for *rehabilitated*	blight
_____	5. synonym for *defect*	digress
_____	6. antonym for *gracious*	ravaged
_____	7. synonym for *skill*	bereft
_____	8. antonym for *progress*	gall
_____	9. synonym for *go-between*	self-evident
_____	10. synonym for *nerve*	competence

C. Journal Freewrite

Before you begin the reading on the next page, take out a journal or sheet of paper and spend some time responding to the following prompt.

TIP: Don't worry about grammar and spelling; just write what comes to mind. The purpose of freewriting is to explore ideas, not to produce a polished work.

Recall a time when someone you know was offended or angered by something you did. However, you didn't think your action or comment was wrong. Were you able to work out the problem? Explain.

Reading 7

from The Remains of the Day

by Kazuo Ishiguro

About the Author
Kazuo Ishiguro
(1954–) was born in
Nagasaki, Japan, and
moved to England with
his parents when he
was five years old. He
has remained there,
gaining recognition as
one of his generation's
leading writers. His nov-
els are about the inner
workings of characters'
minds and how their
feelings are reconciled
with polite British eti-
quette. *The Remains of
the Day*, which is
excerpted here, explores
the character of Mr.
Stevens, a lifelong butler
who is solely concerned
with being a proper ser-
vant to his employer.
The novel won the
Booker Prize in 1989
and was made into a
movie in 1993.

Miss Kenton and my father had arrived at the house at more
or less the same time—that is to say, the spring of 1922—as a
consequence of my losing at one stroke the previous housekeeper and under-butler. This had occurred due to these latter two persons deciding to marry one another and leave the
profession. I have always found such <u>liaisons</u> a serious threat
to the order in a house. Since that time, I have lost numerous
more employees in such circumstances. Of course, one has to
expect such things to occur amongst maids and footmen, and
a good butler should always take this into account in his
planning; but such marrying amongst more senior employees
can have an extremely disruptive effect on work. Of course,
if two members of staff happen to fall in love and decide to
marry, it would be <u>churlish</u> to be <u>apportioning</u> blame; but
what I find a major irritation are those persons—and housekeepers are particularly guilty here—who have no genuine
commitment to their profession and who are essentially
going from post to post looking for romance. This sort of
person is a <u>blight</u> on good professionalism.

But let me say immediately I do not have Miss Kenton in
mind at all when I say this. Of course, she too eventually left
my staff to get married, but I can vouch that during the time
she worked as housekeeper under me, she was nothing less
than dedicated and never allowed her professional priorities
to be distracted.

But I am <u>digressing</u>. I was explaining that we had fallen in
need of a housekeeper and an under-butler at one and the same
time and Miss Kenton had arrived—with unusually good references, I recall—to take up the former post. As it happened,
my father had around this time come to the end of his distinguished service at Loughborough House with the death of his
employer, Mr. John Silvers, and had been at something of a loss
for work and accommodation.[1] Although he was still, of
course, a professional of the highest class, he was now in his
seventies and much <u>ravaged</u> by arthritis and other ailments. It
was not at all certain, then, how he would fare against the

---

[1] a place to live

younger breed of highly professionalized butlers looking for posts. In view of this, it seemed a reasonable solution to ask my father to bring his great experience and distinction to Darlington Hall.[2]

As I remember, it was one morning a little while after my father and Miss Kenton had joined the staff, I had been in my pantry, sitting at the table going through my paperwork, when I heard a knock on my door. I recall I was a little taken aback when Miss Kenton opened the door and entered before I had bidden her to do so. She came in holding a large vase of flowers and said with a smile:

'Mr. Stevens, I thought these would brighten your parlour a little.'

'I beg your pardon, Miss Kenton?'

'It seemed such a pity your room should be so dark and cold, Mr. Stevens, when it's such bright sunshine outside. I thought these would enliven things a little.'

'That's very kind of you, Miss Kenton.'

'It's a shame more sun doesn't get in here. The walls are even a little damp, are they not, Mr. Stevens?'

I turned back to my accounts, saying: 'Merely condensation, I believe, Miss Kenton.'

She put her vase down on the table in front of me, then glancing around my pantry again said: 'If you wish, Mr. Stevens, I might bring in some more cuttings for you.'

'Miss Kenton, I appreciate your kindness. But this is not a room of entertainment. I am happy to have distractions kept to a minimum.'

'But surely, Mr. Stevens, there is no need to keep your room so stark and <u>bereft</u> of colour.'

'It has served me perfectly well thus far as it is, Miss Kenton, though I appreciate your thoughts. In fact, since you are here, there was a certain matter I wished to raise with you.'

'Oh, really, Mr. Stevens.'

'Yes, Miss Kenton, just a small matter. I happened to be walking past the kitchen yesterday when I heard you calling to someone named William.'

'Is that so, Mr. Stevens?'

'Indeed, Miss Kenton. I did hear you call several times for "William." May I ask who it was you were addressing by that name?'

'Why, Mr. Stevens, I should think I was addressing your father. There are no other Williams in this house, I take it.'

'It's an easy enough error to have made,' I said with a small smile. 'May I ask you in future, Miss Kenton, to address my father as "Mr. Stevens"? If you are speaking of him to a third party, then you may wish to call him "Mr. Stevens senior" to distinguish him from myself. I'm most grateful, Miss Kenton.'

With that I turned back to my papers. But to my surprise, Miss Kenton did not take her leave. 'Excuse me, Mr. Stevens,' she said after a moment.

'Yes, Miss Kenton.'

---

[2]the estate where the narrator works

'I am afraid I am not quite clear what you are saying. I have in the past been accustomed to addressing under-servants by their Christian names and saw no reason to do otherwise in this house.'

'A most understandable error, Miss Kenton. However, if you will consider the situation for a moment, you may come to see the inappropriateness of someone such as yourself talking "down" to one such as my father.'

'I am still not clear what you are getting at, Mr. Stevens. You say someone such as myself, but I am as far as I understand the housekeeper of this house, while your father is the under-butler.'

'He is of course in title the under-butler, as you say. But I am surprised your powers of observation have not already made it clear to you that he is in reality more than that. A great deal more.'

'No doubt I have been extremely unobservant, Mr. Stevens. I had only observed that your father was an able under-butler and addressed him accordingly. It must indeed have been most <u>galling</u> for him to be so addressed by one such as I.'

'Miss Kenton, it is clear from your tone you simply have not observed my father. If you had done so, the inappropriateness of someone of your age and standing addressing him as "William" should have been <u>self-evident</u> to you.'

'Mr. Stevens, I may not have been a housekeeper for long, but I would say that in the time I have been, my abilities have attracted some very generous remarks.'

'I do not doubt your <u>competence</u> for one moment, Miss Kenton. But a hundred things should have indicated to you that my father is a figure of unusual distinction from whom you may learn a wealth of things were you prepared to be more observant.'

'I am most indebted to you for your advice, Mr. Stevens. So do please tell me, just what marvelous things might I learn from observing your father?'

'I would have thought it obvious to anyone with eyes, Miss Kenton.'

'But we have already established, have we not, that I am particularly deficient[3] in that respect.'

'Miss Kenton, if you are under the impression you have already at your age perfected yourself, you will never rise to the heights you are no doubt capable of. I might point out, for instance, you are still often unsure of what goes where and which item is which.'

This seemed to take the wind out of Miss Kenton's sails somewhat. Indeed, for a moment, she looked a little upset. Then she said:

'I had a little difficulty on first arriving, but that is surely only normal.'

'Ah, there you are, Miss Kenton. If you had observed my father who arrived in this house a week after you did, you will have seen that his house knowledge is perfect and was so almost from the time he set foot in Darlington Hall.'

---

[3]lacking

Miss Kenton seemed to think about this before saying a little sulkily:

'I am sure Mr. Stevens senior is very good at his job, but I assure you, Mr. Stevens, I am very good at mine. I will remember to address your father by his full title in future. Now, if you would please excuse me.'

After this encounter, Miss Kenton did not attempt to introduce further flowers into my pantry, and in general, I was pleased to observe, she went about settling in impressively. It was clear, furthermore, she was a housekeeper who took her work very seriously, and in spite of her youth she seemed to have no difficulty gaining the respect of her staff.

Understanding the Reading

Complete the next three exercises and see how well you understood the excerpt from *The Remains of the Day*.

Exercise 5.4   Multiple-Choice Questions

Answer the following questions about the reading. Circle the letter of your answer.

TIP: Don't try to answer the questions from memory; go back to the text as often as necessary.

1. Mr. Stevens feels _____ most maids, footmen, and housekeepers.
   A. angry with
   B. charitable toward
   C. inferior to
   D. superior to

2. Mr. Stevens's father and Miss Kenton came to work at Darlington Hall because
   A. he was an invalid and she was his nurse.
   B. he needed employment and a place to stay; she was in love with Stevens.
   C. they both needed employment and a place to stay.
   D. he had been hired as under-butler and she was Mr. Darlington's fiancée.

3. From the context of the story, you can determine that *stark* (middle of page 104) means
   A. unadorned and cold.
   B. cheerful and bright.
   C. antiseptically clean.
   D. decorated in poor taste.

4. Mr. Stevens is the most irritated with Miss Kenton because she
   A. put flowers in his room.
   B. pointed out errors in his bookkeeping.
   C. felt free to come into his pantry without knocking.
   D. did not realize he felt his father should be treated as a superior.

5. When Miss Kenton says, "But we have already established . . . that I am particularly deficient in that respect," she is responding to Mr. Stevens with
   A. humor.
   B. sarcasm.
   C. disrespect.
   D. anger.

Exercise 5.5 Short-Answer Questions

Respond to the following questions in one to two complete sentences. Go back to the text, as you did on the multiple choice.

6. Mr. Stevens says he doesn't blame housekeepers for falling in love with butlers, except under what circumstances?

   _____

   _____

   _____

7. Why does Mr. Stevens think that the under-butler position would be suitable for his father?

   _____

   _____

   _____

8. What are the two reasons Miss Kenton gives for calling Mr. Stevens's father by his first name?

   _____

   _____

   _____

9. At what point during the conversation with Mr. Stevens does Miss Kenton briefly lose her confidence? Why do you think that is?

   _____

   _____

   _____

Respond to the following question in three to four complete sentences. Use details from the text in your answer.

10. Why do you think Mr. Stevens is so concerned with the relationship between Miss Kenton and his father?

_____

_____

_____

_____

_____

Reading Strategy Lesson
Making Inferences and Drawing Conclusions

It is the middle of summer. You've kicked off the covers in your sleep, but you're still uncomfortably warm. You look out your window, and you're sure you can see heat waves rising from the street. Next door, little kids are already splashing in their baby pool and playing with the garden hose. Their mother has never let them do that so early in the day before. You infer that the temperature outside is already higher than it was yesterday at noon. You conclude that it's going to be a scorcher.

When you read, you should make inferences and draw conclusions, just as you do in your daily life. Remember that writers do not always come out and plainly state everything they want you to know. They might *imply* (suggest) things about characters, ideas, or situations, but it is up to you to **infer** (deduce, or logically conclude) what those implications mean.

Making inferences and drawing conclusions about a text involves **evaluating, judging,** and **interpreting**. In your English classes, you have probably spent a lot of time talking about the novels, stories, and poetry that you read. Discussing a piece of writing is a good way to analyze it. You can consider everyone's viewpoint and add your own thoughts. Then you can decide what the book, story, or poem means for you, personally.

When you finish reading something, pause for a few moments and mentally list the author's main points and details. As you consider these main points and details, ask yourself a few questions. They will help you make inferences and then draw some overall conclusions.

• Who or what is the author talking about?

• Is there a hidden meaning behind what the words literally say?

- Is the author hoping for a reaction from me?

- What is the writer's attitude toward the subject? Serious, light-hearted, tongue-in-cheek? How seriously should I take what he or she is saying?

In the excerpt from *The Remains of the Day*, Mr. Stevens gives several examples of what he considers to be Miss Kenton's unacceptable behavior:

- She entered his pantry before he "had bidden her to do so."

- She brought flowers to the room, which he does not want because he is "happy to have distractions kept to a minimum."

- She called his father "William."

- She did not "take her leave" from the pantry when Mr. Stevens was through admonishing her, but stayed to defend her actions.

These examples let us know how Mr. Stevens felt toward Miss Kenton—but what do they **imply** about Mr. Stevens and Miss Kenton? We see that Mr. Stevens is stiff and formal, and not the sort of person we would want for a supervisor. On the other hand, we can infer that Miss Kenton is a perfectly pleasant woman who is actually trying to be kind to the humorless and detached Mr. Stevens.

Exercise 5.7 Practice the Reading Strategy

Read the following excerpts and state what you can infer from them. Then explain what words or phrases led you to your answer.

1. "Lucia looked at her cousin, amazed by the energy with which he spoke, the anxiety in his usually listless face. The change became him, for it showed what he might be, making one regret still more what he was. Before she could speak, he was gone again, to return presently, laughing, yet looking a little angry." (Louisa May Alcott, *Behind a Mask*)

What can you infer about Lucia's cousin *before now*? _____

Explanation: _____

_____

_____

2. "He had risen from his chair and was standing between the parted blinds gazing down into the dull neutral-tinted London street. Looking over his shoulder, I saw that on the pavement opposite there stood a large woman with a heavy fur boa round her neck, and a large curling red feather in a broad-brimmed hat which was tilted in a coquettish Duchess of Devonshire fashion over her ear. From under this great panoply she peeped up in a

nervous, hesitating fashion at our windows, while her body oscillated backward and forward, and her fingers fidgeted with her glove buttons. Suddenly, with a plunge, as of the swimmer who leaves the bank, she hurried across the road, and we heard the sharp clang of the bell." (Sir Arthur Conan Doyle, "A Case of Identity")

What can you infer about the woman across the street? _____

_____

Explanation: _____

_____

_____

3. "Most unpleasant of all was the first minute when, on coming, happy and good-humored, from the theater, with a huge pear in his hand for his wife, he had not found his wife in the drawing-room, to his surprise had not found her in the study either, and saw her at last in her bedroom with the unlucky letter that revealed everything in her hand. She, his Dolly, forever fussing and worrying over household details, and limited in her ideas, as he considered, was sitting perfectly still with the letter in her hand, looking at him with an expression of horror, despair, and indignation." (Leo Tolstoy, *Anna Karenina*)

What can you infer about the letter? _____

_____

Explanation: _____

_____

_____

4. People who eat animals—and yes, that includes birds and fish—are holding the world back from the peace it might attain if this very common form of barbarism were to stop now. Enjoying a meal at the expense of any creature's life simply furthers insensitivity to all living creatures, including human beings.

What can you infer about the author? _____

Explanation: _____

_____

_____

Exercise 5.8 **Apply the Reading Strategy to *The Remains of the Day***

Look back at the excerpt from *The Remains of the Day* on page 103. Then, on the lines provided, list three **inferences** you can make about Mr. Stevens and three you can make about Miss Kenton. Remember, inferences are not stated. They are *implied*.

Inferences about Mr. Stevens:

1. _____

2. _____

3. _____

Inferences about Miss Kenton:

1. _____

2. _____

3. _____

Writing Workshop
Clarifying Ideas with Examples

When you completed the essay in Chapter Four, you used quotations as details to support your position, or thesis. Another way to develop paragraphs is with examples. Examples help you make your points clear, so your argument will be convincing and not be misunderstood.

Read these paragraphs from "On Autumn" by A. A. Milne (best-known for *Winnie the Pooh*). Milne writes about sitting in a restaurant and realizing autumn has arrived.

> Last night the waiter put the celery on with the cheese, and I knew that summer was indeed dead. Other signs of autumn there may be—the reddening leaf, the chill in the early-morning air, the misty evenings—but none of these comes home to me so truly. There may be cool mornings in July; in a year of drought the leaves may change before their time; it is only with the first celery that summer is over.

What does Milne give as **examples** to show autumn is coming? Look at the sentence that begins "Other signs of autumn there may be . . ." and you'll find three. They are "the reddening leaf," "the chill in the early-morning air," and "the misty evenings." The celery is an unexpected example (the personal meaning of autumn for him) and is repeated at the beginning and end of the paragraph.

Exercise 5.9   Practice the Writing Lesson

Here are two more paragraphs from Milne's essay. Read each one and answer the questions that follow.

> A week ago—("A little more cheese, waiter")—a week ago I grieved for the dying summer. I wondered how I could possibly bear the waiting—the eight long months till May. In vain to comfort myself with the thought that I could get through more work in the winter undistracted by thoughts of cricket grounds

and country houses. In vain, equally, to tell myself that I could stay in bed later in the mornings. Even the thought of after-breakfast pipes in front of the fire left me cold. But now, suddenly, I am reconciled to autumn. I see quite clearly that all good things must come to an end. The summer has been splendid, but it has lasted long enough. This morning I welcomed the chill in the air; this morning I viewed the falling leaves with cheerfulness; and this morning I said to myself, "Why, of course, I'll have celery for lunch." ("More bread, waiter.") . . .

1. In this paragraph, what are some examples Milne gives of the things he will be able to do in winter that he cannot do in summer —even though these things do not comfort him?

_____

_____

_____

2. What are some other things about autumn that Milne decides to welcome?

_____

_____

_____

Yet, I can face the winter with calm. I suppose I had forgotten what it was really like. I had been thinking of the winter as a horrid wet, dreary time fit only for professional football. Now I can see other things—crisp and sparkling days, long pleasant evenings, cheery fires. Good work shall be done this winter. Life shall be lived well. The end of the summer is not the end of the world. Here's to October—and, waiter, some more celery.

3. Milne has now reconciled himself to the coming of winter. What are some examples of things to which he is now looking forward?

_____

_____

_____

Here is another example of a well-developed paragraph using examples to support a position. Read the paragraph and analysis. Then go on to Exercise 5.10.

[1]We hated to move because we had excellent neighbors. [2]The Moyers next door were unusually helpful and considerate people who took turns with us driving to the mall and the city pool. [3]When we were on vacation, they watered our lawn, watched our property, and fed our cat. [4]When they were gone,

we did the same for them. [5]The Obreros across the street were also very friendly. [6]Their younger son and my brother were on the same Little League team. [7]In the summer we had cookouts with both families in our back yard, and we also had get-togethers in each other's homes several times a year. [8]We always had a good time. [9]I doubt we will ever find such great neighbors again.

Analysis:

Sentence 1 is the position. The family didn't want to move because their neighbors were excellent.

Sentences 2–7 support the position by providing concrete examples of *how* the neighbors were "excellent."

Sentences 8–9 tie up the paragraph by reinforcing the main position.

Exercise 5.10 Apply the Lesson to Your Own Writing

Choose a position statement from the following list, or create one of your own. Then, on a separate sheet of paper, write and develop a paragraph on your position, using specific, supporting examples. You can use the paragraph about neighbors as a model.

Position Statements:

1. Television caters to many different tastes.
2. Superstitions often influence our behavior.
3. Emergency personnel are vital to our community.
4. One of my major faults is that I tend to procrastinate.
5. We are a nation of wasters.
6. Appearances can be deceiving.
7. We should all try to cut down on the amount of fuel we use.

Exercise 5.11 Apply the Lesson to Revise Your Essay

Reread the essay you completed at the end of Chapter Four on Nuala O'Faolain and happiness. Notice where you can improve your essay by adding more *examples* from her article. Add at least two. Don't write your final draft yet. You will make a few more revisions in Chapter Six.

Grammar Mini-Lesson
Using Appositives Correctly

An **appositive** is a noun or phrase that is placed next to another noun to give additional information about that noun.

On the next page is an example from *The Remains of the Day*.

As it happened, my father had around this time come to the end of his distinguished service at Loughborough House with the death of his employer, *Mr. John Silvers*, and had been at something of a loss for work . . .

"Mr. John Silvers" is an appositive. It gives us more information about Mr. Stevens's father's employer. Without this appositive, we would not know the employer's name.

Examine these additional examples:

Mario Batali, *a famous Italian chef*, owns many restaurants in New York City.

The appositive, *a famous Italian chef*, describes the noun *Mario Batali*.

We were led to victory by Jen, *our team captain*.

The appositive, *our team captain*, tells us more about the noun *Jen*.

Punctuating Appositives

An appositive is set off from the rest of the sentence by commas.

- If the appositive is within the sentence, it is set off by two commas, one before it and one after it:

  Mr. Stevens, *the narrator of the story*, admitted that Miss Kenton was a good housekeeper.

  Miss Kenton, *galled by the butler's criticism of her*, stood up for herself.

- If the appositive comes at the beginning of the sentence, it needs one comma after it:

  A butler for all his adult life, Mr. Stevens was tight-lipped, superior, and controlling.

- If the appositive comes at the end of the sentence, it needs one comma before it:

  The flowers in Mr. Stevens's pantry were brought by Miss Kenton, *the housekeeper*.

- No commas are used when the appositive is so closely associated with the noun it explains that the two are pronounced with no pause between them:

  My sister Ariel planted a garden.

  Mr. Stevens was not appreciative of the flowers *brought to him by Miss Kenton*.

Exercise 5.12 Practice Punctuating Sentences with Appositives

Rewrite each sentence, inserting any necessary punctuation.

1. Roger my friend's cat hides when the doorbell rings.

   _____

2. I went to the gym the meeting place for the track team.

   _____

3. William the Conqueror invaded Britain in A.D. 1066.

   _____

4. The magnolia a southern tree has beautiful flowers.

   _____

5. Didn't my cousin Robert tell you I've been sick?

   _____

Exercise 5.13 Practice Using Appositives for Conciseness

Use an appositive to combine each pair of sentences below into a single sentence.

Example: James rides a motorbike. He is the boy with the red shirt.
   James, the boy with the red shirt, rides a motorbike.

1. Rob hurt his arm. He is our best batter.

   _____

   _____

2. Aldous Huxley wrote *Brave New World*. It is a fascinating novel.

   _____

   _____

3. The builders finished the home by the deadline. The home was a modern condominium.

   _____

   _____

4. The next course was lasagna. It was the main dish.

   _____

   _____

5. Jimmy Carter encouraged the development of alternate energy sources. He was our thirty-ninth president.

   _____

   _____

6. Ronald Reagan was our fortieth president. He won the election by a landslide.

   _____

   _____

7. Sheena jumped up and licked my face. She is my friend's dog.

   _____

   _____

8. We saw Mt. McKinley in Alaska. Natives call it Denali.

   _____

   _____

9. Lauren will play "Maple Leaf Rag." It was composed by Scott Joplin.

   _____

   _____

10. Karate is a system of self-defense. Many people are studying it.

    _____

    _____

Polish Your Spelling

Using Suffixes to Change Adjectives into Nouns

Often when you're writing, you'll want to use a word as a noun instead of using it as an adjective. For example, you might want to discuss *happiness* as a concept (a noun) instead of just describing a person who is *happy* (adjective). Here are some tricks to help you spell the noun forms correctly.

1. You can change some adjectives into nouns by **adding a suffix**.

   - Add *-ness*:

ADJECTIVE		SUFFIX		NOUN
covetous	+	ness	=	covetousness
ripe	+	ness	=	ripeness

   - Add *-ity*:

ADJECTIVE		SUFFIX		NOUN
jovial	+	ity	=	joviality
insane*	+	ity	=	insanity

   Notice that when you add -ity to a word ending in e, *you need to drop the* e.

2. You can change some adjectives into nouns by **dropping a suffix**.

- Drop -*ful*:

ADJECTIVE		SUFFIX		NOUN
beautiful	–	ful	=	beauty
careful	–	ful	=	care

- Drop -*less*:

ADJECTIVE		SUFFIX		NOUN
careless	–	less	=	care
pitiless	–	less	=	pity

- Drop -*ous*:

ADJECTIVE		SUFFIX		NOUN
perilous	–	ous	=	peril
victorious*	–	ous	=	victory

*Notice that if the suffix was added by changing the y to i as in
beautiful, pitiless, and victorious, you need to change the i back to
y to get back to the original noun.*

- Drop -*y*:

ADJECTIVE		SUFFIX		NOUN
healthy	–	y	=	health
icy	–	y	=	ice

3. You can change some adjectives into nouns by **changing a suffix**.

- Change -*ant* to -*ancy* or -*ance*:

ADJECTIVE	NOUN
abundant	abundance
vacant	vacancy
recalcitrant	recalcitrance

- Change -*ent* to -*ence* or -*ency*:

ADJECTIVE	NOUN
corpulent	corpulence
urgent	urgency

Note these spelling irregularities:
1. Replace the *e* that was removed before the suffix was added.

- *awful* changes to *awe*

- *malicious* changes to *malice*

2. Remove one of the doubled consonants.

- *foggy* changes to *fog*

- *muddy* changes to *mud*

Exercise 5.14 Practice Changing Adjectives into Nouns

Turn each adjective into a noun by adding, removing, or changing a suffix.

ADJECTIVE   NOUN

1. important   _____

2. friendly   _____

3. dangerous   _____

4. solid   _____

5. insistent   _____

6. urgent   _____

7. merciful   _____

8. affluent   _____

9. extravagant   _____

10. inferior   _____

Chapter Six

Prereading Guide

Words to know and ideas to consider before you jump into the reading.

A. Essential Vocabulary

Word	Meaning	Typical Use
acrimony (*n*) AK-ri-mo-nee	a feeling of ill will and animosity; hostility	I can't help feeling *acrimony* when I see my old friend; I can't forgive her betrayal.
console (*v*) kun-SOLE	to give comfort; soothe	The mother tried to *console* the baby with a bottle.
contemptuous (*adj*) con-TEMP-choo-us	feeling scorn or disdain; haughty	The rival families were *contemptuous* of one another.
exigent (*adj*) EK-si-jent	1. in need of immediate aid or attention; pressing 2. needing a great deal of physical or mental effort; demanding	There is an *exigent* need for food in the refugee camp. Troops in combat zones face *exigent* circumstances every day.
gratify (*v*) GRAT-i-fy	1. to give satisfaction or pleasure; please 2. (*adj*) gratified: to feel pleased and satisfied	A cookie will *gratify* my sweet tooth. My parents felt *gratified* that I played a solo in the winter concert after they spent so much for lessons.
provident (*adj*) PRAHV-i-dent	planning for the future; far-sighted	It was *provident* of my grandfather to buy that land where the mall will be built.
rapture (*v*) RAP-chur	1. to express strong approval in an emotional way 2. (*n*) a feeling of extreme ecstasy and joy	She *raptured* on and on about her son, although we all knew none of it was true. Sarah was filled with *rapture* when she saw her new bicycle.
revert (*v*) re-VURT	to return to a previous state of being or belief; to regress; to relapse	We enjoyed the holiday fair like little kids, as if we had *reverted* to grade school.

Word	Meaning	Typical Use
treachery (*n*) TRECH-ur-ee	violation of trust and faith; betrayal	Once you've been the victim of someone's *treachery*, it is difficult to trust him or her again.
uproot (*v*) up-ROOT	to force one or more individuals to leave a home; relocate	Brianna was distressed when she learned she would be *uprooted* during her senior year.

B. Vocabulary Practice

Exercise 6.1   Sentence Completion

Using your new vocabulary knowledge, choose the best way to complete the following sentences. Circle the letter of your answer.

1. It was provident of you to _____.
   A. set aside some money
   B. max out your credit card

2. She always seems so contemptuous; she thinks she's _____.
   A. beneath us
   B. better than us

3. My mom says Grandpa's interest in _____ shows he's reverted to his childhood.
   A. swimming
   B. finger painting

4. The _____ of living have increased in the last century.
   A. exigencies
   B. reversions

5. Since they _____, you can sum up their relationship in one word: acrimony.
   A. got together
   B. broke up

6. You cannot help but feel _____ when you hear her incredibly sweet singing.
   A. rapture
   B. acrimony

7. Whenever we'd lose a game, Dad would try to console me by saying, _____.
   A. "Too bad you struck out"
   B. "You played a great game"

8. Because of his treachery, Benedict Arnold was considered a
_____.
   A. hero
   B. traitor

9. Uprooted by the rebellion, the farmers _____.
   A. fought back angrily
   B. moved into the city

10. "I am _____ to be here to speak to you today," said
the politician.
   A. gratified
   B. consoled

Exercise 6.2   Using Fewer Words

Replace the italicized words with a single word from the following
list. The first one has been done for you.

acrimony   rapture   console   treacherous   uprooted

gratified   provident   contempt   reverted   exigent

1. I have good reason for my *feelings of ill*   1. __acrimony__
   will and animosity.

2. I tried to *offer comfort to* Maria, but she   2._____
   remained depressed.

3. Our cat Humphrey feels nothing but *scorn*   3._____
   and disdain for the dog.

4. The people whose house burned down   4._____
   have a(an) *pressing and immediate* need
   for clothing and food.

5. Working Saturdays at the animal shelter   5._____
   gave pleasure and satisfaction to him.

6. If you plan to go to college, it would be   6._____
   a showing of wisdom about the future
   to start looking into possible choices now.

7. My mother showed *strong approval* over   7._____
   my first quilting project.

8. Deciding he had made a bad choice,   8._____
   Brandon *went back* to his previous belief.

9. Cheating on someone you say you love is   9._____
   a(an) *trust-violating* act.

10. *Forced to leave home* at a young age,   10._____
    author Charles Dickens worked in a
    boot-blacking factory.

Exercise 6.3   Synonyms and Antonyms

Fill in the blanks in column A with the required synonyms or antonyms, selecting them from column B. (Remember: A *synonym* is a word similar in meaning to another word. *Autumn* and *fall* are synonyms. An *antonym* is a word opposite in meaning to another word. *Beginning* and *ending* are antonyms.)

	A	B
_____	1. synonym for *hostility*	provident
_____	2. antonym for *agitate*	contemptuous
_____	3. synonym for *precise*	revert
_____	4. antonym for *respectful*	exigent
_____	5. synonym for *regress*	acrimony
_____	6. antonym for *displease*	rapture
_____	7. synonym for *relocate*	console
_____	8. antonym for *unwise*	treachery
_____	9. antonym for *sadness*	uproot
_____	10. antonym for *fidelity*	gratify

C. Journal Freewrite

Before you begin the reading on the next page, take out a journal or sheet of paper and spend some time responding to the following prompt.

TIP: Don't worry about grammar and spelling; just write what comes to mind. The purpose of freewriting is to explore ideas, not to produce a polished work.

> Think of someone to whom you no longer feel close (you don't get along anymore, or perhaps you just grew apart). How do you feel whenever you see this person, or how *would* you feel if you had to spend time with him or her? What would you say to him or her if you could?

Reading 8

from August Is a Wicked Month

by Edna O'Brien

About the Author
Edna O'Brien (1936–) was born in County Clare, Ireland. She moved to London to escape her troubled home life, got married, and wrote her first book, *The Country Girls*, which describes the bleak prospects life held for most Irish girls at the time. O'Brien's novels explore the relationships between men and women, and disappointment in love is a common theme. In this first chapter of *August Is a Wicked Month*, she looks at the feelings of a mother separated for two years from her husband. Today it is the father's turn to take their son.

The weather bureau forecast sun. It was not mistaken. All day for five days it sizzled in the heavens and down below the city of London simmered. People who had hoped for summer wished now for a breeze and a little respite.[1] Only at night did Ellen feel cool. Watering the garden and sitting in the stone alcove. <u>Provident</u> stone. It gave back the warmth taken throughout the hot day and she saw it as something human—the mother who reserves love for when it is most needed. She often sat for an hour, caressing the stone, listening for the sounds of her child if he happened to be sleeping in her house, listening anyhow, which is what one does alone at night in a garden hushed by darkness. It was the best hour, sitting there, warmed, and calm, and a little sad. But next day it would be boiling again. The child's father decided that they would go into the country. They would camp out he said, and make fires and go fishing and do things the boy wanted to do. It only took a day to get the various necessaries and they were ready to leave on Thursday.

In the shade end of the kitchen they sat, drinking tea, she from her mug, he from the blue china cup reserved for guests; hardly speaking. Through the glass half of the kitchen door they watched their child, putting up the tent in the garden. It was already fixed on two poles, a bright blue, flapping back and forth like a flag. The father had done that bit and now the child was putting the pegs in, and giving instruction to George.

"Well into the ground, George," the child said. George was nobody. The child invented him three years before when he was five. It happened that a George came to visit them but very quickly got bored with a child of five and made an excuse about having to go home because of a pain in his head. But the child kept conversing with him after he'd left and held on to him throughout the years.

"It's a beautiful blue," she said, looking through the glare of the sun as the child pulled on a rope and the canvas bellied out.

"They undercharged me," her husband said, piling six-pences, shillings and two-shilling pieces in separate banks on

---

[1]relief

the table, reckoning[2] what he had paid for the tent, the fittings and the two Lilos.[3] Always slow at adding, he reckoned things up when he got home and for some reason he was invariably undercharged. "Because of his <u>contemptuous</u> face," she thought, "because he frightened shop girls and set them astray in their tottings[4] and possibly one or two of them would think him attractive."

"I got away with nine and elevenpence," he said.

"You want me to take it back?" she asked.

"Nonsense." He despised petty honor, but no longer thought it his duty to correct this or any other flaw in her.

"Look," she said and pointed. The tent had swollen out now and as the child pulled on the last bit of rope it rose like a cone of bright blue toward the sky where the light was fiery.

"He's a strong child," she said, "to be able to do it."

"I believe in teaching him these things," her husband said, jumbling the various coins together and putting them in the pocket of his jacket which was spread over the back of his chair. Once when visiting her he hung his jacket on a nail and she went through the pockets for clues, <u>reverting</u> to wifedom again. He must have known. He kept his jacket close to him ever since and picked it up and took it with him even on the short journey through the scullery[5] to the outside lavatory.

"Anything you want for your trip?" she said, guiltily. No, he'd seen to everything. In the boot[6] of the car there was tinned food, Primus stove, sleeping bags, seedless oranges, Elastoplast,[7] disinfectant and various medicines which he'd transferred through a funnel from big economy bottles to littler bottles, suitable for packing. He was far-seeing, careful and <u>exigent</u>. There was nothing left for her to contribute but a tin of shortbread.

"You could come with us," he said flatly as she got out the shortbread and assured him untruthfully that it was homemade. Still cowering. She shook her head to his invitation. It needed a less insipid[8] approach than that to bring her back. They'd separated two years before and the child was shared between their two homes. Out of necessity he invented George. They'd got over the worst part; the <u>acrimony</u> when she first left and when he posted[9] broken combs, half-used compacts and old powder puffs in his campaign to clear out her remains. They'd got over that and settled down to a sort of sullen peace, but they talked now as she always feared they might, like strangers who had never been in love at all.

"He's calling us," she said, relieved to escape. The child was saying, "Mama, Dada, Dada, Mama," in a shrill and happy way. She

---

[2]figuring; calculating
[3]brand name of an air mattress
[4]calculations
[5]a room off a kitchen for storing dishes and doing messy work
[6]trunk
[7]bandages
[8]bland
[9]sent by mail

went out and <u>raptured</u> over the tent and said what a genius he was.

"Now you can take it all down," his father said soberly. He'd got the child to put it up as an exercise.

"I'll help you," she said, kneeling down not so much to help as to get nearer to him, to kiss his clean hair and touch his cheek and take full advantage of the last few minutes of contact. He would love her to join them. He would hug her and say, "Good old Mama," but she couldn't. Anyhow she <u>consoled</u> herself with the thought that he was happy. If she went there would be gloom and she could not bear the thought of night and her husband appointing their sleeping positions —he and her at either end of the new Lilos, the child in between, tossing and turning in the heat. For the last year of their marriage he avoided her in bed and she did not ever want to relive that. The days would be testy—no music, no telephone, no floor to sweep, nothing to fill in the hours of <u>treachery</u> between them. She could not go.

"You'll write me sloppy letters," she said to her son.

"Not sloppy," he said, as he <u>uprooted</u> the pegs, flushed from work and self-importance. Still giving orders to George.

At exactly four minutes to three they set off. She looked down at her watch to appear practical. The sun had gone behind a cloud and the sunshine fell in a spray over the gray motor as they drove away with the child in the back seat squeezed in between a lot of luggage. His father always put him in the back seat in case of accident.

"Goodbye, goodbye," the small hand on the window delivering kisses. The fingers on the glass tapping. The face wrinkled up because it was embarrassed and might also cry.

"Goodbye, goodbye." She could hardly keep her eyes on them.

She came in the house, picked up the underpants and vest that the child had peeled off, held them, looked at them, smelt them, and finally washed them and hung them out to dry. Then she sat at the kitchen table, and put her face on her arm. The sandals he'd discarded were on the table. A prong missing in the buckle of one. His father said to keep them, they might come in useful. They might or they might not. She sat there, feeling, out of habit, for the missing prong, her head on her arm, her arm wet from crying, darkness coming on again. The silverfish that had got in with a grocery order were darting over the floor in search of crumbs and spilt sugar.

"Goodbye, goodbye." They were a long way off now; they might even have pitched tent and settled in for the night, the child fast asleep, the father sitting outside, breathing and <u>gratified</u>, a tarpaulin spread on the grass, because of the dew. He liked the country and was a very light sleeper.

Understanding the Reading

Complete the next three exercises and see how well you understood the excerpt from *August Is a Wicked Month*.

Exercise 6.4 Multiple-Choice Questions

Answer the following questions about the reading. Circle the letter of your answer.

TIP: Don't try to answer the questions from memory; go back to the text as often as necessary.

1. This story takes place
   A. in a backyard.
   B. by a stream.
   C. at a residence in London.
   D. at a campground.

2. Ellen and the child's father say very little to one another because
   A. they are very in tune with one another so no words are necessary.
   B. they prefer to listen to their child talking to his imaginary friend.
   C. they are separated and have little left to say.
   D. the father is mad at Ellen for refusing to come with them.

3. The phrase "went through the pockets for clues, reverting to wifedom again" indicates that Ellen
   A. had always gone through her husband's pockets before doing the laundry.
   B. had suspected her husband of cheating on her when they were married.
   C. was against the separation and wanted to get back together.
   D. was looking for clues that her husband had been under-charged and kept the money.

4. Ellen declines to go on the camping trip mostly because
   A. she dislikes being outdoors.
   B. she wants the father and son to have time alone together.
   C. she knows the atmosphere would be tense and unhappy.
   D. there isn't room in the tent for all three of them.

5. Ellen sits at the kitchen table and cries because
   A. of the sadness and disappointment of her situation.
   B. she is afraid to be alone.
   C. she is angry at her husband.
   D. she cannot afford to buy the child new sandals.

Exercise 6.5   Short-Answer Questions

Respond to the following questions in one to two complete sentences. Go back to the text, as you did on the multiple choice.

6. Why do you think O'Brien included the mother and father's discussion of the tent price? What does this moment show about their personality differences?

   _____

   _____

   _____

7. Why do you think the mother pretends that the shortbread is homemade?

   _____

   _____

   _____

8. Why did the child invent George? Explain.

   _____

   _____

   _____

9. From what point of view is the story told? Explain.

   _____

   _____

   _____

Exercise 6.6   Extending Your Thinking

Respond to the following question in three to four complete sentences. Use details from the text in your answer.

10. Compare and contrast the way the mother and father are affected by the status of their relationship. Pay particular attention to the details O'Brien includes in the last paragraph.

   _____

   _____

   _____

   _____

   _____

   _____

Reading Strategy Lesson
Understanding Character and Conflict

Character

Characters are the people in the story. **Characterization** is the technique the author uses to make the characters seem real to you. The author shows you how a character feels, thinks, and acts so that you can picture the character in your mind.

Just how alive can a character be? Characters whom the British authors Shakespeare and Dickens created centuries ago are particularly memorable. They have lived on far past their creators' deaths. We still feel badly for David Copperfield and hope the Macbeths get their just punishment.

The two main types of characters are the **protagonist** (the person we side with) and the **antagonist** (the person who opposes the protagonist).

Another type of character is the **antihero**. The antihero is a protagonist who is flawed in some way. He or she does not have the characteristics we expect to find in a hero, but we still hope things will turn out well for him or her. Perhaps this person will even change in some dramatic way by the end of the story.

Exercise 6.7 Practice Describing Characters

Use the following character maps to record notes on Ellen and her husband, the two main characters in the O'Brien story. Think about how they look, think, feel, and act. You may need to add some details that you infer.

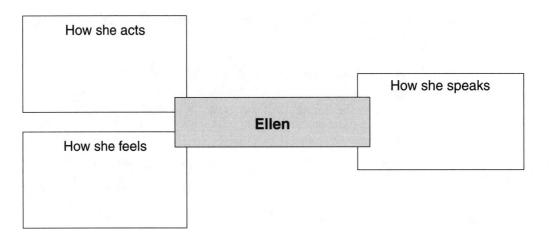

How she acts

How she speaks

Ellen

How she feels

```
┌─────────────────────┐
│   How he acts       │
│                     │
│                     │                    ┌──────────────────────┐
│                     │                    │   How he speaks      │
│                     │   ┌────────────────┤                      │
└─────────────────────┘   │ Ellen's husband│                      │
┌─────────────────────┐   └────────────────┤                      │
│   How he feels      │                    │                      │
│                     │                    └──────────────────────┘
│                     │
│                     │
│                     │
└─────────────────────┘
```

Conflict

Conflict is a struggle between opposing forces. With no conflict, there can be no story. It does not have to be between characters, however. There are several different types of conflict.

- **a character's struggle against nature**

    When one or more characters must overcome an obstacle placed in their path by a natural force, there is a conflict with nature. A storm causes a shipwreck, and the survivors float in a raft. Sharks circle the raft. No land is in sight.

- **a character's struggle against society**

    A character who is in conflict with society may be struggling against poverty, racism, a political or class system, or a social convention. In *To Kill a Mockingbird*, Atticus Finch, the attorney, defends an African-American accused of a crime in a small southern town. Finch and his children are oppressed by most of the townspeople. They are in conflict with their racist society.

- **a character's internal struggle**

    Have you ever wanted to do something you shouldn't and had to struggle with yourself to make your decision? Then you have experienced internal conflict. Internal conflicts center around emotions, morals, or ideas. Should the character follow her heart or her head? Should she do what's right or what's wrong?

- **a character's struggle with another character**

    A conflict between two people is not necessarily a violent one. They may simply engage in a battle of wits, with few words spoken to one another. Think of a detective who is chasing a criminal. They have not met or spoken, but they are in conflict. Likewise, characters may conflict simply because they have different ideas, envy one another, or are struggling for power.

Exercise 6.8 Practice Identifying Conflict

Describe the main conflict evident in the excerpt from *August Is a Wicked Month*. State the type of conflict, who is involved, and what the conflict is about. Can you make inferences about any other conflicts in the story?

_____

_____

_____

_____

_____

_____

Writing Workshop
Achieving Unity

A paragraph has **unity** if it has one main topic and all of the sentences stick to that topic.

For a good example of unity, reread the paragraph from *August Is a Wicked Month* that begins with Ellen asking, "Anything you want for your trip?" (page 124).

Note the characteristics of that paragraph:

1. The first sentence is Ellen's question about whether the husband wants anything for the trip.

2. The other sentences in the paragraph relate to the husband having packed everything they will need. There is a list of the supplies that have been placed in the trunk of the car. All Ellen can contribute is a tin of shortbread.

Now analyze a paragraph on your own. Read this example and decide whether or not you think it is unified.

> Imani has done an exceptional amount of volunteer work. When she was still in middle school, she went to Oakhurst Nursing Home and read to people whose eyesight was failing. The summer of ninth grade, she worked at a camp for children who are physically challenged. When there was no one to coach her little sister's soccer team, Imani took on the job. Imani always gets good grades. She is also very attractive.

This paragraph lacks unity. The last two sentences are off topic; they have nothing to do with the focus of this paragraph, Imani's volunteer work. The sentences should be cut or put into later paragraphs that are specifically about her school performance and attractive appearance.

Exercise 6.9 Apply the Lesson to Your Own Writing

Develop one of the following topic sentences (or one of your own) into a unified paragraph. Your paragraph should have five to six sentences, and each of them should relate to the topic.

Ideas for Topic Sentences:

1. The cards inside magazines are very annoying.
2. _____ is a friend I can depend on.
3. Electricity is indispensable in our daily lives.
4. Airport security is too lax.
5. Failing students should (or should not) lose their driver's licenses.

Write your unified paragraph on a separate sheet of paper.

Grammar Mini-Lesson
Active and Passive Voice

1. An **active verb** describes an action done *by* its subject.
   The weather bureau *forecast* sun.

   (The verb *forecast* is active because it describes an action done *by the weather bureau*. The *weather bureau* is the subject of this sentence.)

2. A **passive verb** describes an action done *to* its subject.
   Sun *was forecast* by the weather bureau.

   (The verb *was forecast* is passive because it describes an action done *to the sun*. *Sun* is the subject of this sentence.)

When you use an active verb, you are writing in the **active voice**. When you use a passive verb, you are writing in the **passive voice**.

Here are some additional examples of active and passive verbs:

    Active: Carelessness *causes* accidents.
    Passive: Accidents *are caused* by carelessness.

    Active: She *will write* the letter.
    Passive: The letter *will be written* by her.

    Active: The children *ate* the chocolates.
    Passive: The chocolates *were eaten* by the children.

Which voice sounds more clear, brief, and natural? The active voice generally works better. (It is particularly essential in news writing, when you want an article to sound lively and current.)

    Compare these sentences:
    Passive: The dog was washed by us.
    Active: We washed the dog.

The second sentence uses fewer words and states the action clearly and simply. The use of the passive verb in the first sentence makes the sentence unnatural sounding and awkward. Think about it. If you gave your dog a bath, would you say, "Guess what! The dog was washed by me!"?

Active verbs are far more common in English than are passive verbs. You should use the active voice whenever possible, especially when the passive voice sounds awkward.

The passive voice does have some uses, however. One good use of passive verbs is to help you avoid the vague pronoun *they*, as in the following:

Poor: *They* grow oranges in Florida.
            (Who are *they*? The sentence is not clear on this
            point. *They* could refer to the people who own a
            particular orange grove or to all of the orange
            growers in Florida.)

Better: Oranges *are grown* in Florida.
            (The focus is on *oranges*, where it belongs—not on
            who grows them.)

You can form the passive voice by adding some form of the verb *to be* to the past participle of a verb. Forms of the verb *to be* are *is*, *was*, *will be*, *has been*, etc. Examples:

is broken   *has been collected*   *was introduced*
will be told   *are being sent*   *were misplaced*

When you write, you should be aware of whether you're using passive or active voice. Always make sure you're using the one that helps you express yourself as clearly and interestingly as possible.

Exercise 6.10 Practice Using Active and Passive Verbs

Improve each of the following sentences by rewriting it with an active or a passive verb, as needed.

Example: An agreement will be entered into by us.

       We will enter into an agreement.

1. Six cookies were eaten by my brother.

2. A second look at Miranda was stolen by Jared.

3. Your help could definitely be used by me.

_____

4. They grow excellent cherries in Washington.

_____

5. A good time will be had by everyone.

_____

6. Their new uniforms were received by the band members.

_____

7. A gold necklace was worn by Jordan.

_____

8. They arrest people who break the curfew in this town.

_____

9. The moon was jumped over by the cow.

_____

10. The sun was blocked out by the clouds.

_____

Exercise 6.11 Apply the Grammar Lesson to Your Own Writing

Reread the essay you wrote for Chapter Four. Check each sentence to see if you used the passive voice where the active voice would be more appropriate. Make any necessary changes. Then write your final draft.

Polish Your Spelling
Turning Verbs into Nouns Using -ION, -ATION, and -URE

Three suffixes for turning verbs (actions) into nouns (things or conditions) are *-ion*, *-ation*, and *-ure*. They all have the same meaning: "act or result of."

VERB		SUFFIX		NOUN
liberate	+	ion	=	liberation
afflict	+	ion	=	affliction
adore	+	ation	=	adoration
consider	+	ation	=	consideration
expose	+	ure	=	exposure
press	+	ure	=	pressure

Exercise 6.12 Practice Turning Verbs into Nouns

Turn the following verbs into nouns by adding *-ion*, *-ation*, or *-ure*. If you have trouble, look back at the examples given.

1. discuss _____

2. seize _____

3. close _____

4. imagine _____

5. construct _____

6. appreciate _____

7. erase _____

8. infect _____

9. perspire _____

10. pollute _____

11. conserve _____

12. expire _____

13. forfeit _____

14. explore _____

15. predict _____

16. separate _____

17. sense _____

18. express _____

19. compose _____

20. resign _____

21. exaggerate _____

22. attract _____

23. observe _____

24. disclose _____

25. confess _____

Unit Two Review

Vocabulary Review

A. Match each word with its definition.

	DEFINITION		WORD
_____	1. a disease or defect that damages or destroys		a. implore
_____	2. to allocate or assign		b. nuptial
_____	3. causing bitterness; troubling		c. recalcitrant
_____	4. to ask desperately or earnestly		d. summon
_____	5. planning for the future		e. apportion
_____	6. relating to marriage or a wedding		f. blight
_____	7. feeling scorn or disdain		g. galling
_____	8. stubborn and uncontrollable		h. gratify
_____	9. to please		i. provident
_____	10. to call up or muster		j. contemptuous

B. Match each word with its synonym.

	SYNONYM		WORD
_____	11. relocate		a. ravage
_____	12. capability		b. self-evident
_____	13. alliance		c. console
_____	14. deviate		d. treachery
_____	15. rigid		e. uproot
_____	16. obvious		f. liaison
_____	17. destroy		g. bereft
_____	18. soothe		h. rigorous
_____	19. betrayal		i. competence
_____	20. grief-stricken		j. digress

C. Match each word with its antonym.

ANTONYM		WORD
_____	21. careless	a. abstracted
_____	22. undemanding	b. churlish
_____	23. sorrow	c. austerity
_____	24. attentive	d. acrimony
_____	25. progress	e. fortuitous
_____	26. polite	f. exigent
_____	27. luxury	g. impeccable
_____	28. good will	h. rapture
_____	29. unfortunate	i. requisite
_____	30. unnecessary	j. revert

Grammar Review

Each sentence below *may* contain an error in the underlined word or phrase. Circle the letter of the error or, if there is no error, mark D.

1. <u>Last night, we went</u> to a Chinese <u>restaurant, Dad got</u>
             A   B
   <u>the same old thing, chicken</u> with broccoli. <u>No error</u>
              C   D

2. <u>Just tell me what</u> time you want to <u>meet and I'll write</u> it
         A   B
   <u>on a sticky note, I'll remember</u> it. <u>No error</u>
             C   D

3. <u>Being, that Leanne</u> was not at <u>home, we didn't</u>
            A   B
   <u>get to see her</u>. <u>No error</u>
       C   D

4. Maya is very <u>health conscious and does not</u> like sugary
                       A
   <u>cereal, so,</u> every <u>morning she eats plain oatmeal instead</u>.
     B   C
   <u>No error</u>
    D

5. <u>Even though my humble friend Amanda</u> did not
                 A
   <u>think she had</u> <u>much talent she</u> won the singing contest.
       B   C
   <u>No error</u>
    D

6. Joe Quigley, one of Alaska's most successful gold miners met
      A   B
   his wife in the town of Kantishna. No error
                   C   D

7. Fannie Quigley an excellent cook, opened a comfort-food
              A   B
   restaurant to feed the hungry miners. No error
                   C   D

8. Each summer, many tourists visits Alaska, the largest state
       A   B   C
   of all fifty. No error
                D

9. My next-door neighbor, Mark, moved there last year with his
          A   B
   family and their dog, a pug. No error
                        C   D

10. He is a hardworking, and accomplished wildlife
                    A
    biologist, a scientist who studies animals. No error
         B   C   D

Spelling Review

A. Change each adjective into an adverb.

1. rigorous   _____

2. impeccable   _____

3. hasty   _____

4. fortuitous   _____

5. abstracted   _____

6. equal   _____

7. suave   _____

8. prolific   _____

9. vague   _____

10. true   _____

B. Change each adjective into a noun.

11. obstinate   _____

12. crafty   _____

13. covetous   _____

14. jovial   _____

15. churlish   _____

16. self-evident   _____

17. competent   _____

18. malicious   _____

19. hesitant   _____

20. harmful   _____

C. Change each verb into a noun.

21. obliterate   _____

22. foreclose   _____

23. interpret   _____

24. contribute   _____

25. civilize   _____

26. expect   _____

27. impress   _____

28. enclose   _____

29. inspire   _____

30. anticipate   _____

Writing Review

Choose one of the topics that follow. On a separate sheet of paper, plan your essay and write your first draft. Then revise and edit your work, and write your final essay.

Several different types of relationships are depicted in the reading selections in this unit. Choose one type and explain what elements are necessary for such a relationship to work in the real world. Use examples and details to support your position. Use at least two quotations from one or more of the selections in your essay.

OR

Choose a type of relationship and write an essay comparing and contrasting a good one with a poor one. For example, you might compare good/bad boss-employee relationships. Write from personal experience and observation. Include specific examples and details to support your statements.

Unit Two Extension Activities

 SPEAK/LISTEN

Genre Switch

In "Chasing the Evanescent Glow," Nuala O'Faolain describes her view of personal happiness. Rewrite the article as a speech, poem, or advice column, pretending you are O'Faolain and you are guiding others in their pursuit of happiness. What, if anything, can we do to feel satisfied? Read your work out loud to your class.

 EXPLORE

From Page to Screen: Exploring a Director's Decisions

Watch the movie version of *The Remains of the Day* (1993). How is Mr. Stevens depicted? Is he the same as you pictured him? Are the characters' relationships as you imagined? Write a reaction to the movie versus the story. (Or write about how *you* would produce it if you could—whom you would cast and why, and how you would have the actors play the parts.)

 WRITE

Loneliness or Solitude?

Both O'Faolain and the mother Ellen in *August Is a Wicked Month* spend time alone. Is there a difference between loneliness and solitude? Look up both words in a dictionary. Then write two paragraphs explaining how each experience affects you. Do they feel the same?

OR

Recalling an Unpleasant Encounter

Imagine it is Miss Kenton's day off, and she's met a friend, another housekeeper, for lunch in London. You are at the next table and overhear their conversation. Write their discussion about Miss Kenton's encounter with Mr. Stevens in drama form. Example: Miss Kenton: Audrey, you won't believe what Mr. Stevens! Audrey: What has he done now?

CONNECT

Text-to-Text Connections

Compare the theme of separation in *The Bay of Angels* and *August is a Wicked Month*. Is the separation between mother and child depicted as a natural occurrence, or as the result of something else? How do Zoë and Ellen cope with being left alone? Use textual evidence in your answer.

UNIT THREE

Other Places, Other Times

Chapter Seven

Prereading Guide
Words to know and ideas to consider before you jump into the reading.

A. Essential Vocabulary

Word	Meaning	Typical Use
distinction (*n*) dis-TINK-shun	1. a difference that distinguishes one thing from others; dissimilarity 2. honor, merit, worthiness	It's important to make *distinctions* between what is possible and what is not. General Schwarzkopf served the armed forces with *distinction*.
exquisite (*adj*) ex-QUIZ-it	1. of extraordinary charm, beauty, or design; elegant 2. intensely felt; acute	I think the movie won an Oscar because of its *exquisite* costuming. He was in such *exquisite* pain that he finally agreed to go to the dentist.
habitable (*adj*) HAB-i-tuh-bul	suitable for living in or on; occupiable	There are lots of dead trees on our farm, and the birds find them quite *habitable*.
idiom (*n*) ID-ee-um	1. an expression that cannot be understood by knowing only what the words literally mean; colloquialism 2. dialect	The expression, "He's all bark and no bite," is an *idiom*. "All y'all" is an *idiom* that means "everybody" in the dialect of the American South.
ingenious (*adj*) in-GENE-ee-us	marked by creativity or inventiveness; innovative	If George Washington Carver had not been *ingenious*, we might not be able to enjoy peanut butter.
intonation (*n*) in-tone-AY-shun	the pattern of changes in pitch in a singing or speaking voice; inflection	My French teacher says I have to work on my *intonation*.
linguistic (*adj*) lin-GWIST-ik	1. relating or pertaining to language 2. (*n*) linguistics: the study of language; language characteristics	The guidance counselor said that with my *linguistic* ability, I could become a translator. My aunt has a master's degree in *linguistics*.
oscillation (*n*) oss-il-AY-shun	back and forth movement; swaying	The *oscillation* of the hypnotist's pendulum put him in a trance.

Word	Meaning	Typical Use
singular (*adj*) SING-yoo-lur	1. exceptional or remarkable; extraordinary 2. individual or unique; unusual	We may not win many football games, but our band is *singular*. She leads a *singular* life that few would understand.
tumult (*n*) TOO-mult	disorder and uproar; commotion	What was the *tumult* in the cafeteria about? The food isn't that bad.

B. Vocabulary Practice

Exercise 7.1   Sentence Completion

Using your new vocabulary knowledge, choose the best way to complete the following sentences. Circle the letter of your answer.

1. The intonation is what makes the _____ unique.
   A. baseball game
   B. song

2. He has a knack for linguistics and _____ his foreign language classes.
   A. does not understand
   B. does well in

3. _____ might be habitable for penguins, but not for people.
   A. Antarctica
   B. The Yukon

4. I need to think of an ingenious reason for _____.
   A. an extension on my homework
   B. going to school

5. _____ is an idiom.
   A. "That's how the cookie crumbles"
   B. "These cookies are crumbly"

6. With his _____ designs, Frank Lloyd Wright was a singular architect.
   A. ordinary
   B. unique

7. One obvious distinction between the two students is that one is a boy and the other is _____.
   A. a girl
   B. named after a grandparent

8. When _____ began gathering near the Capitol Building, the police prepared for a tumultuous evening.
   A. tourists
   B. protesters

9. The little boutique was filled with _____ items, all finely made by hand.
   A. exquisite
   B. run-of-the-mill

10. Emily didn't want to learn piano; something about the relentless _____ of the metronome got on her nerves.
    A. transition
    B. oscillation

Exercise 7.2 Using Fewer Words

Replace the italicized words with a single word from the following list.

exquisite	distinction	habitable	idioms	ingenious
intonations	linguistics	oscillation	singular	tumult

1. Phrases like "have a ride out" and "acting a bit cheeky" are typical English *expressions or colloquialisms*.

   1._____

2. My sister is always doing something wrong; she keeps our family in *disorder and uproar*.

   2._____

3. No one is like my uncle—he's a(an) *exceptional and remarkable* individual.

   3._____

4. They did a great deal of work on the old house and made it more *suitable for living*.

   4._____

5. The *back-and-forth movement* of the clock's pendulum made a soothing ticktock sound.

   5._____

6. The bride wore her grandmother's *extraordinarily beautiful* sapphire necklace.

   6._____

7. She's in Africa studying *something related to languages*.

   7._____

8. "Silicon Valley Uptalkers" is an article about the *variations of voice pitch* of young people who live in the area.

   8._____

9. Even as a child, Josh had *creative and innovative* schemes.

   9._____

10. Her GPA was 3.9, and she graduated with *merit and honor*.

    10._____

Exercise 7.3 Synonyms and Antonyms

Fill in the blanks in column A with the required synonyms or antonyms, selecting them from column B. (Remember: A *synonym* is a word similar in meaning to another word. An *antonym* is a word opposite in meaning to another word.)

	A	B
_____	1. synonym for *colloquialism*	exquisite
_____	2. antonym for *flawed*	intonation
_____	3. antonym for *similarity*	oscillation
_____	4. antonym for *unlivable*	tumult
_____	5. antonym for *ordinary*	linguistics
_____	6. synonym for *swaying*	distinction
_____	7. synonym for *language study*	habitable
_____	8. synonym for *inventive*	singular
_____	9. synonym for *commotion*	idiom
_____	10. synonym for *inflection*	ingenious

C. Journal Freewrite

Before you begin the reading on the next page, take out a journal or sheet of paper and spend some time responding to the following prompt.

TIP: Don't worry about grammar and spelling; just write what comes to mind. The purpose of freewriting is to explore ideas, not to produce a polished work.

Have you ever traveled somewhere where the culture and lifestyle were surprisingly different from your own? What surprised you, and what did you learn? Or think of a place you'd *like* to go and imagine how the natives' ways might differ from your own.

from The Aran Islands

by J. M. Synge

About the Author
John Millington Synge (pronounced sing) **(1871–1909)** is best known as a dramatist who brought his native Irish dialect and folklore to the stage. After graduating from Trinity College in 1892, he joined a group of Irish expatriates studying in Paris. There, the poet William Butler Yeats encouraged Synge to write about his own people and their culture. His play *Riders to the Sea* was based on his research in the Aran Islands, three islands west of the Irish mainland where residents still speak Gaelic and hold folk festivals honoring ancient Irish traditions. This reading is a nonfiction prose excerpt from Synge's Aran Islands research.

I am settled at last on Inishmaan in a small cottage with a continual drone of Gaelic coming from the kitchen that opens into my room.

Early this morning the man of the house came over for me with a four-oared curagh[1]—that is, a curagh with four rowers and four oars on either side, as each man uses two—and we set off a little before noon.

It gave me a moment of exquisite satisfaction to find myself moving away from civilisation in this rude canvas canoe of a model that has served primitive races since men first went to sea.

We had to stop for a moment at a hulk that is anchored in the bay, to make some arrangement for the fish-curing of the middle island, and my crew called out as soon as we were within earshot that they had a man with them who had been in France a month from this day.

When we started again, a small sail was run up in the bow, and we set off across the sound with a leaping oscillation that had no resemblance to the heavy movement of a boat.

The sail is only used as an aid, so the men continued to row after it had gone up, and as they occupied the four cross-seats I lay on the canvas at the stern and the frame of slender laths, which bent and quivered as the waves passed under them.

When we set off it was a brilliant morning of April, and the green, glittering waves seemed to toss the canoe among themselves, yet as we drew nearer this island a sudden thunderstorm broke out behind the rocks we were approaching, and lent a momentary tumult to this still vein of the Atlantic.

We landed at a small pier, from which a rude track leads up to the village between small fields and bare sheets of rock like those in Aranmor. The youngest son of my boatman, a boy of about seventeen, who is to be my teacher and guide, was waiting for me at the pier and guided me to his house, while the men settled the curagh and followed slowly with my baggage.

---

[1]a primitive type of canoe made of canvas and wood

My room is at one end of the cottage, with a boarded floor and ceiling, and two windows opposite each other. Then there is the kitchen with earth floor and open rafters, and two doors opposite each other opening into the open air, but no windows. Beyond it there are two small rooms of half the width of the kitchen with one window apiece.

The kitchen itself, where I will spend most of my time, is full of beauty and <u>distinction</u>. The red dresses of the women who cluster round the fire on their stools give a glow of almost Eastern richness, and the walls have been toned by the turf-smoke to a soft brown that blends with the grey earth-colour of the floor. Many sorts of fishing-tackle, and the nets and oil-skins of the men, are hung upon the walls or among the open rafters; and right overhead, under the thatch,[2] there is a whole cowskin from which they make pampooties.[3]

Every article on these islands has an almost personal character, which gives this simple life, where all art is unknown, something of the artistic beauty of medieval life. The curaghs and spinning-wheels, the tiny wooden barrels that are still much used in the place of earthenware, the home-made cradles, churns, and baskets, are all full of individuality, and being made from materials that are common here, yet to some extent peculiar to the island, they seem to exist as a natural link between the people and the world that is about them.

The simplicity and unity of the dress increases in another way the local air of beauty. The women wear red petticoats and jackets of the island wool stained with madder,[4] to which they usually add a plaid shawl twisted round their chests and tied at their back. When it rains they throw another petticoat over their heads with the waistband round their faces, or, if they are young, they use a heavy shawl like those worn in Galway. Occasionally other wraps are worn, and during the thunderstorm I arrived in I saw several girls with men's waistcoats buttoned round their bodies. Their skirts do not come much below the knee, and show their powerful legs in the heavy indigo[5] stockings with which they are all provided.

The men wear three colours: the natural wool, indigo, and a grey flannel that is woven of alternate threads of indigo and the natural wool. In Aranmor many of the younger men have adopted the usual fisherman's jersey, but I have only seen one on this island.

As flannel is cheap—the women spin the yarn from the wool of their own sheep, and it is then woven by a weaver in Kilronan for fourpence a yard—the men seem to wear an indefinite number of waistcoats and woollen drawers one over the other. They are usually surprised at the lightness of my own dress, and one old man I spoke to for a minute on the pier, when I came ashore, asked me if I was not cold with 'my little clothes.'

As I sat in the kitchen to dry the spray from my coat, several men who had seen me walking up came in to me to talk to me, usually

_____

[2]roof made of woven grass, straw, or other plant material
[3]shoes or slippers
[4]red plant dye
[5]dark blue

murmuring on the threshold, 'The blessing of God on this place,' or some similar words.

The courtesy of the old woman of the house is <u>singularly</u> attractive, and though I could not understand much of what she said—she has no English—I could see with how much grace she motioned each visitor to a chair, or stool, according to his age, and said a few words to him till he drifted into our English conversation.

For the moment my own arrival is the chief subject of interest, and the men who come in are eager to talk to me.

Some of them express themselves more correctly than the ordinary peasant, others use the Gaelic <u>idioms</u> continually and substitute 'he' or 'she' for 'it,' as the neuter pronoun is not found in modern Irish.

A few of the men have a curiously full vocabulary, others know only the commonest words in English, and are driven to <u>ingenious</u> devices to express their meaning. Of all the subjects we can talk of war seems their favourite, and the conflict between America and Spain is causing a great deal of excitement. Nearly all the families have relations who have had to cross the Atlantic, and all eat of the flour and bacon that is brought from the United States, so they have a vague fear that 'if anything happened to America,' their own island would cease to be <u>habitable</u>.

Foreign languages are another favourite topic, and as these men are bilingual they have a fair notion of what it means to speak and think in many different idioms. Most of the strangers they see on the islands are philological students, and the people have been led to conclude that <u>linguistic</u> studies, particularly Gaelic studies, are the chief occupation of the outside world.

'I have seen Frenchmen, and Danes, and Germans,' said one man, 'and there does be a power a Irish books along with them, and they reading them better than ourselves. Believe me there are few rich men now in the world who are not studying the Gaelic.'

They sometimes ask me the French for simple phrases, and when they have listened to the <u>intonation</u> for a moment, most of them are able to reproduce it with admirable precision.

Understanding the Reading

Complete the next three exercises and see how well you understood the excerpt from *The Aran Islands*.

Exercise 7.4   Multiple-Choice Questions

Answer the following questions about the reading. Circle the letter of your answer.

TIP: Don't try to answer the questions from memory; go back to the text as often as necessary.

1. From context, you can determine that philological students study
   A. what people do for a living in Ireland.
   B. Gaelic books and Irish traditions.
   C. language and its development.
   D. logic and mathematics.

2. Who is "the man who had been in France" in paragraph 4?
   A. one of the crew members
   B. a friend the author brought along
   C. the captain of the large boat
   D. the author

3. Which statement is true?
   A. The author is very interested in the islanders' language.
   B. The islanders are haughty and contemptuous.
   C. The author feels frightened and threatened by the islanders.
   D. The author is repulsed by the islanders' simplicity.

4. The man who mentioned the author's "little clothes" was referring to his
   A. having brought only one suit of clothes with him.
   B. clothes being lighter weight than the islanders'.
   C. clothes being obviously too small for him.
   D. clothes being a different color than those on Inishmaan.

5. From context, you can infer that Galway, Kilronan, and Aranmor are
   A. names of some of the island's residents.
   B. other islands in the Aran group.
   C. names of companies that make flannel cloth.
   D. other places in Ireland.

Exercise 7.5 Short-Answer Questions

Respond to the following questions in one to two complete sentences. Go back to the text, as you did on the multiple choice.

6. Why do you think one man told the author, "Believe me there are few rich men now in the world who are not studying the Gaelic"?

   _____

   _____

   _____

7. In what ways does the author equate *simplicity* with *beauty* in this passage?

   _____

   _____

   _____

8. The islanders fear that "if anything happened to America" they could no longer live on Inishmaan. Do you think this is a common fear in other nations? Explain.

_____

_____

_____

9. Synge tells us that the men on the island are excited about the war between Spain and America. The war took place from 1898 to 1899 and began in part because the United States supported Cuba in its efforts to gain independence from Spain. Why would the circumstances of the war interest residents of the Aran Islands—Irish people who were subjects of Britain?

_____

_____

_____

Exercise 7.6   Extending Your Thinking

Respond to the following question in three to four complete sentences. Use details from the text in your answer.

10. The theme of this unit is "Other Places, Other Times." What contributed to the narrator's feeling that he was in "another place, another time," even though he was still in his native Ireland?

_____

_____

_____

_____

_____

_____

Reading Strategy Lesson
Distinguishing Fact from Opinion

Who Is Telling the Truth?

Many nonfiction pieces you read contain a mixture of factual information and the author's opinions, especially in newspapers, in magazines, or on the Internet. Authors frequently disguise their opinions as fact, to make their arguments seem more believable. As a reader, it is important that you read critically and frequently ask yourself, "Is this an expression of fact or opinion?" "Is this worded to sound like something it isn't?" "Can I believe this?"

Here is an example of deceptive wording:

> Jessica started going to the Smith Learning Center in October. In December, her grades had greatly improved.

You hear testimonials like this all the time in TV commercials. Each sentence might be true on its own, but when they're put together, they can be quite misleading. Perhaps Jessica's grades did go up, but we don't know if that had anything to do with the Smith Learning Center. Maybe she started studying more, turned in late assignments, or completed extra credit work. Or maybe her grades improved in subjects different from the ones for which she got extra help at the center. We don't even know how often she frequented the center. It is the center's *position* that they deserve credit for her success, but it is not necessarily true or verifiable.

Distinguishing opinion from fact can be very challenging. To learn more about the center, you could do further research. You would need to carefully consider your sources. If they are biased—written by people who work for the center, for example—you might find yourself right back where you started. While you know there are at least two sides to the story, you still don't know which one to believe.

When you do online research, there are so many sources of information at your disposal that it becomes particularly difficult to determine which ones are valid or biased. Here are some tips to help you distinguish facts from opinions on the Internet.

The Internet: Proceed with Caution

Every day, we rely more and more on the Internet for information. It is true that it offers tremendous amounts of dependable information and opportunities to learn a great deal. It is also true that anyone can post "information" or comments that are completely untrue and misleading. Blogs and chat rooms are obvious examples where people are simply spouting their opinions—so you at least know you should carefully filter anything you find there. On the other hand, there are legitimate-looking Web sites that are also replete with lies. Before you trust the information on a Web site:

- Check the URL extension: ".com" means "commercial," the site is a business; ".gov" means the site is maintained by the federal government; ".org" means the source of the site is an organization. While none of these extensions guarantee that their information is accurate, they do give you a clue to the site's purpose. If it is likely that the site owners/operators want to influence your opinion or convince you to buy something, bear that in mind.

- Explore what kind of evidence is given for the information on the Web site. Is it from a reliable source or study, or does it seem to be just one person's ideas?

- See if the Web site has sections like "About Us" and "Contact Us." Is there a physical address in the contact information? Is there a phone number? Are there names of people associated with the Web site?

- Double-check your information by looking at several other Web sites and other types of media, such as newspapers, encyclopedias, and so forth.

Getting at the Truth

The sharing of honest and well-reasoned disagreements is healthy. Freedom of speech is one of the most treasured of American rights. Unfortunately, the result of freedom of speech can be misleading information. Ultimately, it is up to you to learn the truth.

No one has the time to research every article or statement he or she hears. Therefore, it's helpful to have a reading strategy you can apply whenever you need to separate fact from opinion.

REMEMBER:
- A fact is something that can be proved, based on objective information.
- An opinion expresses a view, an idea, or a belief that cannot be proved.

Opinion

You can suspect that an article you are reading is mostly based on opinion if you find

- words that express judgments or evaluations about something or someone, especially in absolutes (for example, *best, only, biggest, worst, fastest, smartest, most, evil*).

- key phrases that indicate the writer is giving an opinion, such as "I believe," "I think," "In my opinion," "I suggest."

- phrases that indicate others agree with the writer, such as "many believe" or "most feel." (Ask yourself, *How many? Most of whom?*)

- attempts to make the reader feel foolish for not agreeing. Watch for phrases like "Anyone who believes otherwise is not being realistic," "You will have to admit," "You should," "You ought to," "Like thousands of others."

- words that express a degree of uncertainty, such as *might, may, could, possibly, up to, as much as,* or *probably*.

The questions on the following page will help you determine the reliability of something you're reading.

Fact

- Can the facts be verified? Trusted?

- Who produced the facts, and how did they get them? Are the facts truly relevant to the point?

- Is the author experienced or educated in this field?

- Is the article objective, or does it seem like it may be biased?

- Does the writer give sources for the facts presented? Are these sources reliable?

- If the facts come from a study, who funded it? How many people did it involve? What kinds of people were chosen to participate?

- Has the author countered the claims of the other side?

- Do the facts prove the author's claim or merely suggest that it is true?

- Does the author use qualifying words or phrases such as *relatively*, *most*, or *only*?

Exercise 7.7 Practice the Reading Strategy

Indicate whether each statement is fact or opinion by writing F or O on the blank.

_____ 1. Everyone enjoys a roller coaster ride. Even people who scream are having fun.

_____ 2. The first roller coaster was built in Russia in the 1700s. It was actually two long ice slides. Riders had to climb to the tops of the slides on wooden stairs.

_____ 3. The Mauch Chunk Switchback Railway in Pennsylvania was America's first roller coaster. People raced down a long incline in a railway car.

_____ 4. It's too bad the MCR no longer runs.

_____ 5. In 1884, La Marcus Adna Thompson built the first true American roller coaster at Coney Island in Brooklyn, New York. Then he and a man named John Miller teamed up to build the first real "scream machines."

_____ 6. Probably every town in America wanted one of their coasters.

_____ 7. Cedar Point Amusement Park in Sandusky, Ohio, has 16 roller coasters. It's called "the roller coaster capital of the world."

_____ 8. Some roller coasters there are just too scary for any intelligent person.

_____ 9. Roller coasters do not have engines. After they get to the top of the first hill, they work completely by inertia and gravity.

_____ 10. Gravity pulls the coaster cars down, and inertia keeps them moving.

Exercise 7.8 Apply the Reading Strategy to Analyze Articles

The two articles that follow are on the same topic. However, each provides a different slant. Read the articles, underlining statements of opinion twice and statements of fact once. Circle any qualifiers or seemingly deceptive wording. Then answer the questions.

Article 1
Better Beach Health Spotlighted in New U.S. Data

(Washington, D.C.—July 27, 2005) U.S. beaches have become more-enjoyable places for Americans to play, thanks to improved water monitoring and state and local actions to address sources of pollution.

EPA's most recent data on beach closings and advisories show that only four percent of beach days were lost in 2004 due to advisories or closures triggered by monitoring for bacteria. Most of the closures were relatively short in duration. More than 2,700 closings were two days or less, and only 59 closings lasted more than 30 days.

The number of beaches monitored has more than tripled—3,574 in 2004, compared with 1,021 in 1997, the first year EPA began collecting beach-monitoring program data. Of the beaches reported to EPA in 2004, 942, or 26 percent, had at least one advisory or closing during the 2004 season.

The differences are attributable both to greater state participation in the program and also to improved measurement and monitoring made possible by grant money from EPA. For the past five years, EPA has provided nearly $42 million in grants to 35 coastal and Great Lakes states and territories. The grants help improve water monitoring and fund public-information programs that alert beach-goers about the health of their beaches.

"The small percentage of beach days lost in 2004 is encouraging," said Assistant Administrator for Water Benjamin H. Grumbles. "Reducing exposure to disease-causing bacteria in beach water will help protect all Americans, especially children, who are more susceptible to pathogens. Finding the sources of pollution will help keep beach-goers safe at their favorite recreational spots. Federal dollars have gone a long way to help states identify problems."

1. Is the first sentence of the article fact or opinion? Explain your answer.

_____

_____

_____

2. Does the article tell how many actual days beaches were closed or warnings (advisories) were posted? If so, what is the exact number?

_____

_____

_____

3. Are there any words or phrases in this article that give an impression of something without being specific? Explain.

_____

_____

_____

4. Does the article compare beach closings to the previous year? If so, where?

_____

_____

_____

5. What phrases are used in this article to create a positive feeling about the safety of the nation's beaches?

_____

_____

_____

Article 2
Beach Closings Climb in 2004
According to the National Resources Defense Council's annual report, U.S. beach closings and advisories related to pollution numbered higher than ever in 2004. There were almost 20,000 days of closings and advisories across the country at beaches on the oceans, bays, and the Great Lakes. This represents an increase of 9 percent over 2003.

One reason for the difference is increased monitoring and higher standards for bacteria testing. New testing policies and practices mandated by a 2000 federal law are beginning to show true levels of beach water pollution. The BEACH Act of 2000 required coastal and Great Lakes states to begin regularly monitoring beach water by 2004 and advising the public when it is unsafe to enter.

While monitoring has increased, there is another alarming trend. Normally, beach water is polluted by sewage discharges and runoff from streets after rains or during the spring melt. In 2004, 73 percent of the closings and advisories were ascribed to "unknown sources."

Until 2001, laws protecting wetlands and headwaters that filter water before it flows into lakes and oceans helped keep beach waters cleaner. Many of these protections were rolled back, and there have been proposals to lessen sewage treatment requirements. Contaminated storm water from new development is allowed to pollute rivers that flow into lakes and seas, and federal funding for clean water programs has been cut.

The large number of closings and advisories in 2004 is clear evidence that pollution controls need to be tightened, not relaxed.

1. Does this article mention the total number of beach closings in 2004? If so, what is it?

   _____

   _____

   _____

2. Why does this article talk about the waterways leading into the lakes and oceans?

   _____

   _____

   _____

3. Are there any words or phrases in this article that give an impression of something without being specific? Explain.

   _____

   _____

   _____

4. What is the general tone of this article regarding the safety of the nation's beaches?

   _____

   _____

   _____

5. Compare the two articles. Which article do you believe is more factual? Explain your reasoning.

   _____

   _____

   _____

Writing Workshop
Using Fact and Opinion

In the Reading Strategy Lesson, you learned that it is not always easy to distinguish fact from opinion, and that writers can make opinions sound as convincing as facts.

When you write a persuasive or explanatory essay, you know that you need to support your statements with facts. However, this doesn't mean you can't express an opinion. In fact, when you respond to an essay prompt, you begin with a thesis statement that *gives* your opinion or position. Then you give factual evidence to support your thesis.

Suppose you are given the following essay topic:

> J. M. Synge wrote the play *Riders to the Sea* after his research in the Aran Islands. Audiences disliked the play because they thought he was making fun of simple Irish country people. You have read part of his research about the Aran Islands. *Do you think he intended to mock the people he met?* Explain your answer.

The italicized words in the prompt tell you that you need to answer the question, "Do you think he intended to mock the people he met?" In other words, you need to give your opinion. Then you need to back it up with facts from the reading selection. Your thesis statement could read something like this:

> In his play *Riders to the Sea*, J. M. Synge intended to mock the people he met in the Aran Islands.
>
> OR
>
> In his play *Riders to the Sea*, J. M. Synge did not intend to mock the people he met in the Aran Islands.

Notice that the **thesis statement** directly addresses the italicized sentence in the prompt.

To continue the essay, you would need to go back to the reading and find some facts to support your opinion. For example, if you felt that Synge was making fun of the people, you might choose these facts:

1. They were very impressed that Synge had been to France, which is only across the English Channel. He is showing that the people have never been anywhere.
2. The islanders took him to Inishmaan in a primitive canoe.
3. The kitchen has an earth floor, and the walls are stained with smoke.
4. Synge calls their lifestyle "medieval."
5. Synge makes fun of the men's "indefinite number of waist-coats."
6. He points out how they call objects "he" and "she."

Exercise 7.9 Practice the Writing Lesson

Suppose you saw Synge's visit to the island of Inishmaan in a completely different way. An opposing case can be made for every one of the points listed above. Briefly describe an opposite view for each item. The first one has been done for you.

1. They were very impressed that Synge had been to France, which is only across the English Channel. He is showing that the people have never been anywhere.

   Opposing view: <u>Synge was charmed by the islanders' isolation.</u>

2. The islanders took him to Inishmaan in a primitive canoe.

   Opposing view: _____

3. The kitchen has an earth floor, and the walls are stained with smoke.

   Opposing view: _____

4. Synge calls their lifestyle "medieval."

   Opposing view: _____

5. Synge makes fun of the men's "indefinite number of waistcoats."

   Opposing view: _____

6. He points out how they call objects "he" and "she."

   Opposing view: _____

Exercise 7.10 Apply the Lesson to Your Own Writing

Choose one of the following topics. Brainstorm by making a T-chart or list of arguments for *both* sides (come up with three to five points for each side). When you're done brainstorming, write a detailed paragraph from the pro viewpoint. Include at least three of the points you came up with. Then write a detailed paragraph from the con viewpoint in the same way.

Topics:
1. Should juveniles who commit violent crimes be tried as adults?
2. Should motorcycle helmets be required in every state?
3. Should school cafeterias get rid of fast food and vending machines that sell junk food?
4. Can the assassination of a dictator be justified?
5. Are beauty contests harmful?
6. Do reality shows bring out the best in those involved?

Grammar Mini-Lesson
Using *Who, Whom, Who's,* and *Whose*

It is easy to get confused about when to use *who, whom, who's,* and *whose.* Well, *who* wouldn't be? Review the rules on the following page and then complete Exercise 7.11.

1. **Who** is used as a **subject** (the person or thing doing the verb in the sentence).

> "My mistress, **who** had kindly commenced to instruct me . . ."
> (Here, *who* is the subject of the verb *had commenced*. We're talking about a person *who* (*subj*) commenced to do something (*v*).)

> **Who** is absent?
> (*Who* is the subject of the verb *is*. We're talking about a person *who* (*subj*) is (*v*) absent.)

2. **Whom** is used as an **object**.

- as an object of a verb (the person or thing *receiving* the verb in the sentence)
  Frederick Douglass made friends of the boys **whom** he met in the street.
  (Here, *whom* is the object of the verb *met*. Douglass *met* (*v*) the *boys* (*obj*); the boys *whom* he met.)

  > **Whom** did you see?
  > (*Whom* is the object of the verb *did see*. This one is trickier because it's a question. If you're not sure whether to use *who* or *whom* in a question, try answering it. You *saw* (*v*) the *singers* (*obj*); the singers *whom* you saw.)

- as an object of a preposition (*from, to, with, next to, above, around*, etc.)
  Dan is the student with **whom** I changed places.
  (*Whom* is the object of the preposition *with*.)

  > From **whom** did you get the information?
  > (*Whom* is the object of the preposition *from*.)

3. **Whose** indicates ownership.
  The girl **whose** watch you found is my cousin.
  (*Whose* indicates ownership of *watch*.)

  > **Whose** glove is this?
  > (*Whose* indicates ownership of *glove*.)

CAUTION: Do not confuse *whose* with the contraction *who's* meaning "who is."

> *Who's* (*Who is*) absent?

Exercise 7.11 Practice Using *Who, Whom, Whose,* and *Who's*

Fill in the blank with the correct choice. The first one has been done for you.

1. Frederick Douglass gave bread to the hungry lads, <u>who</u> in return gave him the more valuable bread of knowledge.

2. To _____ should we send the check?

3. I could not tell _____ answer was correct.

4. _____ should we ask?

5. _____ on the telephone?

6. This is my sister Megan, _____ is in the ninth grade.

7. _____ turn is it?

8. Do you know by _____ the book was written?

9. At the entrance I met a teacher _____ I had a year ago.

10. _____ was elected?

Exercise 7.12 Apply the Lesson to Create Your Own Sentences

Follow the guidelines for each section.

I. Write three sentences using *who* correctly.

1._____
2._____
3._____

II. Write three sentences using *whom* correctly.

4._____
5._____
6._____

III. Write two sentences using *whose* correctly.

7._____
8._____

IV. Write two sentences using *who's* correctly.

9._____
10._____

Polish Your Spelling
When to Use -ABLE or -IBLE and -ABILITY or -IBILITY

-ABLE or -IBLE?

Should you use *-able* or *-ible* to complete *imagin - - - -*?

If you know there is an *-ation* word beginning with the letters *imagin* (for example, *imagination*), use *-able*.

Answer: *Imaginable*

Because nouns like *presentation, application, irritation,* and *adoration* exist, the corresponding adjectives are spelled *presentable, applicable, irritable,* and *adorable*.

Exception: *sensible* ends in *-ible*, despite the existence of *sensation*.

Except for this hint, there is no easy way to tell whether an adjective ends in *-able* or *-ible*. Therefore, study the following:

Frequently Used -ABLE Adjectives

acceptable	conceivable	disposable	miserable
advisable	consumable	excusable	perishable
applicable	dependable	hospitable	predictable
available	desirable	imaginable	presentable
believable	despicable	intolerable	probable

Frequently Used -IBLE Adjectives

convertible	feasible	invisible	plausible
digestible	flexible	irresistible	possible
divisible	horrible	legible	responsible
edible	incredible	negligible	sensible
eligible	inexhaustible	permissible	terrible

Note: The suffixes *-able* and *-ible* do not change when a prefix is added or removed.

> un + predict*able* = unpredict*able*
> improb*able* – im = prob*able*
> ir + respons*ible* = irrespons*ible*
> inexhaust*ible* – in = exhaust*ible*

-ABILITY OR -IBILITY?

Nouns ending in *-ability* come from adjectives ending in *-able*.
Nouns ending in *-ibility* come from adjectives ending in *-ible*.

ADJECTIVE	NOUN
advisable	advisability
responsible	responsibility

Exercise 7.13 Practice the Spelling Rules

A. The following adjectives have either *-able* or *-ible* omitted. Write the complete adjective on the line.

Example: undepend   <u>undependable</u>

1. unavail   _____

2. indigest   _____

3. miser   _____

4. imposs   _____

5. horr   _____

B. The following nouns have either *-ability* or *-ibility* omitted. Write the complete noun on the line.

Example: undepend   <u>undependability</u>

6. dur   _____

7. elig   _____

8. perish   _____

9. inflex   _____

10. present   _____

Chapter Eight

Prereading Guide
Words to know and ideas to consider before you jump into the reading.

A. Essential Vocabulary

Word	Meaning	Typical Use
conjecture (*v*) cun-JECK-shur	1. to guess; to arrive at a conclusion using guesswork; to surmise 2. (*n*) a guess	Since the lights were on, we *conjectured* that you were at home. You were there, so we had made the right *conjecture*.
derelict (*adj*) DAIR-i-likt	1. abandoned or discarded, usually due to poor condition; deserted 2. neglectful of one's responsibilities; delinquent 3. (*n*) a person or thing that has been outcast or rejected	The *derelict* boat has been slowly decaying on the vacant lot for years. She was *derelict* in learning her lines for the play. It was hard to believe that the homeless *derelict* was once a wealthy CEO.
excessive (*adj*) ek-CESS-iv	beyond what is usual or necessary; extreme	People usually get rid of an old car when repair costs become *excessive*.
gesticulate (*v*) jess-TICK-yu-late	to make hand motions while talking; gesture	My sister looked comical sitting alone, talking on her cell phone, and *gesticulating*.
intimation (*n*) in-ti-MAY-shun	a subtle clue or indication; implication	The dark clouds were an *intimation* that it would rain.
portal (*n*) POR-tul	a foyer or doorway, often a large and impressive one; entranceway	The *portals* of heaven are often called "the pearly gates."
precocious (*adj*) pre-KO-shus	developing abilities at an early age, especially mental skills; advanced	Everyone laughed when the *precocious* four-year-old told his aunt, "I'm grateful for your hospitality."
shrill (*adj*) SHRIHL	1. having a high-pitched sound; piercing 2. (*v*) to make a high piercing sound or cry	"I'm not going, and that's that," said Nicole in a *shrill* voice. The siren *shrilled* in the distance.
uneasiness (*n*) un-EAZ-ee-ness	the state of being restless or worried; anxiety	Arum was filled with *uneasiness* when the teacher passed out the tests.

Word	Meaning	Typical Use
utmost (*adj*) UT-mowst	to the greatest degree possible; maximum	Drivers were warned to drive with the *utmost* care on the slick streets.

B. Vocabulary Practice

Exercise 8.1   Sentence Completion

Using your new vocabulary knowledge, choose the best way to complete the following sentences. Circle the letter of your answer.

1. Listening to a shrill voice can be very _____.
   A. relaxing
   B. unpleasant

2. Excessive rain often causes _____.
   A. flooding
   B. storms

3. We are dealing with matters of utmost danger. Ordinary safety measures _____.
   A. will not suffice
   B. must be followed

4. When you are _____, there is no need to conjecture.
   A. in doubt
   B. certain

5. Heather's uneasiness over the tryouts _____.
   A. helped her sleep soundly
   B. kept her awake

6. Austin was a _____ when he was sixteen. He is that precocious.
   A. sophomore at the university
   B. freshman in high school

7. "Do you still wear earrings?" my friend asked, _____ that she was considering buying me jewelry for my birthday.
   A. declaring
   B. intimating

8. The derelict car was sold for _____.
   A. scrap
   B. almost $15,000

9. Tracy improved her _____ by learning to gesticulate.
   A. concentration
   B. public speaking

10. The lavishly decorated portal was the _____ of the tour of the mansion.
    A. beginning
    B. end

Exercise 8.2   Using Fewer Words

Replace the italicized words with a single word from the following list.

conjectured	excessive	shrill	uneasiness	utmost
portal	gesticulate	derelict	intimation	precocious

1. What is the reason for your *restlessness and worry?*   1._____

2. The president's visit received the *greatest possible* publicity.   2._____

3. When we saw Sam's car, we *arrived at the conclusion* that he had returned home.   3._____

4. The electric saw made a(an) *high-pitched and piercing* sound.   4._____

5. The snow this past winter was *beyond what is usual.*   5._____

6. The *subtle hint* was that he wanted to ask me out.   6._____

7. If my grandfather can't *make hand motions,* he can't talk.   7._____

8. *Advanced beyond her years,* Alyssa played the violin at age five.   8._____

9. The *outcast vagrant* was a sad sight.   9._____

10. Wait for me by the *entrance or doorway.*   10._____

Exercise 8.3   Synonyms and Antonyms

Fill in the blanks in column A with the required synonyms or antonyms, selecting them from column B. (Remember: A *synonym* is a word similar in meaning to another word. An *antonym* is a word opposite in meaning to another word.)

	A	B
_____	1. synonym for *maximum*	conjecture
_____	2. synonym for *advanced*	excessive
_____	3. synonym for *hint*	shrill
_____	4. synonym for *extreme*	uneasiness
_____	5. antonym for *responsible*	utmost
_____	6. synonym for *piercing*	portal
_____	7. synonym for *entranceway*	gesticulate
_____	8. antonym for *fact*	derelict
_____	9. antonym for *comfort*	intimation
_____	10. synonym for *gesture*	precocious

C. Journal Freewrite

Before you begin the reading on the next page, take out a journal or sheet of paper and spend some time responding to the following prompt.

TIP: Don't worry about grammar and spelling; just write what comes to mind. The purpose of freewriting is to explore ideas, not to produce a polished work.

Imagine that you are having a very odd dream. As you are dreaming you are actually wishing you would wake up. The only problem is this: You find out you're already awake. Briefly describe a dream you've had and how you would deal with the situation if you woke up and found it was real. (If you can't remember a dream, use your imagination.)

from Gulliver's Travels

by Jonathan Swift

About the Author
Jonathan Swift
(1667–1745) was an Irish poet and political writer known for being a master of satire—using wit, irony, or sarcasm to expose someone's or something's vices or foolish behaviors. His poems, stories, political pamphlets, and novels mock leading literary, religious, and political figures of his time. One of his best-known works, *Gulliver's Travels* (which he published under the name "Lemuel Gulliver"), was well received as escapist fantasy. Beneath the story, however, is a satire of political parties and courts, social conditions, and the pompous class activities Swift had spent most of his life condemning.

Reader's Tip: In this excerpt, Gulliver, the only survivor of a shipwreck, is cast up on the shore of an unknown land, where a strange adventure befalls him. Keep in mind that Gulliver's Travels *is a satire. The characters symbolize people in English government and society.*

I then advanced forward near half a mile, but could not discover any sign of houses or inhabitants; at least I was in so weak a condition, that I did not observe them. I was extremely tired, and with that, and the heat of the weather, and about half a pint of brandy that I drank as I left the ship, I found myself much inclined to sleep. I lay down on the grass, which was very short and soft, where I slept sounder than ever I remember to have done in my life, and, as I reckoned, above nine hours; for when I awake, it was just daylight. I attempted to rise, but was not able to stir: For as I happened to lie on my back, I found my arms and legs were strongly fastened on each side to the ground; and my hair, which was long and thick, tied down in the same manner. I likewise felt several slender ligatures across my body, from my armpits to my thighs. I could only look upwards, the sun began to grow hot, and the light offended my eyes. I heard a confused noise about me, but in the posture I lay, could see nothing except the sky. In a little time I felt something alive moving on my left leg, which advancing gently forward over my breast, came almost up to my chin; when bending my eyes downwards as much as I could, I perceived it to be a human creature not six inches high, with a bow and arrow in his hands, and a quiver at his back. In the mean time, I felt at least forty more of the same kind (as I <u>conjectured</u>) following the first. I was in the <u>utmost</u> astonishment, and roared so loud, that they all ran back in a fright; and some of them, as I was afterwards told, were hurt with the falls they got by leaping from my sides upon the ground. However, they soon returned, and one of them, who ventured so far as to get a full sight of my face, lifting up his hands and eyes by way of admiration, cried out in a <u>shrill</u> but distinct voice, *Hekinah Degul*: The others repeated the same words several times, but

I then knew not what they meant. I lay all this while, as the reader may believe, in great <u>uneasiness</u>; At length, struggling to get loose, I had the fortune to break the strings, and wrench out the pegs that fastened my left arm to the ground; for, by lifting it up to my face, I discovered the methods they had taken to bind me; and, at the same time, with a violent pull, which gave me <u>excessive</u> pain, I a little loosened the strings that tied down my hair on the left side, so that I was just able to turn my head about two inches. But the creatures ran off a second time, before I could seize them; whereupon there was a great shout in a very shrill accent, and after it ceased, I heard one of them cry aloud, *Tolgo Phonac*; when in an instant I felt above an hundred arrows discharged on my left hand, which pricked me like so many needles; and besides they shot another flight into the air, as we do bombs in Europe, whereof many, I suppose, fell on my body (though I felt them not) and some on my face, which I immediately covered with my left hand. When this shower of arrows was over, I fell a-groaning with grief and pain, and then striving again to get loose, they discharged another volley larger than the first, and some of them attempted with spears to stick me in the sides; but, by good luck, I had on me a buff jerkin,[1] which they could not pierce. I thought it the most prudent method to lie still, and my design was to continue so till night, when my left hand being already loose, I could easily free myself: and as for the inhabitants, I had reason to believe I might be a match for the greatest armies they could bring against me, if they were all of the same size with him that I saw.

---

[1]close-fitting leather tunic or vest

Understanding the Reading

Complete the next three exercises and see how well you understood the excerpt from *Gulliver's Travels*.

Exercise 8.4   Multiple-Choice Questions

Answer the following questions about the reading. Circle the letter of your answer.

TIP: *Don't try to answer the questions from memory; go back to the text as often as necessary.*

1. From context, you can determine that *ligatures* (p. 149) means
   A. ligaments or tendons.
   B. heavy chains.
   C. a tightly braided rope.
   D. something used to tie something else.

2. *Tolgo Phonac* most likely means
   A. "Run away quickly!"
   B. "Here comes Tolgo!"
   C. "Let the arrows fly!"
   D. "This man is a giant!"

3. When Gulliver says, ". . . but I then knew not what they meant," you can infer that
   A. he would have to look in a dictionary to see what *Hekinah Degul* meant.
   B. *Hekinah Degul* is the name of the little people's leader.
   C. Gulliver will stay with the little people long enough to learn their language.
   D. *Hekinah Degul* means something bad will happen.

4. Gulliver plans to
   A. wait until night to free himself and sneak away.
   B. catch some of the little humans and take them back to Ireland.
   C. use his personal experience to prove the existence of leprechauns.
   D. wait until night to free himself and easily fight off anyone who interferes.

Exercise 8.5   Short-Answer Questions

Respond to the following questions in one to two complete sentences. Go back to the text, as you did on the multiple choice.

5. Think back to the author sidebar about Jonathan Swift and the Reader's Tip. If Gulliver symbolizes a moral middle-class Englishman, and the tiny men symbolize politicians, what connection can you draw between their relative sizes and their behaviors?

   _____

   _____

   _____

6. What is the satirical symbolism of the little men tying up Gulliver while he was asleep?

   _____

   _____

   _____

7. What do you think happens next in this story?

   _____

   _____

   _____

Exercise 8.6 Extending Your Thinking

Respond to the following question in three to four complete sentences. Use details from the texts in your answer.

8. Both Gulliver and Synge visited unusual islands. How does Gulliver's imaginary experience on the island of tiny men compare to Synge's actual experience on the island of Inishmaan? Whose experience would you rather have? Why?

_____

_____

_____

_____

_____

_____

_____

from The Time Machine

by H. G. Wells

About the Author
Herbert George Wells (1866–1946) was an English novelist best known for his popular science fiction. He was concerned about the future of the world and the survival of human civilization, and he envisioned the future as a nightmare taken over by technology and alien empires. In 1928, he wrote *The Open Conspiracy: Blue Prints for a World Revolution*, advocating a global civilization. His novel *The War of the Worlds* was made into a motion picture in 1960, and in 2004 Steven Spielberg adapted the story for a remake. This is an excerpt from his first novel, *The Time Machine*, published in 1894.

Reader's Tip: In this story, an inventor in Victorian England has created a machine that he hopes will take him back in time to correct the errors of the past. Instead, he is propelled into the year 802,701.

A queer thing I soon discovered about my little hosts, and that was their lack of interest. They would come to me with eager cries of astonishment, like children, but like children they would soon stop examining me and wander away after some other toy. The dinner and my conversational beginnings ended, I noted for the first time that almost all those who had surrounded me at first were gone. It is odd, too, how speedily I came to disregard these little people. I went out through the portal into the sunlit world again as soon as my hunger was satisfied. I was continually meeting more of these men of the future, who would follow me a little distance, chatter and laugh about me, and, having smiled and gesticulated in a friendly way, leave me again to my own devices.

The calm of evening was upon the world as I emerged from the great hall, and the scene was lit by the warm glow of the setting sun. At first things were very confusing. Everything was so entirely different from the world I had known—even the flowers. The big building I had left was situated on the slope of a broad river valley, but the Thames had shifted perhaps a mile from its present position. I resolved to mount to the summit of a crest perhaps a mile and a half away, from which I could get a wider view of this our planet in the year Eight Hundred and Two Thousand Seven Hundred and One A.D. For that, I should explain, was the date the little dials of my machine[1] recorded.

As I walked I was watching for every impression that could possibly help to explain the condition of ruinous splendour in which I found the world—for ruinous it was. A little way up the hill, for instance, was a great heap of granite, bound together by masses of aluminium, a vast labyrinth of

---

[1] the time machine

precipitous walls and crumpled heaps, amidst which were thick heaps of very beautiful pagoda-like plants—nettles possibly but wonderfully tinted with brown about the leaves, and incapable of stinging. It was evidently the <u>derelict</u> remains of some vast structure, to what end built I could not determine. It was here that I was destined, at a later date, to have a very strange experience—the first <u>intimation</u> of a still stranger discovery—but of that I will speak in its proper place.

Looking round with a sudden thought, from a terrace on which I rested for a while, I realized that there were no small houses to be seen. Apparently the single house, and possibly even the household, had vanished. Here and there among the greenery were palace-like buildings, but the house and the cottage, which form such characteristic features of our own English landscape, had disappeared.

"Communism," said I to myself.

And on the heels of that came another thought. I looked at the half-dozen little figures that were following me. Then, in a flash, I perceived that all had the same form of costume, the same soft hairless visage, and the same girlish rotundity[2] of limb. It may seem strange, perhaps, that I had not noticed this before. But everything was so strange. Now, I saw the fact plainly enough. In costume, and in all the differences of texture and bearing that now mark off the sexes from each other, these people of the future were alike. And the children seemed to my eyes to be but the miniatures of their parents. I judged, then, that the children of that time were extremely <u>precocious</u>, physically at least, and I found afterwards abundant verification of my opinion.

Seeing the ease and security in which these people were living, I felt that this close resemblance of the sexes was after all what one would expect; for the strength of a man and the softness of a woman, the institution of the family, and the differentiation of occupations are mere militant necessities of an age of physical force; where population is balanced and abundant, much childbearing becomes an evil rather than a blessing to the State; where violence comes but rarely and off-spring are secure, there is less necessity—indeed there is no necessity—for an efficient family, and the specialization of the sexes with reference to their children's needs disappears. We see some beginnings of this even in our own time, and in this future age it was complete. This, I must remind you, was my speculation at the time. Later, I was to appreciate how far it fell short of the reality.

———
[2]soft roundness

Understanding the Reading

Complete the next three exercises and see how well you understood the excerpt from *The Time Machine*.

Exercise 8.7   Multiple-Choice Questions

Answer the following questions about the reading. Circle the letter of your answer.

TIP: Don't try to answer the questions from memory; go back to the text as often as necessary.

1. From context, you can determine that *visage* (p. 174) means
   A. device for gripping things.
   B. small ear.
   C. face.
   D. leg.

2. Where does this story take place?
   A. a spaceship traveling through a time warp
   B. England in A.D. 802,701
   C. medieval England
   D. another planet in modern times

3. The different strengths of males and females are unnecessary in the society described because
   A. everyone does the same job.
   B. there is little violence and the people are happy and secure.
   C. either parent can meet the children's needs.
   D. both B and C.

4. The narrator describes his surroundings as "ruinous splendour" because
   A. things from the past were in ruins, but the place had its own grandeur.
   B. the small beings thought it was splendid to ruin things from the past.
   C. the place was a disaster area.
   D. English cottages no longer existed.

Exercise 8.8   Short-Answer Questions

Respond to the following questions in one to two complete sentences. Go back to the text, as you did on the multiple choice.

5. How are the little people in Wells's world of the future different from those Gulliver encountered in the previous reading?

   _____

   _____

   _____

6. What do you think would have to happen to allow the inhabitants of a far-in-the-future world to live in "ease and security"?

_____

_____

_____

7. While both stories in this chapter are fiction, which place—the one created by Wells or the one created by Swift—is less likely ever to exist? Why?

_____

_____

_____

Exercise 8.9   Extending Your Thinking

Respond to the following question in three to four complete sentences. Use details from the text in your answer.

8. Explain what you think Wells means by "where population is balanced and abundant, much childbearing becomes an evil rather than a blessing to the State" (last paragraph).

_____

_____

_____

_____

_____

_____

Reading Strategy Lesson
Thinking About Setting

When writers create a story, one of the first decisions they have to make involves the **setting**—where and when it will take place. The **setting** is both the *time* and *place* in which the events of the story occur. The time may be a historical period, such as the Middle Ages or the early twentieth century, or it may be much more specific: a certain year, date, or even part of a day. In a similar way, the place may be general or specific. For example, *England* or *an island country* are general settings. *London, England*, and *Hawaii* are more specific. *Buckingham Palace* and *Waikiki Beach* are even more specific.

The setting affects the story's details. If a story is set in 1830, the characters will be writing letters or sending messages by foot or horseback to one another, not sending e-mails or telephoning as they might if it were set in today's world. A story that takes place in a spaceship is going to be much different from one that takes place in a covered wagon.

When you read, try to picture the setting. This will help you gain a fuller understanding of what is happening in the story.

Exercise 8.10 Practice the Reading Strategy

Read the following passage. Underline the clues that tell you about the setting.

> Despite the blinding blizzard, the animals had to be tended. Jeremiah tied a rope to the railing of the porch, tied the other end to his belt, and headed in the direction of the barn. He thought he could see the merest shadow of the wagon they'd brought all the way from Kentucky to the Nebraska Territory, and he knew if he got to the wagon, he could see the barn. He would never be able to go to sleep knowing he'd left Bessie unmilked and loyal Tom and Sadie, the best horses in the territory, wondering why they had no hay or oats.

Since travel was by horse and wagon and Nebraska was not yet a state, you know this is not modern times, but somewhere in the late 1800s. There is a barn, a cow, and horses, so this must be a farm. It is snowing, so the story must take place in the winter. You should have underlined *blizzard*, *barn*, *wagon*, *Nebraska Territory*, *unmilked*, and *horses*.

Exercise 8.11 Apply the Reading Strategy to *Gulliver's Travels* and *The Time Machine*

Answer the following questions in complete sentences.

1. Gulliver, the only survivor of a shipwreck, is cast up on the shore of an unknown land, where a strange adventure befalls him.

What is the setting? _____

2. Read these sentences from *The Time Machine*:

The big building I had left was situated on the slope of a broad river valley, but the Thames had shifted perhaps a mile from its present position. I resolved to mount to the summit of a crest perhaps a mile and a half away, from which I could get a wider view of this our planet in the year Eight Hundred and Two Thousand Seven Hundred and One A.D. For that, I should explain, was the date the little dials of my machine recorded.

What do these sentences tell you about the setting of the story? Underline the clues and write your answer on the lines.

_____

_____

_____

Writing Workshop
Using a Variety of Sentence Structures

Read the following passage, paying close attention to the different sentence structures.

> The undisguised open-mouthed attention of the entire party was fixed on the homely, negative personality of Mr. Cornelius Appin. Of all her guests, he was the one who had come to Lady Blemley with the vaguest reputation. Someone had said he was "clever," and he had got his invitation in the moderate expectation, on the part of his hostess, that some portion at least of his cleverness would be contributed to the general entertainment. Until teatime that day she had been unable to discover in what direction, if any, his cleverness lay. He was neither a wit nor a croquet champion, a hypnotic force nor a begetter of amateur theatricals. Neither did his exterior suggest the sort of man in whom women are willing to pardon a generous measure of mental deficiency, he had subsided into mere Mr. Appin, and the Cornelius seemed a piece of transparent baptismal bluff. (Saki, "Tobermory")

Let's look at the sentence structures in the paragraph. The first sentence is an average-length simple sentence that includes several adjectives to make it interesting: *undisguised*, *open-mouthed*, *entire*, *homely*, *negative*. In just one sentence, the author has conveyed several ideas. Now read the second sentence:

> Of all her guests, he was the one who had come to Lady Blemley with the vaguest reputation.

It begins and ends with a prepositional phrase. It is a simple enough sentence, yet it introduces the hostess of the party (Lady Blemley) and implies that she has her doubts about Mr. Appin.

Look at the third sentence:

> Someone had said he was "clever," and he had got his invitation in the moderate expectation, on the part of his hostess, that some portion at least of his cleverness would be contributed to the general entertainment.

This is a more complicated sentence. The author could have simply said:

> Lady Blemley had invited Mr. Appin mostly because she thought he would be entertaining.

This sentence would provide us with about the same information, but it would be almost the same length as the two previous sentences.

Sentence structure variety is like seeing a variety of scenery as you ride along on a bus or train. If the scenery varies—even if that "scenery" is people or buildings—you look out the window with more interest. If it stays the same, you are likely to go to sleep. Similarly, sentence variety can keep your readers more interested and engaged in your work.

Let's look at how you can vary sentence structure.

1. Combine Shorter Sentences

The dog ran. The gate was open. The dog ran into the road. It was almost hit by a car. A neighbor stopped. He called the dog. He took the dog home. He shut the gate. He shut it firmly.

Does this remind you of something you read in grade school? When you first learned to read, the sentences were short and the words repeated because that made learning easier. As a writer, though, you generally don't want to sound that choppy. One way to avoid this is to combine your shorter sentences. For example:

The dog ran through the open gate and into the road, almost getting hit by a car. A neighbor stopped and called the dog, took him home, and shut the gate firmly as he left.

While this is smoother, we could still improve it by adding some descriptive words and changing some of the more common words into more interesting ones:

The frisky dog dashed through the open gate, narrowly missed by a speeding car. Fortunately, a passing neighbor called the little terrier and took her home, making especially sure the gate was firmly closed before he went on.

Compare the "mental scenery" of the original sentence with this one. Which is more alive? Don't be discouraged if you think something you've written lacks luster and life. Try combining your sentences and adding and changing words. Published writers and editors do it all the time, and so can you!

Exercise 8.12 Practice the Writing Lesson

Combine the simple sentences into one sentence and rewrite it on the lines. You may want to add or change words to make the final sentence more interesting.

1. Coastal storms sometimes sweep in from the Atlantic. They come with little warning. They can cause a lot of damage.

   _____

   _____

2. It was the critical moment. She could not respond. It was unfortunate. She was paralyzed with fright.

   _____

   _____

3. Eric changed his seat. It was against my wishes. He took his belongings with him.

_____

_____

4. The cheerleaders boosted our morale. They did it at the roughest moments. They inspired us to fight back.

_____

_____

5. A drenched motorcyclist stood beside his bike. He was in the shelter of the overpass. He watched the downpour.

_____

_____

2. Vary Sentence Beginnings

Another way to add variety to your sentence structure is to vary the way you begin each sentence. The normal word order of the English sentence is *subject-predicate*. The predicate consists of the verb and the words used with it to make a statement about the subject.

Example: The guards worked overtime without protest, expecting extra compensation.

However, if you begin all of your sentences with the subject ("The guards"), your writing will seem monotonous. For variety, try starting some of your sentences in a different way. Here are three ways you could vary the above sentence:

A. Begin with an adverb.
   Tirelessly, the guards worked overtime without protest, expecting extra compensation.

B. Begin with a prepositional phrase.
   Without protest, the guards worked overtime, expecting extra compensation.

C. Begin with a participial phrase.
   Expecting extra compensation, the guards worked overtime without protest.

WRITER'S HINT: Do you notice a slight difference in meaning among these three sentences? How you choose to begin not only affects structure but also affects your content—what part or idea you're emphasizing.

Exercise 8.13 Practice the Writing Lesson

Rewrite each sentence three times.

- On Line A, begin the sentence with an adverb.
- On line B, begin the sentence with a prepositional phrase.
- On line C, begin the sentence with a participial phrase.

If you get stuck, look back at the example from the lesson.

1. Courtney always lends me her notes without the slightest hesitation, knowing that I will take good care of them.

   A. _____

   _____

   B. _____

   _____

   C. _____

   _____

2. Three patients sat nervously in the outer office, waiting to see the dentist.

   A. _____

   _____

   B. _____

   _____

   C. _____

   _____

3. Benjamin usually turns on his TV before bedtime, hoping to be allowed to stay up.

   A. _____

   _____

   B. _____

   _____

   C. _____

   _____

4. Martinez is obviously the team's best pitcher at the moment, unbeaten in his last thirteen games.

   A. _____

   _____

   B. _____

   _____

   C. _____

   _____

5. Sydney often has a snack before dinner, insisting that she is starving.

A. _____

_____

B. _____

_____

C. _____

_____

Exercise 8.14 Apply the Lesson to Revise a Passage

Here is the continuation of the passage about Mr. Applin. Read and revise it, by combining the sentences in italics on the lines provided. You may also want to add descriptive words and change common phrases to more lively ones.

1. *Now he was claiming to have launched on the world a discovery. It was better than the invention of gunpowder. It was better than the printing press. It made steam locomotion seem trivial.*

_____

_____

_____

_____

2. "Here and there among cats," said Mr. Applin, "one comes across an outstanding superior intellect, just as one does among the ruck of human beings, and when I made the acquaintance of Tobermory a week ago, I saw at once that I was in contact with a 'Beyond—cat' of extraordinary intelligence. With Tobermory, as you call him, I have reached the goal."

   Sir Wilfred went in search of Tobermory. The party-goers found seats at the table. They did not expect much. They assumed Mr. Applin was something like a ventriloquist or magician.

_____

_____

_____

_____

3. *The cat, Tobermory, came into the room. Lady Blemley jokingly asked if he would like some milk. Toby seemed to nod. Then he surprised everyone. He said "I don't mind if I do."*

_____

_____

_____

_____

4. *They watched him drink. Nobody said a word. Then Toby sighed. He sat back. He looked at the people gathered at the table.*

_____

_____

_____

_____

5. "What do you think of human intelligence?" asked Mavis.
"You put me in an embarrassing position," said Tobermory.
He did not look embarrassed. "I remember when Lady Blemley suggested inviting you. Sir Wilfred said you were a brainless woman. Lady Blemley said she hoped you were thick enough to buy their old car. It won't start half the time. Just so you know."

_____

_____

_____

_____

6. "Wouldn't you like to go and see if cook has your dinner ready?" suggested Lady Blemley hurriedly, affecting to ignore the fact that it was at least two hours to Tobermory's dinnertime.
"Thanks," said Tobermory, "not quite so soon after tea."
"Adelaide!" said Mrs. Cornett, "Do you mean to encourage that cat to go out and gossip about us in the servants' hall?"
The panic spread. People began remembering that Toby was often around when they visited. He often sat on the windowsill in the parlor. Lady Blemley and her friends took tea in the parlor. They also gossiped about one another in the parlor.

_____

_____

_____

_____

At this point, the chronicle mercifully ceased. Tobermory had caught a glimpse of the big yellow Tom from the Rectory working his way through the shrubbery, and had vanished in a flash through the open French window.
Clovis broke the dominating silence. "He won't turn up tonight. He's probably in the local newspaper office at the present moment, dictating the first installment of his reminiscences."

Exercise 8.15 Apply the Lesson to Your Own Writing

Look back at the paragraphs you wrote for Exercise 7.10 on page 159. Choose one side (pro or con) and write a persuasive essay in response to the topic. Focus on using a variety of sentence structures as you write.

Grammar Mini-Lesson
Using *Which, Who,* and *That*

Which, who, and *that* are pronouns that *relate back* to a previous word. Therefore, we call them **relative pronouns**.

Jonathan Swift wrote
> I lay down on the grass, *which* was very short and soft . . .

In this sentence, *which* is a relative pronoun because it relates back to the noun *grass*.

The word to which a relative pronoun relates or refers is called its **antecedent**. In the example, *grass* is the antecedent of the pronoun *which*.

Note the following:
1. Use *which* if its antecedent is a thing.
   > . . . my hair, *which* was long and thick...

2. Use *who* if its antecedent is a person.
   > . . . one of them, *who* ventured so far as to get a full sight of my face . . .

3. Use *that* if its antecedent is either a thing or a person.
   > This is the bus *that* goes downtown.

Using *that* can help you emphasize something specific or important. "This is the bus *that* goes downtown" means that this is *the specific bus that goes downtown,* as opposed to all the others that don't.

Exercise 8.16 Practice Identifying Pronouns and Antecedents

Underline the relative pronoun once and the antecedent twice.

Example: I just finished reading the rest of <u>August Is a Wicked Month</u>, <u>which</u> I enjoyed very much.

1. I looked at the half dozen little figures that were following me.

2. We were waiting for some friends who had promised to meet us after school.

3. The players who were chosen were Mike, Derek, Andrew, and me.

4. I got the idea from a carpenter who repaired our building.

5. There is the mosquito that has been driving me nuts! Got him!

Check your answers. Compare them with a partner's. Do you have the same answers? Do the relative pronouns you underlined once refer back to the words or phrases you underlined twice?

Exercise 8.17 Practice Using Relative Pronouns

Enter the correct choice: *who*, *which*, or *that*.

1. First, I want to remind everyone of the book sale, _____ is scheduled for Saturday.

2. Now let's talk about the book _____ we read for this month.

3. How many of you are the same students _____ were at last month's meeting?

4. Who will get in touch with the members _____ were absent from this meeting?

5. We need to make sure they get the information _____ we discussed.

Polish Your Spelling
Contractions and Possessives

Many spelling mistakes are caused by confusion with contractions and possessives. *Do you need an apostrophe? Do you need an extra s? Does the apostrophe go before or after the s?* The following lesson will help clarify the punctuation rules so you can spell with more confidence.

1. Contractions
Jonathan Swift wrote
   I attempted to rise, but was not able to stir.

Another way to write this sentence is
   I attempted to rise, but *wasn't* able to stir.

The contraction *wasn't* is another way of saying "was not." The *apostrophe* takes the place of the *o* in the word *not*, and the two words are put together to make one word.
   An apostrophe takes the place of one letter in these examples: *isn't, couldn't, hadn't, wouldn't, it's, she's,* and *he's.*

H. G. Wells wrote

> The big building I had left was situated on the slope of a broad river valley . . .

Wells could have used the contraction *I'd* instead of "I had." The apostrophe in *I'd* replaces the letters ha in *had*.

An apostrophe can take the place of several letters in a contraction, for example in *who've* (who have), *they'd* (they had), *we've* (we have), and *can't* (cannot). When you want to change two words into a contraction, simply substitute an apostrophe for the letters that are left out.

A WRITER'S DECISIONS

Why do you think Swift and Wells decided to write out the words instead of using contractions? Think about how contractions affect tone. Is there a difference in sound between "We cannot come to your party" and "We can't come to your party"? In general, writing out the words sounds more formal. Keep this in mind in your own writing—spell out words when you want to sound more polished; use contractions when you can be more casual.

---

2. Possessive Pronouns

The H. G. Wells sentence continues

> . . . but the Thames had shifted perhaps a mile from its present position.

In this sentence, *its* is a possessive pronoun that refers to *position*. The *position* belongs to the Thames River.

Why did Wells write *its* and not *it's*? Because the latter option is a contraction (*it's* = *it* + *is*). If he had chosen *it is*, the sentence would read

> . . . but the Thames had shifted perhaps a mile from *it is* present position.

He needed to use the possessive form, *its*.

To improve your spelling and writing, learn these **possessive pronouns** and their use:

POSSESSIVE PRONOUN	MEANING	USE
my and *mine*	belonging to me	It is *my* fault. The fault is *mine*.
your and *yours*	belonging to you	Is this *your* jacket? Is this jacket *yours*?
his	belonging to him	Ali lost *his* key. Is this key *his*?

her and *hers*	belonging to her	This is *her* pen. This is *hers*.
its	belonging to it	A bird left *its* nest.
our and *ours*	belonging to us	Are these *our* tickets? Are these tickets *ours*?
their and *theirs*	belonging to them	Given them *their* share. You have yours; give them *theirs*.

You can see from the list that *no apostrophe* is used with a possessive pronoun. Pay special attention to those ending in *s*. Like all other possessive pronouns, they are never written with an apostrophe.

      yours   hers   ours   theirs

3. Possessive Nouns

On the other hand, **possessive nouns** do take apostrophes: the *boy's* keys, the *horse's* mane, the *car's* engine, the football *player's* helmet, the *children's* toys, the *students'* homework.

Note again the use of the apostrophe in a possessive noun but not in a possessive pronoun:

These notes are *Emily's*. (possessive *noun*—needs an apostrophe)

These notes are *hers*. (possessive *pronoun*—no apostrophe)

Exercise 8.18 Practice Distinguishing Between Contractions and Possessives

I. Replace the words in parentheses with a contraction expressing the same idea.

1. Most people (who have) _____ read *The Time Machine* found it fascinating.

2. (It is) _____ extremely thought provoking.

3. H. G. Wells (did not) _____ have a high opinion of the Victorian society in which he lived.

4. (I have) _____ seen the movie of *The Time Machine*.

5. It (was not) _____ much like the book and was disappointing.

II. In the blank, write the choice that makes the sentence correct.

6. Let me know when (you're, your) _____ done reading the introduction.

7. (It's, Its) _____ important to read it before you continue.

8. Is the book (her's, hers) _____ ?

9. These are my keys. Where are (your's, yours) _____ ?

10. Have you met my (sisters, sister's) _____ friend?

Chapter Nine

Prereading Guide
Words to know and ideas to consider before you jump into the reading.

A. Essential Vocabulary

Word	Meaning	Typical Use
calamity (*n*) ka-LA-mi-tee	1. a state of distress caused by serious disaster or loss 2. a disaster or other serious event involving loss and lasting pain or affliction	The family was in a *calamity* after the storm destroyed their home. Hurricane Katrina was a *calamity* we will never forget.
counsel (*n*) KOWN-sell	1. advice 2. lawyer engaged in the trial of a case; attorney	"You would not have made this error if you had followed my *counsel*," the coach said. Before answering the question, the witness conferred with his *counsel*.
discourse (*n*) DIS-course	talk; conversation; communication of ideas by talking	Having a face-to-face *discourse* can help you avoid the kinds of misunderstandings that happen in e-mails.
earnestly (*adv*) UR-nest-lee	in a serious manner; wholeheartedly	I looked her in the eye and answered her questions *earnestly*.
importunity (*n*) im-por-TU-nih-tee	an urgent or persistent request or demand	Joe finally listened to the teacher's *importunities* and brought up his grade.
precipitate (*v*) pre-SI-pi-tate	1. to cause or bring about, usually suddenly 2. to fall or arrive suddenly into a state or condition	Responding to him in that tone of voice will surely *precipitate* an argument. Don't *precipitate* yourself into a state of misery—think positively!
prevail (*v*) pre-VEIL	1. urge successfully (usually with *on* or *upon*); persuade 2. gain the advantage; win; triumph	The leader's inspiring speech *prevailed* upon the people to take action. In spite of the odds, the team *prevailed* in the end.
propensity (*n*) pro-PEN-si-tee	a strong preference or natural inclination; leaning	Although I sometimes wear light colors, I have a *propensity* toward blacks and browns.

Word	Meaning	Typical Use
prophetic (*adj*) pro-FE-tick	having the characteristics of a *prophecy* (prediction of the future); foretelling future events; predictive	I had a feeling I would get that job; I had a *prophetic* dream about it two nights before.
vicissitudes (*n*) vi-SI-si-tudez	changes or fluctuations that occur naturally or by chance (and can result in hardships)	Sometimes it's hard to stay calm in face of all the *vicissitudes* of daily life.

B. Vocabulary Practice

Exercise 9.1   Sentence Completion

Using your new vocabulary knowledge, choose the best way to complete the following sentences. Circle the letter of your answer.

1. That was a long discourse. I did not know you could _____ so much.
   A. run
   B. talk

2. The magazine precipitated a scandal when it published that _____.
   A. correction box
   B. shocking photo

3. He was surprised by the vicissitudes of the past few years; he hadn't expected things to _____.
   A. change
   B. stay the same

4. Listening to all of the coach's importunities made me _____.
   A. feel proud
   B. realize we had work left to do

5. When you needed counsel, there was no one to _____ you.
   A. advise
   B. recommend

6. The _____ is the one who prevails.
   A. loser
   B. winner

7. In the past I _____, but now I am working earnestly.
   A. was very serious
   B. joked most of the time

8. They were _____ after last year's calamity.
   A. cheerful
   B. devastated

9. I have a propensity toward home-cooked meals, so I almost _____ go out to dinner.
   A. always
   B. never

10. What the coach said last year was prophetic. We have just won the championship, _____.
    A. as he had predicted
    B. in spite of his doubts

Exercise 9.2 Using Fewer Words

Replace the italicized words with a single word from the following list.

precipitate   counsel   prophetic   earnestly   discourse

prevail   importunities calamity   vicissitudes propensity

1. She talked to him *in a serious manner* about her feelings.

   1._____

2. I don't like trying new things; I have a(an) *natural inclination* toward the comfortable and familiar.

   2._____

3. Many people made donations to help them recover from the *serious, misfortunate event*.

   3._____

4. If you ignore your parents' *urgent, serious requests*, you may be punished.

   4._____

5. Do you think the *natural, visible changes* of nature are beyond human control?

   5._____

6. I fell asleep during his *lengthy communication of ideas* on the history of ballpoint pens.

   6._____

7. Mentioning such a controversial issue will surely *quickly bring about* an argument.

   7._____

8. If you practice hard, you will *gain the advantage*.

   8._____

9. He had a meeting with his *lawyer engaged in the trial of a case* before their court date.

   9._____

10. I had a(an) *predictive of the future* dream about winning that trip.

    10._____

Exercise 9.3   Synonyms and Antonyms

Fill in the blanks in column A with the required synonyms or antonyms, selecting them from column B. (Remember: A *synonym* is a word similar in meaning to another word. An *antonym* is a word opposite in meaning to another word.)

	A	B
_____	1. synonym for *changes*	prevail
_____	2. synonym for *conversation*	importunity
_____	3. antonym for *jokingly*	prophetic
_____	4. antonym for *indifference*	precipitate
_____	5. synonym for *distress*	earnestly
_____	6. synonym for *predictive*	propensity
_____	7. antonym for *lose*	calamity
_____	8. synonym for *advice*	counsel
_____	9. synonym for *demand*	discourse
_____	10. synonym for *incite*	vicissitudes

C. Journal Freewrite

Before you begin the reading on the next page, take out a journal or sheet of paper and spend some time responding to the following prompt.

TIP: Don't worry about grammar and spelling; just write what comes to mind. The purpose of freewriting is to explore ideas, not to produce a polished work.

> Think of a time you made a decision of which your parents or guardian did not approve. How did they express their displeasure? Did they try to convince you to change your mind? How? What tactics did you use to try to get them on your side?

from Robinson Crusoe

by Daniel Defoe

About the Author
Daniel Defoe
(1660–1731) wrote
more than 500 books,
pamphlets, articles, and
poems. He is considered
the first of the great
eighteenth-century
English novelists. In
1702, he became a
secret agent, publishing
political and social articles that promoted or
criticized various issues.
In his more personal
writings, he defended
religious freedom and
called for improved edu-
cation and better treat-
ment of the poor. When
he was 59, Defoe began
writing novels. *Robinson
Crusoe* is his most
famous.

Being the third son of the family and not bred to any trade,
my head began to be filled very early with rambling
thoughts. My father, who was very ancient, had given me a
competent share of learning, as far as house-education and a
country free school generally go, and designed me for the
law; but I would be satisfied with nothing but going to sea;
and my inclination to this led me so strongly against the will,
nay, the commands of my father, and against all the
entreaties and persuasions of my mother and other friends,
that there seemed to be something fatal in that <u>propensity</u> of
nature, tending directly to the life of misery which was to
befall me.

My father, a wise and grave man, gave me serious and
excellent <u>counsel</u> against what he foresaw was my design. He
called me one morning into his chamber, where he was con-
fined by the gout,[1] and expostulated very warmly with me
upon this subject. He asked me what reasons, more than a
mere wandering inclination, I had for leaving father's house
and my native country, where I might be well introduced,
and had a prospect of raising my fortune by application and
industry, with a life of ease and pleasure. He told me it was
men of desperate fortunes on one hand, or of aspiring, superior fortunes on the other, who went abroad upon adventures, to rise by enterprise, and make themselves famous in
undertakings of a nature out of the common road; that these
things were all either too far above me or too far below me;
that mine was the middle state, or what might be called the
upper station of low life, which he had found, by long experience, was the best state in the world, the most suited to
human happiness, not exposed to the miseries and hardships,
the labour and sufferings of the mechanic part of mankind,
and not embarrassed with the pride, luxury, ambition, and
envy of the upper part of mankind. He told me I might judge
of the happiness of this state by this one thing – viz.[2] that this
was the state of life which all other people envied; that kings

---

[1] a disease causing painful swelling and inflammation of a joint
[2] abbreviation of *videlicet*: that is to say; namely

have frequently lamented the miserable consequence of being born to great things, and wished they had been placed in the middle of the two extremes, between the mean and the great; that the wise man gave his testimony to this, as the standard of felicity,[3] when he prayed to have neither poverty nor riches.

He bade me observe it, and I should always find that the <u>calamities</u> of life were shared among the upper and lower part of mankind, but that the middle station had the fewest disasters, and was not exposed to so many <u>vicissitudes</u> as the higher or lower part of mankind; nay, they were not subjected to so many distempers and uneasinesses, either of body or mind, as those were who, by vicious living, luxury, and extravagances on the one hand, or by hard labour, want of necessaries, and mean or insufficient diet on the other hand, bring distemper upon themselves by the natural consequences of their way of living; that the middle station of life was calculated for all kind of virtue and all kind of enjoyments; that peace and plenty were the handmaids of a middle fortune; that temperance, moderation, quietness, health, society, all agreeable diversions, and all desirable pleasures, were the blessings attending the middle station of life; that this way men went silently and smoothly through the world, and comfortably out of it, not embarrassed with the labours of the hands or of the head, not sold to a life of slavery for daily bread, nor harassed with perplexed circumstances, which rob the soul of peace and the body of rest, nor enraged with the passion of envy, or the secret burning lust of ambition for great things; but, in easy circumstances, sliding gently through the world, and sensibly tasting the sweets of living, without the bitter; feeling that they are happy, and learning by every day's experience to know it more sensibly.

After this he pressed me <u>earnestly</u>, and in the most affectionate manner, not to play the young man, nor to <u>precipitate</u> myself into miseries which nature, and the station of life I was born in, seemed to have provided against; that I was under no necessity of seeking my bread; that he would do well for me, and endeavour to enter me fairly into the station of life which he had just been recommending to me; and that if I was not very easy and happy in the world, it must be my mere fate or fault that must hinder it; and that he should have nothing to answer for, having thus discharged[4] his duty in warning me against measures which he knew would be to my hurt; in a word, that as he would do very kind things for me if I would stay and settle at home as he directed, so he would not have so much hand in my misfortunes as to give me any encouragement to go away; and to close all, he told me I had my elder brother for an example, to whom he had used the same earnest persuasions to keep him from going into the Low Country[5] wars, but could not <u>prevail</u>, his young desires prompting him to run into the army, where he was killed; and though he said he would not cease to pray for me, yet he would venture to say to me, that if I did

---

[3]happiness
[4]relieved or released from an obligation/duty by performing an appropriate action
[5]Netherlands, Belgium, and Luxembourg

take this foolish step, God would not bless me, and I should have leisure hereafter to reflect upon having neglected his counsel when there might be none to assist in my recovery.

I observed in this last part of his <u>discourse</u>, which was truly <u>prophetic</u>, though I suppose my father did not know it to be so himself—I say, I observed the tears run down his face very plentifully, especially when he spoke of my brother who was killed: and that when he spoke of my having leisure to repent,[6] and none to assist me, he was so moved that he broke off the discourse, and told me his heart was so full he could say no more to me.

I was sincerely affected with this discourse, and, indeed, who could be otherwise? and I resolved not to think of going abroad any more, but to settle at home according to my father's desire. But alas! a few days wore it all off; and, in short, to prevent any of my father's further <u>importunities</u>, in a few weeks after I resolved to run quite away from him. However, I did not act quite so hastily as the first heat of my resolution prompted; but I took my mother at a time when I thought her a little more pleasant than ordinary, and told her that my thoughts were so entirely bent upon seeing the world that I should never settle to anything with resolution enough to go through with it, and my father had better give me his consent than force me to go without it; that I was now eighteen years old, which was too late to go apprentice to a trade or clerk to an attorney; that I was sure if I did I should never serve out my time, but I should certainly run away from my master before my time was out, and go to sea; and if she would speak to my father to let me go one voyage abroad, if I came home again, and did not like it, I would go no more; and I would promise, by a double diligence, to recover the time that I had lost.

This put my mother into a great passion; she told me she knew it would be to no purpose to speak to my father upon any such subject; that he knew too well what was my interest to give his consent to anything so much for my hurt; and that she wondered how I could think of any such thing after the discourse I had had with my father, and such kind and tender expressions as she knew my father had used to me; and that, in short, if I would ruin myself, there was no help for me; but I might depend I should never have their consent to it; that for her part she would not have so much hand in my destruction; and I should never have it to say that my mother was willing when my father was not.

Though my mother refused to move it to my father, yet I heard afterwards that she reported all the discourse to him, and that my father, after showing a great concern at it, said to her, with a sigh, "That boy might be happy if he would stay at home; but if he goes abroad, he will be the most miserable wretch that ever was born: I can give no consent to it."

———
[6]to be sorry; to feel or show regret

Understanding the Reading

Complete the next three exercises and see how well you understood the reading from *Robinson Crusoe*.

Exercise 9.4   Multiple-Choice Questions

Answer the following questions about the reading. Circle the letter of your answer.

TIP: Don't try to answer the questions from memory; go back to the text as often as necessary.

1. The father
   A. does not try to influence Robinson's thinking.
   B. has stopped mourning for Robinson's elder brother.
   C. is not able to hide his feelings.
   D. makes no predictions about Robinson's future.

2. The passage suggests that the Crusoe family is
   A. not poor.
   B. unable to pay its debts.
   C. highly respected.
   D. large.

3. The phrase "to play the young man" (beginning of paragraph 4) most likely means to act
   A. after careful consideration.
   B. recklessly.
   C. like a coward.
   D. selfishly.

4. Which statement about the father is *not* supported by the reading?
   A. He expresses himself with considerable skill.
   B. He is convinced that his advice to his son is absolutely correct.
   C. He is worried about his son's future.
   D. He is determined not to help a son who disregards his advice.

5. Which would make the best title for the excerpt?
   A. A Dutiful Son
   B. Thirst for Adventure
   C. A Warning
   D. A Father's Blessing

Exercise 9.5   Short-Answer Questions

Respond to the following questions in one to two complete sentences. Go back to the text, as you did on the multiple choice.

6. Briefly summarize three of the father's reasons why Crusoe should stay home.

_____

_____

_____

7. How would you describe the father's tone when speaking to his son? What words in the text make this clear?

_____

_____

_____

8. How does Crusoe feel about his father's advice? Describe his emotions in your own words.

_____

_____

_____

9. Predict what you think is most likely to happen later. What clues in the text helped you make this prediction?

_____

_____

_____

Exercise 9.6 Extending Your Thinking

Respond to the following question in three to four complete sentences. Use details from the texts in your answer.

10. Every narrator or character in this unit found himself in an adventure, or contemplating one. Compare *two* narrators. What reasons do they have for wanting to take or winding up on a journey?

_____

_____

_____

_____

_____

Reading Strategy Lesson

Cause-and-Effect Relationships

Life itself is a series of causes and effects:

CAUSES ⟶	EFFECTS
stay up too late	sleep through your alarm
miss the bus	late for school
miss the first-period test	need to schedule a make-up time
take make-up test	miss basketball practice

You can see how a cause leads to an effect, which then becomes a cause leading to another effect in a chain reaction. In literature, cause-and-effect relationships are the heart and soul of plot—the events that make up a story. Identifying these relationships in a text will help you read with greater understanding.

Let's look at the causes and effects in the *Robinson Crusoe* excerpt you just read.

CAUSES ⟶	EFFECTS
Robinson Crusoe has a thirst for adventure.	He decides to go see the world.
His father calls him into his office.	Crusoe momentarily agrees to stay home.
Crusoe gets another urge to go away.	He approaches his mother.
His mother tells his father everything.	The father refuses to give his consent.

The rest of the book is made up of more causes and effects. Everything that happens can be linked to something else and is a result of all that went before. As you may have predicted, Robinson Crusoe does go on an adventure and winds up shipwrecked on a desert island. If he had not wanted to see the world, he might have stayed in London and never gotten into this situation.

Exercise 9.7   Practice the Reading Strategy

The following paragraph summarizes some of the things that happen to Robinson Crusoe later in the novel, on the desert island. Read the paragraph. Then, on a separate sheet of paper, create a cause-and-effect map like the one in the example.

> The first thing Crusoe had to do was figure out what he was going to eat and drink, and what he could use to build a shelter. He was able to get to the wrecked ship, and he found many things that could be salvaged to use on the island, including a blank journal. He was very lonely, so he began to write in the journal, keeping track of everything he did each

day. He found he could be very inventive when he needed to be and was able to create the things he needed out of what was at hand. He built a canoe, but it was too heavy to move. Then he built a small boat and was able to navigate around the island. He built a summer home in a more fertile area. He often wondered if he deserved his situation because he had disobeyed his parents and gone off to sea. After 15 years alone, Crusoe found a naked footprint. He worried night and day about who had made the print, and whether the person would be friendly or not if they ever met.

Now create your own cause-and-effect map.

Writing Workshop
Cause-and-Effect Essays

In the previous section, you saw how literature is often developed using cause and effect. Cause and effect can also be a useful way to develop an expository essay.

Cause-and-Effect Essays

While a storyteller relies on imagination and creativity to invent a convincing series of related events, a cause-and-effect essay must be supported with facts and details.

If you are asked to do this type of writing, the prompt usually asks for only the causes *or* the effects of some action or issue. For example:

What were the **causes** of the American Revolutionary War?

- Stamp Act
- Townshend Acts
- economic upheaval
- British occupation of the colonies

What were the **effects** of the American Revolutionary War?

- American independence from England
- eight years of war, death, and deprivation
- fear and mistrust between neighbors
- the U.S. Constitution

Since life is so driven by cause-and-effect relationships, the number of possible topics for essays developed by cause and/or effect is almost unlimited. For example:

What are some **causes** of problems between parents and teenagers?
What are some **effects** of problems between parents and teenagers?

What are the **causes** of environmental destruction?
What **effect** can one person have on the environment?

What **causes** romantic relationships to end?
What are the **effects** of romantic relationships ending?

What **causes** leaves to turn in the fall?
What are the **effects** of the change of colors?

Sort Out the Impact of Your Causes

Some causes are **necessary** causes, that is, the event could not happen otherwise. In the last example above, when leaves begin to die in the fall, hidden pigments become visible and the leaves change color. This cannot happen unless the leaves die.

Other causes are **contributory**. This means that they help produce an effect, but they can't create the effect alone. In the autumn leaves example, there are several contributory causes to leaf die-off: Age, lack of water, and less sunlight and warmth are all contributory causes.

A third type of cause is **sufficient** cause. This is a cause that can produce an effect, but it is not the only one that can do it. Frost is a sufficient cause of leaf die-off—but the same effect can be seen from a combination of contributory causes.

When you write a cause-and-effect essay, take into consideration *all* the possible causes and effects. This will make your essay more interesting, give you more to write about, and help you to create a solid and well-reasoned piece of writing.

Exercise 9.8 Apply the Lesson to Your Own Writing

Think about issues, processes, or events that are important to you. Choose one, and list some possible causes *or* effects on a separate sheet of paper, using an essay map like the one on the next page. (If you can't think of a topic of your own, use one of the examples above.) Make sure you choose a topic for which you can think of at least five to ten causes or effects. Write your topic in the middle and your causes or effects in the circles. Add more circles if necessary.

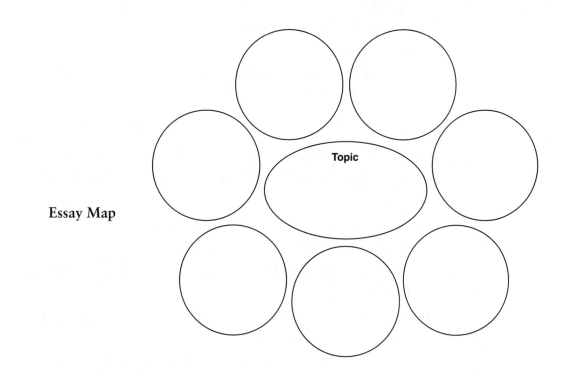

Essay Map

Topic

Grammar Mini-Lesson
Avoiding Double Negatives

The use of double negatives is a very common mistake. Once you understand what you are really saying or writing when you use a double negative, it will be easier to stop.

Question: Crusoe did not have _____ hope of surviving. (*no* or *any?*)

Answer: Crusoe did not have *any* hope of surviving.

Explanation: In making a negative statement, we use only one negative word. Since the sentence already contains one negative word, *not*, it is a mistake to choose *no*, which is also a negative word. In fact, choosing *no* would change the meaning of the sentence. If he did not have "*no* hope," then he must have had *some* hope that he would survive.

Also correct: He had *no* hope of surviving.

Explanation: In this case, *no* may be used, since the sentence contains no other negative word.

Here are some negative words. Be careful to use only one of them in each negative statement.

no	not	nobody
scarcely	only	hardly
barely	nothing	neither
nowhere	but (when it means	words ending in *n't*
none	*only*)	(meaning *not*)
never	no one	

Exercise 9.9 Practice Using Negatives Correctly

Complete each sentence by choosing the correct word in parentheses and writing it on the line. Look back at the list of negative words if you need help.

1. I didn't know _____ about it. (anything, nothing)

2. Abby has hardly _____ clothes she likes. (any, no)

3. Try to find some fresh berries for dessert; we couldn't find _____. (any, none)

4. Where are Alex and Chloë? I haven't seen _____ of them. (either, neither)

5. Our teacher did not fail _____ on that test. (anybody, nobody)

6. You got yourself into this. You don't have _____ else to blame. (no one, anyone)

7. Isaiah's little dog _____ barely a foot tall. (is, isn't)

8. Most of us haven't _____ gone camping. (never, ever)

9. He _____ but two sheets of paper left. (had, hadn't)

10. She told us that she _____ nothing to do with Tiffany anymore. (didn't have, had)

Exercise 9.10 Practice Using One Negative for Clarity

Each sentence is one correct way of making a negative statement. On the line, write the same statement in another equally correct way. The first two are done for you as examples.

1. You have not answered any of my questions.
   You have answered none of my questions.

2. Don't mention it to anyone.
   Mention it to no one.

3. There are no eggs left.

   _____

4. I didn't want either of them.

   _____

5. She had never been to the city before.

   _____

6. They didn't have anybody to mow their lawn.

   _____

7. He has nothing to do today.

_____

8. I looked for errors but I found none.

_____

9. We are not getting anywhere.

_____

10. There aren't any signs of improvement.

_____

Polish Your Spelling
Words Ending in -ANCE and -ENCE

In *Robinson Crusoe*, the father says that people who live with "*extravagances*" bring "distemper upon themselves by the natural *consequences* of their way of living . . ." Notice that although the nouns *extravagances* and *consequences* have similar endings, the former is spelled "-ances," and the latter is spelled "-ences." It is easy to get such endings confused when you're writing. Avoid spelling mistakes by studying the most commonly used *-ance* and *-ence* nouns. Here are some to review:

-ANCE		-ENCE	
abundance	endurance	adherence	indifference
allegiance	extravagance	adolescence	indolence
appliance	ignorance	affluence	indulgence
assistance	importance	audience	insolence
attendance	observance	coherence	interference
brilliance	perseverance	confidence	negligence
compliance	reliance	consequence	occurrence
defiance	repentance	impatience	permanence
disturbance	resemblance	incompetence	vehemence
elegance	resistance	independence	violence

Exercise 9.11 Practice Spelling -ANCE and -ENCE Nouns

Write the missing letter in column A and the complete word in column B.

A	B
1. repent__nce	_____
2. compli__nce	_____
3. indiffer__nce	_____
4. adolesc__nce	_____
5. self-confid__nce	_____
6. persever__nce	_____
7. incoher__nce	_____
8. occurr__nce	_____
9. appli__nce	_____
10. eleg__nce	_____

Unit Three Review

Vocabulary Review

A. Match each word with its definition.

	DEFINITION		WORD
_____	1. marked by creativity		a. oscillation
_____	2. relating to language		b. precocious
_____	3. back and forth movement		c. intimation
_____	4. beyond what is usual		d. linguistic
_____	5. to make hand motions		e. discourse
_____	6. subtle clue or indication		f. excessive
_____	7. developing early		g. ingenious
_____	8. having a high-pitched sound		h. shrill
_____	9. conversation		i. calamity
_____	10. a serious, unfortunate event		j. gesticulate

B. Match each word with its synonym.

	SYNONYM		WORD
_____	11. colloquialism		a. portal
_____	12. inflection		b. utmost
_____	13. commotion		c. prophetic
_____	14. entranceway		d. precipitate
_____	15. maximum		e. intonation
_____	16. advice		f. vicissitudes
_____	17. cause		g. importunities
_____	18. demands		h. idiom
_____	19. changes		i. counsel
_____	20. predictive		j. tumult

C. Match each word with its antonym.

ANTONYM	WORD
_____ 21. lose	a. exquisite
_____ 22. indifference	b. prevail
_____ 23. jokingly	c. habitable
_____ 24. fact	d. uneasiness
_____ 25. comfort	e. earnestly
_____ 26. flawed	f. singular
_____ 27. unlivable	g. conjecture
_____ 28. unoriginal	h. distinction
_____ 29. similarity	i. propensity
_____ 30. responsible	j. derelict

Grammar Review

The underlined portions of the paragraph may or may not contain errors. If there is an error, circle the letter of the best correction in the answer choices. If there is no error, choose D.

A New Phenomena Hits the U.S.

On February 7 1964, four young men
     (1)
arrived in the United States from their hometown of Liverpool, Britain. John Lennon, Paul McCartney, George Harrison, and Ringo Starr, known
              (2)
collectively as the Beatles, have came to
    (2)   (3)
New York for an appearance on the Ed
   (3)
Sullivan Show. One of their songs "I Want
            (4)   (5)
to Hold your hand" was a hit single in the
   (5)

1. A. On February 7, 1964,
   B. On February 7, 1964
   C. On February 7 1964
   D. no change
2. A. Starr known collectively as the Beatles,
   B. Starr, known collectively as the Beatles
   C. Starr, known collectively, as the Beatles,
   D. no change
3. A. have come to New York
   B. comes to New York
   C. had come to New York
   D. no change
4. A. One of their songs,
   B. One of there songs
   C. One of they're songs,
   D. no change
5. A. "I Want To Hold Your Hand,"
   B. I Want to Hold Your Hand,"
   C. "I want to hold your hand,"
   D. no change

U.S, <u>nobody realized how popular they will</u>
(6)

<u>become. Including the Beatles themselves.</u>
(6)   (7)

Their music structure was simple and seemed <u>to lift the nation's spirits</u>. Just a
(8)

few months before, President John F. Kennedy had been assassinated. This new pop music—and the long-haired, <u>fun-loving Beatles themselfs</u>—were
(9)

<u>just what Americans' needed.</u>
(10)

6. A. nobody realized how popular they would become.
   B. and nobody realized how popular they would become.
   C. but nobody realized how popular they would become.
   D. no change

7. A. The Beatles themselves included.
   B. Even the Beatles themselves was surprised by their U.S. success.
   C. Even the Beatles themselves were surprised by their U.S. success.
   D. no change

8. A. to lift the nation's spirits'.
   B. to lift the nations spirits.
   C. to lift the nations' spirits.
   D. no change

9. A. fun-loving Beatles themselves
   B. fun-loving Beatles theirselves
   C. fun-loving Beatles theirselfs
   D. no change

10. A. just what American's needed.
    B. just what Americans needed.
    C. just what Americans have needed.
    D. no change

Spelling Review

A. Add *-ible*, *-able*, *-ibility*, or *-ability* and write the correctly spelled word on the line.

1. permiss + suffix to make an adjective   _____

2. ador + suffix to make a noun   _____

3. sens + suffix to make an adjective   _____

B. Replace the words in parentheses with a contraction and write it on the line.

4. (It is) _____ past midnight.

5. Let me know when (you are) _____ ready to leave.

6. (Who is) _____ riding with us?

7. (I am) _____ not enjoying this party anyway.

C. Fill in the missing letter to form a correctly spelled word.

8. abund____nce

9. viol____nce

10. resist____nce

Writing Review

Choose one of the following topics. Plan your essay and write your first draft. Then revise and edit, and produce a final draft. Make sure you identify your audience, purpose, and task before you begin planning. Use specific details and examples to support your statements.

In *The Aran Islands*, *Gulliver's Travels*, and *The Time Machine*, the authors describe adventures that take place in unusual or faraway places. Choose one of the selections. Evaluate the information in the piece. Which parts *are* or *could be* true? Which parts could not be true?

OR

Choose two of the selections in this unit. Compare the narrators' attitudes and reactions to being on an adventure. How did they feel? What were they thinking? What did they do?

SPEAK/LISTEN
Talk Show

Work with a small group and imagine you are a production team
for a TV talk show. First, choose one of the readings from this unit.
Imagine that the narrator has returned from his adventure. Time-
machine technology allows him to be a special guest on your show.
Compose a list of questions for your guest. Then choose a show
host and someone to play the role of the returning adventurer. Help
your guest plan answers to the questions. Present your three- to
five-minute show segment to the class.

EXPLORE
Appreciating a Full Text

Choose one of the reading selections from this unit. Use the Internet
to find out more information about the piece and its author. (Things
to consider include, but are not limited to, the following: When was
it written? What is the historical/cultural context? How was it
received? What is the full plot?) Write two paragraphs summarizing
your findings. Be sure to cite your sources.

WRITE
Survival Stories

A number of stories and novels are centered around characters on
deserted islands. Some examples you may have read are *The Cay*,
Treasure Island, and *Island of the Blue Dolphins*. Why do you
think people are so fascinated with stories about island survival?
Would you like to try being a "survivor?" Explain.

CONNECT
Literature and Social Action

Like H. G. Wells, you are concerned about the future. You decide you
must wake people up to what is happening around them. With a small
group, research a social issue on the Internet. Create a name for the
organization you will form and decide what your group's mission and
actions should be. Then design a poster announcing its first meeting.
The poster should give enough information about your group's goals
that people will be encouraged to attend. Possible issues include the
destruction of the environment, or epidemics such as AIDS or the
West Nile virus.

Acts of Love and Kindness

Chapter Ten

Prereading Guide

Words to know and ideas to consider before you jump into the reading.

A. Essential Vocabulary

Word	Meaning	Typical Use
diminutive (*adj*) di-MIN-yoo-tiv	extremely small; tiny	Mice are *diminutive* creatures that frighten much larger ones.
genial (*adj*) JEEN-e-ul	friendly and agreeable; pleasant	Dylan is *genial* and enjoyable to be around.
interminable (*adj*) in-TUR-min-uh-bul	seemingly endless; relentless	The trip across the ocean seemed *interminable*.
methodical (*adj*) meh-THOD-i-kul	having a regular pattern; systematic	Zach cleaned his room in a *methodical* way, starting in one corner and working his way around.
oblivion (*n*) o-BLIV-e-un	lack of awareness or memory; forgetfulness	When she fell off her skateboard, she hit her head hard and entered a frightening state of *oblivion*.
precaution (*n*) pre-KAW-shun	an action taken ahead of time to avoid a bad outcome; fore-thought	Before doing surgery, medical personnel take many *precautions* to avoid infection or other problems.
spasmodic (*adj*) spaz-MOD-ik	1. involving jerky muscular con-tractions that are involuntary; convulsive 2. occurring in spells; irregular	When my dog sleeps, her muscles often have *spasmodic* move-ments, as if she is dreaming. The attacks are *spasmodic*, so it is not easy to predict when another will occur.
tether (*n*) TETH-ur	a tie or rope holding something back; restraint	The horse broke its *tether* and ran across the field.
throes (*n*) THROWZ	a painful experience; struggle	They were still in the *throes* of recovering from one hurricane when another one hit.
unperturbed (*adj*) un-pur-TURBD	serene and unruffled; calm	It was quite likely that Juan had broken his leg, but he seemed *unperturbed* as the EMTs loaded him into the ambulance.

B. Vocabulary Practice

Exercise 10.1 Sentence Completion

Using your new vocabulary knowledge, choose the best way to complete the following sentences. Circle the letter of your answer.

1. I hope you take the precaution of wearing _____ when you skate.
   A. knee pads
   B. a new shirt

2. Methodical people work systematically and get things done _____.
   A. eventually
   B. efficiently

3. Although their relationship was generally _____, they had spasmodic arguments.
   A. good
   B. unpleasant

4. Amanda, one of the most genial girls I know, has _____ friends.
   A. few
   B. many

5. Many women in the throes of childbirth are _____.
   A. unperturbed
   B. in pain

6. In *Gulliver's Travels*, Gulliver was tied down by an army of _____ humans.
   A. ordinary
   B. diminutive

7. You are _____ to take dogs to the park, but they must be on a tether.
   A. allowed
   B. not allowed

8. Joel _____ the evening at the opera; it seemed interminable.
   A. enjoyed
   B. loathed

9. Unperturbed by her opponent's outstanding record, Lauren was sure she would _____ the tennis match.
   A. win
   B. lose

10. Ryan seemed to live in a world of oblivion, _____ of his surroundings.
    A. aware
    B. unaware

Exercise 10.2 Using Fewer Words

Replace the italicized words with a single word from the following list.

methodically genial   throes   spasmodic precautions
unperturbed   interminable oblivious tether   diminutive

1. In the *painful experience* of bankruptcy,   1._____
   Mr. Tucker lost his vacation home and
   second car.

2. You'll have to use a(an) *tie or rope* to   2._____
   keep the lumber from falling off the truck.

3. No matter what happens, my cousin seems   3._____
   to remain *calm and unruffled*.

4. Aaron seemed *unaware and forgetful*   4._____
   of his mother's request that he make his
   bed in the morning.

5. We need to take *actions ahead of time* to   5._____
   prevent the demolition of the building from
   harming other structures.

6. Some diseases involve *involuntary jerking*   6._____
   muscle movements.

7. My sister is *extremely small*—only five feet   7._____
   tall and 90 pounds.

8. Ahmad, who is unusually *pleasant and*   8._____
   friendly, is very popular.

9. The *seemingly endless* racket of the   9._____
   jackhammer outside was annoying, to say
   the least.

10. Each evening, she studied her French *with*   10._____
    a regular system.

Exercise 10.3 Synonyms and Antonyms

Fill in the blanks in column A with the required synonyms or antonyms, selecting them from column B. (Remember: A *synonym* is a word similar in meaning to another word. An *antonym* is a word opposite in meaning to another word.)

	A	B
_____	1. synonym for *struggle*	diminutive
_____	2. synonym for *convulsive*	genial
_____	3. antonym for *anxious*	interminable
_____	4. antonym for *disagreeable*	methodical
_____	5. antonym for *disorderly*	oblivion
_____	6. synonym for *restraint*	precaution
_____	7. synonym for *relentless*	spasmodic
_____	8. antonym for *awareness*	throes
_____	9. antonym for *huge*	tether
_____	10. synonym for *forethought*	unperturbed

C. Journal Freewrite

Before you begin the reading on the next page, take out a journal or sheet of paper and spend some time responding to the following prompt.

TIP: Don't worry about grammar and spelling; just write what comes to mind. The purpose of freewriting is to explore ideas, not to produce a polished work.

Imagine that you have been given a wonderful and unexpected gift with which you are completely delighted. Describe what that gift is, why it is so special, and how you feel about the person who gave it to you.

from West With the Night

by Beryl Markham

About the Author

Beryl Markham (1902–1986) moved with her family to a farm in Kenya, Africa, at the age of four. The British had brought horse racing with them to Kenya, so Markham trained and raced horses and had her own stable of winners. She began writing stories about her unusual life, and in 1942 published *West With the Night*, the book from which this excerpt is taken. The book was not a big seller at first, but it was rediscovered and republished in 1983. Critics called it "a lost masterpiece."

At eight-thirty Otieno knocks.

'Come quickly. She is lying.'

Knives, twine, disinfectant—even anaesthetic—are all ready in my foaling-kit, but the last is <u>precaution</u>. As an Abyssinian, Coquette should have few of the difficulties that so often attend a Thoroughbred mare. Still, this is Coquette's first. First things are not always easy. I snatch the kit and hurry through the cluster of huts, some dark and asleep, some wakeful with square, yellow eyes. Otieno at my heels, I reach the stable.

Coquette is down. She is flat on her side, breathing in <u>spasmodic</u> jerks.

Horses are not voiceless in pain. A mare in the <u>throes</u> of birth is almost helpless, but she is able to cry out her agony. Coquette's groans, deep, tired, and a little frightened, are not really violent. They are not hysterical, but they are infinitely expressive of suffering, because they are unanswerable.

I kneel in the grass bedding and feel her soft ears. They are limp and moist in the palm of my hand, but there is no temperature. She labours heavily, looking at nothing out of staring eyes. Or perhaps she is seeing her own pain dance before them.

The time is not yet. We cannot help, but we can watch. We three can sit cross-legged—Toombo near the manger, Otieno against the cedar planking, myself near the heavy head of Coquette—and we can talk, almost tranquilly, about other things while the little brush of flame in the hurricane lamp paints experimental pictures on the wall.

'Wa-li-hie!' says Toombo.

It is as solemn as he ever gets. At the dawning of doomsday he will say no more. A single 'Walihie!' and he has shot his philosophic[1] bolt. Having shot it, he relaxes and grins, <u>genially</u>, into himself.

The labouring of Coquette ebbs and flows in <u>methodical</u> tides of torment. There are minutes of peace and minutes of anguish, which we all feel together, but smother, for ourselves, with words.

---

[1] related to intellectual inquiry and wisdom

Unit Four Acts of Love and Kindness   **217**

Otieno sighs. 'The Book talks of many strange lands,' he says. 'There is one that is filled with milk and with honey. Do you think this land would be good for a man, Beru?'

Toombo lifts his shoulders. 'For which man?' he says. 'Milk is not bad food for one man, meat is better for another, *ooji* is good for all. Myself, I do not like honey.'

Otieno's scowl is mildly withering. 'Whatever you like, you like too much, Toombo. Look at the roundness of your belly. Look at the heaviness of your legs!'

Toombo looks. 'God makes fat birds and small birds, trees that are wide and trees that are thin, like wattle. He makes big kernels and little kernels. I am a big kernel. One does not argue with God.'

The theosophism[2] defeats Otieno; he ignores the globular[3] Jesuit slouching <u>unperturbed</u> under the manger, and turns again to me.

'Perhaps you have seen this land, Beru?'

'No.' I shake my head.

But then I am not sure. My father has told me that I was four when I left England.

Leicestershire. Conceivably it could be the land of milk and honey, but I do not remember it as such. I remember a ship that sailed <u>interminably</u> up the hill of the sea and never, never reached the top. I remember a place I was later taught to think of as Mombasa, but the name has not explained the memory. It is a simple memory made only of colours and shapes, of heat and trudging people and broad-leaved trees that looked cooler than they were. All the country I know is this country—these hills, familiar as an old wish, this veldt,[4] this forest. Otieno knows as much.

'I have never seen such a land, Otieno. Like you, I have read about it. I do not know where it is or what it means.'

'That is a sad thing,' says Otieno; 'it sounds like a good land.'

Toombo rouses himself from the stable floor and shrugs. 'Who would walk far for a kibuyu[5] of milk and a hive of honey? Bees live in every tenth tree, and every cow has four teats. Let us talk of better things!'

But Coquette talks first of better things. She groans suddenly from the depth of her womb, and trembles. Otieno reaches at once for the hurricane lamp and swells the flame with a twist of his black fingers. Toombo opens the foaling-kit.

'Now.' Coquette says it with her eyes and with her wordless voice. 'Now—perhaps now——'

This is the moment, and the Promised Land is the forgotten one.

I kneel over the mare waiting for her foal to make its exit from <u>oblivion</u>. I wait for the first glimpse of the tiny hooves, the first sight of the sheath—the cloak it will wear for its great début.

---

[2]religious idea based on mystical insight
[3]spherical; round
[4]open grazing land in southern Africa
[5]a gourd used by natives to carry and store milk

It appears, and Coquette and I work together. Otieno at one of my shoulders, Toombo at the other. No one speaks because there is nothing to say.

But there are things to wonder.

Will this be a colt or a filly? Will it be sound and well-formed? Will its new heart be strong and stubborn enough to snap the tethers of nothingness that break so grudgingly? Will it breathe when it is meant to breathe? Will it have the anger to feed and to grow and to demand its needs?

I have my hands at last on the tiny legs, on the bag encasing them. It is a strong bag, transparent and sleek. Through it I see the diminutive hooves, pointed, soft as the flesh of sprouted seeds—impotent hooves, insolent in their urgency to tread the tough earth.

Gently, gently, but strong and steady, I coax the new life into the glow of the stable lamp, and the mare strains with all she has. I renew my grip, hand over hand, waiting for her muscles to surge with my pull. The nose—the head, the whole head—at last the foal itself, slips into my arms, and the silence that follows is sharp as the crack of a Dutchman's whip—and as short.

'Walihie!' says Toombo.

Otieno smears sweat from under his eyes; Coquette sighs the last pain out of her.

I let the shining bag rest on the pad of trampled grass less than an instant, then break it, giving full freedom to the wobbly little head.

I watch the soft, mouse-coloured nostrils suck at their first taste of air. With care, I slip the whole bag away, tie the cord and cut it with the knife Otieno hands me. The old life of the mare and the new life of the foal for the last time run together in a quick christening of blood, and as I bathe the wound with disinfectant, I see that he is a colt.

He is a strong colt, hot in my hands and full of the tremor of living.

Coquette stirs. She knows now what birth is; she can cope with what she knows. She lurches to her feet without gracefulness or balance, and whinnies once—so this is mine! So this is what I have borne! Together we dry the babe.

When it is done, I stand up and turn to smile at Otieno. But it is not Otieno; it is not Toombo. My father stands beside me with the air of a man who has observed more than anyone suspected. This is a scene he has witnessed more times than he can remember; yet there is bright interest in his eyes—as if, after all these years, he has at last seen the birth of a foal!

He is not a short man nor a tall one; he is lean and tough as a riem.[6] His eyes are dark and kind in a rugged face that can be gentle.

'So there you are,' he says—'a fine job of work and a fine colt. Shall I reward you or Coquette—or both?'

Toombo grins and Otieno respectfully scuffs the floor with his toes. I slip my arm through my father's and together we look down on the awkward, angry little bundle, fighting already to gain his feet.

---

[6]a leather strap or belt

'Render unto Cæsar,' says my father; 'you brought him to life. He shall be yours.'

A bank clerk handles pounds of gold—none of it his own—but if, one day, that fabulous faery everyone expects, but nobody ever meets, were to give him all this gold for himself—or even a part of it—he would be no less overjoyed because he had looked at it daily for years. He would know at once (if he hadn't known it before) that this was what he had always wanted.

For years I had handled my father's horses, fed them, ridden them, groomed them, and loved them. But I had never owned one.

Now I owned one. Without even the benefit of the good faery, but only because my father said so, I owned one for myself. The colt was to be mine, and no one could ever touch him, or ride him, or feed him, or nurse him—no one except myself.

I do not remember thanking my father; I suppose I did, for whatever words are worth. I remember that when the foaling-box was cleaned, the light turned down again, and Otieno left to watch over the newly born, I went out and walked with Buller beyond the stables and a little way down the path that used to lead to Arab Maina's.

I thought about the new colt, Otieno's Promised Land, how big the world must be, and then about the colt again. What shall I name him?

Who doesn't look upward when searching for a name? Looking upward, what is there but the sky to see? And seeing it, how can the name or the hope be earthbound? Was there a horse named Pegasus that flew? Was there a horse with wings?

Yes, once there was—once, long ago, there was. And now there is again.

Understanding the Reading

Complete the next three exercises and see how well you understood the excerpt from *West With the Night.*

Exercise 10.4 Multiple-Choice Questions

Answer the following questions about the reading. Circle the letter of your answer.

TIP: Don't try to answer the questions from memory; go back to the text as often as necessary.

1. From context, you can infer that Otieno and Toombo are
   A. children of people who work on the farm.
   B. African natives who work for the author's father.
   C. a veterinarian and his assistant.
   D. the author's brothers.

2. Coquette's groans are "infinitely expressive of suffering" because
   A. they are violent and terrifying.
   B. she is so exhausted.
   C. there is no way to explain to her what is happening.
   D. the author feels especially close to this horse.

3. Which statement is *true*?
   A. Otieno and Toombo are not friends.
   B. Otieno enjoys joking with Toombo.
   C. Toombo is hurt and insulted by Otieno's remarks.
   D. The author tries to keep peace between Otieno and Toombo.

4. At the moment the foal is delivered, the author is primarily concerned with
   A. whether it will be a colt or a filly.
   B. whether it will be able to run fast and win races.
   C. what color it will be.
   D. whether it will be strong and healthy.

5. The author names her new colt Pegasus because
   A. she sees the constellation by that name in the sky.
   B. she named him after another horse she once had.
   C. the colt was born with small wings.
   D. the name symbolizes hope.

Exercise 10.5 Short-Answer Questions

Respond to the following questions in one to two complete sentences. Go back to the text, as you did on the multiple choice.

6. How do Toombo and Otieno differ in their ideas about "the land of milk and honey"?

   _____
   _____
   _____

7. To what does the author compare a bank clerk receiving pounds of gold? Why is this an appropriate comparison?

   _____
   _____
   _____

8. How do you picture the author's future interactions with the colt?

   _____
   _____
   _____

9. Markham uses vivid, specific adjectives and other descriptive language to help readers form mental pictures of how things look. Find and explain one example of this language.

_____

_____

_____

Exercise 10.6 Extending Your Thinking

Respond to the following question in three to four complete sentences. Use details from the text in your answer.

10. The theme of this unit is "Acts of Love and Kindness." Describe how at least two of the characters in this excerpt express either love or kindness.

_____

_____

_____

_____

_____

_____

Reading Strategy Lesson
Understanding Cultural Context

What Is Cultural Context?

You have already learned how to define words by looking at them within a reading selection. By seeing how the words relate to the text—looking at them in **context**—you can make a better decision about what they mean.

When you read a story, article, or poem written during a different time period or about a foreign country, it is very helpful to know something about the historical, social, and political elements of the reading. This is its **cultural context**.

West With the Night was written by a woman who grew up in Kenya, a country on the southeast coast of Africa. As you know from the reading, her father operated a farm there. But she was born in England—so why did she end up in Kenya? The following information will help you answer that question.

In 1888, Great Britain took over land on the southeastern coast of Africa and called it Imperial British East Africa. In 1920, the land became a British colony and was named Kenya. By 1902, Europeans were already being encouraged to farm in the new territory. They were able to acquire large parcels of land, and the weather in Kenya was especially favorable for farming.

This meant that many of the native people, particularly the Kikuyu, simply lost their land. They had two choices: move to the capital (Nairobi) to find employment, or stay on the land that had been theirs and work for the European farmers. In 1918, the European settlers, who wanted more cheap farm labor, convinced the British government to pass laws that virtually forced native Africans to become farm laborers. The laws called for higher taxes on Africans, and the only way they could get the money was by working on the settlers' farms. Native Africans were not allowed to vote or become members of the colony's governing council.

Native Africans began to rebel against the way they were being treated. From 1952 to 1956, a group of Kikuyus called the Mau Mau began killing European settlers and the African natives who were loyal to them. British soldiers were sent in to quell the rebellion, killing about 12,000 Africans and imprisoning 100,000 more. Pressure against Britain continued, however, and in 1963 Kenya became independent.

Exercise 10.7 Practice the Reading Strategy

You now know a little bit more about Kenya. Look back at the introductory material about Beryl Markham. Then answer the following questions.

1. What do you think motivated Beryl Markham's father to move his family to Kenya?

   _____

   _____

2. What is the most likely reason that Toombo and Otieno were working on the farm?

   _____

   _____

3. Would Otieno and Toombo be likely to joke with Beryl's father the way they did with one another? Why or why not?

   _____

   _____

4. When Beryl's father enters the barn, "Toombo grins and Otieno respectfully scuffs the floor with his toes." Which of the two seems to be more submissive to Mr. Markham? How do you know?

_____

_____

5. Since Beryl had known no other life than that on the farm in Kenya, how do you suppose she regarded the natives who worked there? Explain your answer.

_____

_____

Exercise 10.8 Apply the Reading Strategy

Following are three proverbs that come from the Kikuyu culture. Interpret each proverb with reference to the information excerpt you read on page 222.

1. People who have not secret agreement are beaten by a single club.

_____

_____

2. He who seeks his goat with the man who ate it, is certain not to find it.

_____

_____

3. A piece of land is not a little thing.

_____

_____

Writing Workshop
Defining and Incorporating Your Own Cultural Context

What Is American Cultural Context?

The 1991 Nobel Prize winner Nadine Gordimer said that she had learned she could not be a successful writer until she wrote about the civil and political unrest in her native South Africa, and about the people it affected. Gordimer explained that South African writers ". . . have to enter through the tragedy of our own particular place."

In the previous unit, J. M. Synge traveled to a remote part of Ireland so he could write plays about the language, customs, and lifestyles of Irish country people. He wanted to write in the **cultural context** of Ireland.

In the excerpt you just read, Beryl Markham described an evening of her life as a settler's daughter in Kenya. She wrote in the **cultural context** of a colonial Kenyan farm.

But what about American writers?

- William Faulkner, Carson McCullers, and Harper Lee all wrote about life in the American South. *To Kill a Mockingbird* described the atmosphere of a small southern town in the 1960s. In order to fully appreciate a book about the American South, you should know the cultural context of the book's events.

- Sherman Alexie, N. Scott Momaday, Louise Erdrich, and Joy Harjo all write about life in Native American families and communities.

- Sandra Cisneros, Judith Ortiz Cofer, and Rudolfo Anaya tell their stories from the viewpoints of Hispanic Americans.

- Other American writers discuss life in New York City, Los Angeles, New England, or the Midwest. Or they write from their own cultural viewpoint—the unique experience of being African-American, Asian, Jewish, or Muslim.

Keeping all this in mind, how would you define **American cultural context?**

Of course, this is a big country. There are many different cultural contexts. If you live on a ranch in Texas, your perception of America will be different from that of someone who lives in a large city like Chicago or Atlanta. If you own the ranch, your context will be different than if you are a maid at the ranch house. If you read a book that takes place in Alaska or Hawaii, it is helpful to know something about the location and what makes life there different from where you live and yet still American. Fortunately, television and film, as well as magazines, newspapers, and the Internet, help us to tune in to what life is like in other areas of our country. Reading literature written by authors from diverse backgrounds enhances our understanding of other ethnic groups.

Exercise 10.9 Practice the Writing Lesson

Think about the two locations on the table on the next page. What are your associations with each place? Unless you have visited both of them yourself, you will need to rely on what you've learned from various sources to fill in both sides of the T-square. Suggestions for comparison are given on the table, but you should add anything else you think of.

Ranch or farm in the West	New York City or other large city
animals:	animals:
vehicles:	vehicles:
number of people you see:	number of people you see:
buildings:	buildings:
people wear:	people wear:
jobs:	jobs:
people talk:	people talk:
entertainment:	entertainment:
weather:	weather:

If you read a story that takes place in one of these locations, you would be able to picture some of the things you listed—for example, places, people, and weather. If you wanted to write a story about one of these places, you would need to include its cultural context in order to make it seem realistic.

Now that you have contrasted two locations in America, you're ready to go onto the next exercise that has you define your own personal cultural context. To do this, you will have to think about the customs, foods, styles of dress, social customs, crafts, movies, TV shows, and so forth that surround you in your area and are part of a typical week in your world.

Exercise 10.10 Apply the Lesson to Your Own Writing

On a separate sheet of paper, draw a circle and write "My cultural context" in the middle. Then make a cluster map around it, listing the things you feel are truly expressive of your part of America. Your map should include references to things like local landmarks, people, jobs, dialect, foods, crafts, and festivals. You may also want to include some insights about your ethnic group. Then, use your map to write at least three paragraphs describing a scene typical of your life in your neighborhood. Try to include not only what you see but also what you hear, smell, taste, and feel. It can be as simple as what you see sitting on your porch on a Saturday afternoon, taking a walk or a bike ride, or going to the mall.

As you write, consider the following: What do people say? How are they dressed? What do they eat and drink? What kinds of people do you see on the street? Are they friendly or not?

You can extend this activity by writing a story that takes place in the neighborhood you have described—a story that takes place in your very own personal cultural context.

Grammar Mini-Lesson
Good or *Well?*

In the Markham story, Otieno asks the author about "the land of milk and honey." "Do you think this land would be *good* for a man, Beru?" he says.

1. *Good* is an adjective. It describes a noun (a person, place, or thing), not an action.

> This is a *good* dinner.   (adjective modifying the noun *dinner*)

> The food tastes *good*.   (adjective modifying the noun *food*)

2. *Well* also can be an adjective, meaning "healthy" or "not ill."

> I'm so glad to hear you are *well*.   (adjective modifying the pronoun *you*)

> My uncle is not a *well* person.   (adjective modifying the noun *person*)

3. In other contexts, *well* is an adverb, modifying a verb. Here are some more examples of the use of *well* as an adverb:

> Alexa dances *well*.   (adverb modifying the verb *dances*)

> I did *well* on the test.   (adverb modifying the verb *did*)

> Things are going *well* for me.   (adverb modifying the verb *are going*)

4. Note that both of the following are correct, but they do not have the same meaning:

> I feel *good*.   (This means "I am happy" or "I'm in an excellent mood.")

> I feel *well*.   (This means "I feel healthy" or "I'm in good health.")

Exercise 10.11 Practice Using *Good* and *Well* Correctly

On the blank, write either *good* or *well* to complete the sentence correctly.

1. I didn't do too _____ in the tryouts for the baseball team.

2. Paolo has a fever; he is not _____.

3. Even though it's old, the car still runs _____.

4. I felt _____ when I learned I had passed all my finals.

5. The food on this menu all looks _____ to me.

6. My little brothers do not behave very _____ when I have friends over.

7. That is really _____ news.

8. She's only an acquaintance; I do not know her _____.

9. I think this milk has gone sour; it doesn't smell _____.

10. Since his knee injury, Chris has not been able to play as _____ as before.

Exercise 10.12 Apply the Lesson to Create Your Own Sentences

Write five sentences using *well* correctly and five sentences using *good* correctly.

1. _____

2. _____

3. _____

4. _____

5. _____

6. _____

7. _____

8. _____

9. _____

10. _____

Polish Your Spelling
Adding the Suffixes -OR and -ER to Create New Words

The suffixes *-or* and *-er* have the same meaning: "one who."

imitate + or = imitator (one who imitates)

observe + er = observer (one who observes)

But how can you tell whether a noun ends in *-or* or *-er*?

1. If you can trace the noun to a verb of at least two syllables ending in *ate*, use *-or* with that noun.

Examples:

imitate	imitator
create	creator
demonstrate	demonstrator
investigate	investigator

Exception:

debate *debater*

2. Aside from the above clue, there is no easy way to tell whether a noun ends in -*or* or -*er*. That is why you need to study the most frequently used -*or* and -*er* nouns.

-OR		-ER	
ambassador	juror	buyer	owner
author	mayor	defender	player
contributor	monitor	interpreter	pleader
creditor	possessor	invader	pretender
debtor	professor	laborer	printer
editor	senator	manufacturer	purchaser
governor	supervisor	offender	reporter
janitor	tailor	organizer	supporter

3. Also study these few nouns that end in -*ar*:
    beggar   burglar   liar   scholar

Exercise 10.13 Practice the Rules for Adding -OR and -ER

Change each word below by adding -*or*, -*er*, or -*ar*. Write the complete word on the line.

1. janit___   _____

2. burgl___   _____

3. ambassad___   _____

4. organiz___   _____

5. schol___   _____

6. may___   _____

7. report___   _____

8. senat___   _____

9. translat___   _____

10. invad___   _____

Chapter Eleven

Prereading Guide
Words to know and ideas to consider before you jump into the reading.

A. Essential Vocabulary

Word	Meaning	Typical Use
accommodate (*v*) uh-KOM-uh-date	1. to make fit; adapt; adjust	When we moved, it took a while to *accommodate* myself to my new school.
	2. to have space for; hold without crowding; contain	The new hotel can *accommodate* two hundred guests.
appeal (*n*) uh-PEEL	1. call for help; plea; earnest request	Thousands of volunteers responded to the hospital's *appeal* for blood donors.
	2. (*v*) to make a request or plea	The attorney said he would *appeal* the case to a higher court.
attire (*v*) uh-TIRE	1. to put clothing on; dress	All the boys at the prom were *attired* in tuxedos.
	2. (*n*) clothing	Her choice of *attire* was striking.
confidence (*n*) KON-fih-dens	feeling of trust; faith; reliance	Have *confidence* in my brother's promise; he always keeps his word.
curiosity (*n*) kure-ee-OSS-i-tee	1. eager desire to know; inquisitiveness	You can satisfy your *curiosity* on a variety of topics by conducting Internet research.
	2. strange or rare object; rarity	Many people visit antiques shops in search of *curiosities*.
deceit (*n*) dee-SEET	the act of misleading or lying; a trick; cheating	Wise businesses treat their customers fairly because they know that in the long run, *deceit* does not pay.
delicate (*adj*) DELL-i-cut	easily hurt or damaged; frail; sickly	If you drop this camera, you will probably damage it because it has a very *delicate* mechanism.
frankness (*n*) FRANK-ness	openness and honesty in expressing what one thinks	I appreciate your *frankness* in telling me what you didn't like about my speech.
involuntary (*adj*) in-VOL-un-tare-ee	not subject to control by the will; automatic; instinctive	You can't stop a sneeze or a yawn because they are *involuntary* acts.

Word	Meaning	Typical Use
timidly (*adv*) TIM-id-lee	in a fearful or shy manner; hesitantly	When it seemed that there might be a fight, most of the bystanders *timidly* withdrew to safe ground.

B. Vocabulary Practice

Exercise 11.1 Sentence Completion

Using your new vocabulary knowledge, choose the best way to complete the following sentences. Circle the letter of your answer.

1. _____ is usually an involuntary remark.
   A. "Ouch!"
   B. "Okay"

2. To _____ is to practice deceit.
   A. pretend to be older than you are
   B. come late to a quiz

3. The manager was attired _____.
   A. after a long day
   B. in a business suit

4. An _____ is an appeal with which most of us are familiar.
   A. SOS
   B. I.O.U.

5. I was _____ to follow the path as my eyes accommodated themselves to the dark.
   A. unable
   B. able

6. If you behave timidly, others may think you are _____.
   A. scared
   B. rude

7. Her curiosity shows that she is _____.
   A. eager to learn
   B. not interested

8. A _____ is extremely delicate.
   A. mountaintop
   B. spider's web

9. Aidan must have confidence in you; he _____.
   A. never lends you anything
   B. gave you his car keys

10. The child's frankness _____ the truth.
    A. prevented us from learning
    B. helped us learn

Exercise 11.2 Using Fewer Words

Replace the italicized words with a single word from the following list.

frankness	involuntary	accommodate	appeal	delicate
timidly	attired	deceit	confidence	curiosity

1. Her *feeling of trust* in Matt was gone after she learned he had lied to her.

   1._____

2. Do you think the restaurant will *have space for* the whole team?

   2._____

3. Sometimes it hurts to hear the truth, but you can count on Jessie for her *openness and honesty in expressing her opinion*.

   3._____

4. "Sir, can you help me find my way home?" the girl asked *in a fearful manner*.

   4._____

5. Her health is *easily hurt or damaged*, so make sure she dresses warmly.

   5._____

6. Jordan got up, *put garments on* herself, and headed for the gym.

   6._____

7. The digestive process is *not subject to control by the will*.

   7._____

8. Trevor's *eager desire to know* about geology led him to a career in the oil exploration field.

   8._____

9. Marissa's *call for help* was answered quickly by emergency services.

   9._____

10. Because of his constant *acts of lying*, we soon stopped believing anything he said.

    10._____

Exercise 11.3 Synonyms and Antonyms

Fill in the blanks in column A with the required synonyms or antonyms, selecting them from column B. (Remember: A *synonym* is a word similar in meaning to another word. An *antonym* is a word opposite in meaning to another word.)

	A	B
_____	1. synonym for *adapt*	appeal
_____	2. synonym for *plea*	confidence
_____	3. antonym for *courageously*	delicate
_____	4. antonym for *controlled*	accommodate
_____	5. antonym for *honesty*	frankness
_____	6. synonym for *inquisitiveness*	involuntary
_____	7. synonym for *frail*	timidly
_____	8. synonym for *outspokenness*	attire
_____	9. antonym for *doubt*	curiosity
_____	10. synonym for *dress*	deceit

C. Journal Freewrite

Before you begin the reading on the next page, take out a journal or sheet of paper and spend some time responding to the following prompt.

TIP: Don't worry about grammar and spelling; just write what comes to mind. The purpose of freewriting is to explore ideas, not to produce a polished work.

> Suppose you are walking on a street in town one evening and a little girl about seven years old stops you and tells you she is lost. Describe the situation.

from The Old Curiosity Shop

by Charles Dickens

About the Author
**Charles Dickens
(1812–1870)** faced
many hardships in his
early life. His father was
sent to debtors' prison,
and his family had to
pay the debts. Dickens,
twelve at the time, was
sent to work in a shoe-
blacking factory. There
he developed an under-
standing of the troubles
of the poor and working
classes. Later, as a journalist and writer, he was
a strong voice for
England's lowest
classes. His works are
still widely read—you
may be familiar with *A
Tale of Two Cities, Great
Expectations,* or *A
Christmas Carol.* This
excerpt is from his novel
The Old Curiosity Shop.
Dickens describes his
narrator's encounter
with Little Nell and her
grandfather.

One night I had roamed into the City, and was walking slowly on in my usual way, musing upon a great many things, when I was arrested by an inquiry, the purport[1] of which did not reach me, but which seemed to be addressed to myself, and was preferred in a soft sweet voice that struck me very pleasantly. I turned hastily round and found at my elbow a pretty little girl, who begged to be directed to a certain street at a considerable distance, and indeed in quite another quarter of the town.

"It is a very long way from here," said I, "my child."

"I know that, sir," she replied <u>timidly</u>. "I am afraid it is a very long way, for I came from there to-night."

"Alone?" said I, in some surprise.

"Oh, yes, I don't mind that, but I am a little frightened now, for I had lost my road."

"And what made you ask it of me? Suppose I should tell you wrong?"

"I am sure you will not do that," said the little creature, "you are such a very old gentleman, and walk so slow yourself."

I cannot describe how much I was impressed by this <u>appeal</u> and the energy with which it was made, which brought a tear into the child's clear eye, and made her slight figure tremble as she looked up into my face.

"Come," said I, "I'll take you there."

She put her hand in mine as confidingly as if she had known me from her cradle, and we trudged away together; the little creature <u>accommodating</u> her pace to mine, and rather seeming to lead and take care of me than I to be protecting her. I observed that every now and then she stole a curious look at my face, as if to make quite sure that I was not deceiving her, and that these glances (very sharp and keen they were too) seemed to increase her <u>confidence</u> at every repetition.

For my part, my <u>curiosity</u> and interest were at least equal to the child's, for child she certainly was, although I thought

---

[1]significance

it probable from what I could make out, that her very small and <u>del-icate</u> frame imparted a peculiar youthfulness to her appearance. Though more scantily <u>attired</u> than she might have been, she was dressed with perfect neatness, and betrayed no marks of poverty or neglect.

"Who has sent you so far by yourself?" said I.

"Someone who is very kind to me, sir."

"And what have you been doing?"

"That, I must not tell," said the child firmly.

There was something in the manner of this reply which caused me to look at the little creature with an <u>involuntary</u> expression of surprise; for I wondered what kind of errand it might be that occasioned her to be prepared for questioning. Her quick eye seemed to read my thoughts, for as it met mine she added that there was no harm in what she had been doing, but it was a great secret—a secret which she did not even know herself.

This was said with no appearance of cunning or <u>deceit</u>, but with an unsuspicious <u>frankness</u> that bore the impress[2] of truth. She walked on as before, growing more familiar with me as we proceeded and talking cheerfully by the way, but she said no more about her home, beyond remarking that we were going quite a new road and asking if it were a short one.

While we were thus engaged, I revolved in my mind a hundred different explanations of the riddle and rejected them every one. I really felt ashamed to take advantage of the ingenuousness[3] or grateful feeling of the child for the purpose of gratifying my curiosity. I love these little people; and it is not a slight thing when they, who are so fresh from God, love us. As I had felt pleased at first by her confidence I determined to deserve it, and to do credit to the nature that had prompted her to repose it in me.

There was no reason, however, why I should refrain from seeing the person who had inconsiderately sent her to so great a distance by night and alone, and as it was not improbable that if she found herself near home she might take farewell of me and deprive me of the opportunity, I avoided the most frequented ways and took the most intricate, and thus it was not until we arrived in the street itself that she knew where we were. Clapping her hands with pleasure and running on before me for a short distance, my little acquaintance stopped at a door and, remaining on the step till I came up, knocked at it when I joined her.

A part of this door was of glass unprotected by any shutter, which I did not observe at first, for all was very dark and silent within, and I was anxious (as indeed the child was also) for an answer to our summons. When she had knocked twice or thrice there was a noise as if some person were moving inside, and at length a faint light appeared through the glass which, as it approached very slowly, the bearer having to make his way through a great many scattered arti-

---

[2]imprint
[3]innocence

cles, enabled me to see both what kind of person it was who advanced and what kind of place it was through which he came.

It was an old man with long grey hair, whose face and figure as he held the light above his head and looked before him as he approached, I could plainly see. Though much altered by age, I fancied I could recognize in his spare and slender form something of that delicate mould which I had noticed in the child. Their bright blue eyes were certainly alike, but his face was so deeply furrowed[4] and so very full of care, that here all resemblance ceased.

The place through which he made his way at leisure was one of those receptacles for old and curious things which seem to crouch in odd corners of this town and to hide their musty treasures from the public eye in jealousy and distrust. There were suits of mail standing like ghosts in armour here and there, fantastic carvings brought from monkish cloisters, rusty weapons of various kinds, distorted figures in china and wood and iron and ivory: tapestry and strange furniture that might have been designed in dreams. The haggard[5] aspect of the little old man was wonderfully suited to the place; he might have groped among old churches and tombs and deserted houses and gathered all the spoils with his own hands. There was nothing in the whole collection but was in keeping with himself, nothing that looked older or more worn than he.

As he turned the key in the lock, he surveyed me with some astonishment which was not diminished when he looked from me to my companion. The door being opened, the child addressed him as grandfather, and told him the little story of our companionship.

"Why, bless thee, child," said the old man, patting her on the head, "how couldst thou miss thy way? What if I had lost thee, Nell!"

"I would have found my way back to YOU, grandfather," said the child boldly; "never fear."

The old man kissed her, then turning to me and begging me to walk in, I did so. The door was closed and locked. Preceding me with the light, he led me through the place I had already seen from without, into a small sitting-room behind, in which was another door opening into a kind of closet, where I saw a little bed that a fairy might have slept in, it looked so very small and was so prettily arranged. The child took a candle and tripped into this little room, leaving the old man and me together.

"You must be tired, sir," said he as he placed a chair near the fire, "how can I thank you?"

"By taking more care of your grandchild another time, my good friend," I replied.

"More care!" said the old man in a shrill voice, "more care of Nelly! Why, who ever loved a child as I love Nell?"

He said this with such evident surprise that I was perplexed what answer to make, and the more so because coupled with something fee-

---

[4]wrinkled
[5]worn-down

Unit Four Acts of Love and Kindness   **237**

ble and wandering in his manner, there were in his face marks of deep and anxious thought which convinced me that he could not be, as I had been at first inclined to suppose, in a state of dotage or imbecility.[6]

"I don't think you consider—" I began.

"I don't consider!" cried the old man interrupting me, "I don't consider her! Ah, how little you know of the truth! Little Nelly, little Nelly!"

It would be impossible for any man, I care not what his form of speech might be, to express more affection than the dealer in curiosities did, in these four words. I waited for him to speak again, but he rested his chin upon his hand and shaking his head twice or thrice fixed his eyes upon the fire.

_____

[6]He was neither senile nor feeble-minded.

Understanding the Reading

Complete the next three exercises and see how well you understood the excerpt from *The Old Curiosity Shop*.

Exercise 11.4 Multiple-Choice Questions

Answer the following questions about the reading. Circle the letter of your answer.

TIP: Don't try to answer the questions from memory; go back to the text as often as necessary.

1. The word *betrayed*, as used in the phrase, "betrayed no marks of poverty or neglect," means
   A. treacherously disclosed.
   B. concealed.
   C. showed.
   D. covered up.

2. The narrator's attitude toward the child includes all of the following *except*
   A. surprise.
   B. suspicion.
   C. concern.
   D. admiration.

3. Which statement is *false*?
   A. The child observes the narrator closely.
   B. The narrator observes the child closely.
   C. The child makes no attempt to suppress her true feelings.
   D. The excerpt makes little use of dialogue.

4. Dickens's purpose for writing *The Old Curiosity Shop* was most likely to
   A. expose child neglect as a social problem.
   B. warn children not to go out alone.
   C. satirize politicians.
   D. reveal how crime rings operate.

5. The last two paragraphs of the reading indicate that
   A. the old man is not going to say another word to the narrator.
   B. the narrator might have learned more had he not insulted the old man.
   C. the old man is tired and about to fall asleep.
   D. there is much more to the story than the reader can imagine at this point.

Exercise 11.5 Short-Answer Questions

Respond to the following questions in one to two complete sentences. Go back to the text, as you did on the multiple choice.

6. What clues or direct information about Nell's personality does Dickens provide?

   _____

   _____

   _____

7. Nell indicates that her errand is a secret she cannot tell but that no harm is done by it. How does the narrator react to this information?

   _____

   _____

   _____

8. Which lines in the reading do you find most surprising? Why?

   _____

   _____

   _____

9. How did the narrator's expectations of the child's caretaker compare to his impressions of the old man once he actually met him?

   _____

   _____

   _____

Exercise 11.6 Extending Your Thinking

Respond to the following question in three to four complete sentences. Use details from the text in your answer.

10. The theme of this unit is "Acts of Love and Kindness." Do you think the act of kindness described in this story would be likely to happen in a large city today? Why or why not?

_____

_____

_____

_____

_____

_____

Reading Strategy Lesson
Identifying Tone and Mood

Identifying the **tone** and **mood** of a piece of literature can enhance your appreciation of the author's purpose and theme.

Tone and mood are often confused. An easy way to remember the difference is this: You speak in many different tones of voice. Your tone creates an atmosphere or mood. For example, if you are having a disagreement with a friend or sibling in angry tones, the mood will be tense.

Tone

You can think of tone as the narrator's "tone of voice" or attitude toward the subject. Is his or her voice conversational, friendly, amused, ironic, angry, contemptuous, gloomy, sad, happy? There are as many tones as there are emotional states, and if you listen to the narrator's voice, you should be able to detect how he or she feels about the subject. Remember, too, that the narrator's tone may be informal and unemotional. If there seems to be a lack of feeling about the subject, the tone is likely more formal.

Mood

Mood is the overall atmosphere or frame of mind that the story evokes in the reader. Mood develops out of the narrator's tone. Mood can also be described using emotions: joyful, sorrowful, depressing, romantic, idealistic, fanciful, mysterious, foreboding, and so forth.

How to Identify Tone

First, you must identify the point of view from which the story is written. *The Old Curiosity Shop* is told in the first person. The unnamed narrator uses the words *I*, *me*, and *mine*.

Next, look for clues that tell you the narrator's basic feelings toward his subject. While it's true that the narrator is concerned about the little girl being out alone at night, concern is not his over-all tone. He is a bit suspicious of what sort of errand she has been on, but suspicion is not the overriding tone, either. These are emotions that pass. We need to look for clues that are repeated. Pay special attention to the italicized words:

> For my part, my *curiosity* and *interest* were at least equal to the child's . . .

> I *wondered* what kind of errand it might be that occasioned her to be prepared for questioning.

> While we were thus engaged, I revolved in my mind a hundred different explanations of the *riddle* and rejected them every one. I really felt ashamed to take advantage of the ingenuousness or grateful feeling of the child for the purpose of *gratifying my curiosity*.

> There was *no reason, however, why I should refrain from seeing the person* who had inconsiderately sent her to so great a distance by night and alone . . .

Which of these words best describes the narrator's tone?

amused   curious   suspicious   ironic

The best choice here is *curious*. In fact, the narrator was so curious to find out where the little girl lived, and with whom, that he "avoided the most frequented ways and took the most intricate" so that she would not realize where she was too quickly and run home before he could satisfy his curiosity.

How to Identify Mood

To identify mood, you need only ask yourself, "What sort of atmosphere has the narrator created?" Using the narrator's tone as a tip, you may find that you, too, are curious about why Nell is out so late alone. There is a certain mystery about the little girl's errand. The mood is *mysterious*. Perhaps, since the narrator is so curious, he will solve the riddle.

Exercise 11.7 Practice the Reading Strategy

Read each excerpt on pages 242 and 243, underlining phrases that alert you to its tone and mood. Then answer the questions.

Dark spruce forest frowned on either side of the frozen waterway. The trees had been stripped by a recent wind of their white covering of frost, and they seemed to lean towards each other, black and ominous, in the fading light. A vast silence reigned over the land. The land itself was a desolation, lifeless, without movement, so lone and cold that the spirit of it was not even that of sadness. There was a hint in it of laughter, but of a laughter more terrible than any sadness—a laughter that was mirthless as the smile of the sphinx, a laughter cold as the frost and partaking of the grimness of infallibility. It was the masterful and incommunicable wisdom of eternity laughing at the futility of life and the effort of life. It was the Wild, the savage, frozen-hearted Northland Wild. (Jack London, *White Fang*)

1. The **tone** of this passage can best be described as
   A. severe.
   B. sunny.
   C. positive.
   D. formal.

2. The **mood** of this passage can best be described as
   A. hopeful.
   B. joyful.
   C. ominous.
   D. terrifying.

When Mary Lennox was sent to Misselthwaite Manor to live with her uncle everybody said she was the most disagreeable-looking child ever seen. It was true, too. She had a little thin face and a little thin body, thin light hair and a sour expression. Her hair was yellow, and her face was yellow because she had been born in India and had always been ill in one way or another. Her father had held a position under the English Government and had always been busy and ill himself, and her mother had been a great beauty who cared only to go to parties and amuse herself. . . . She had not wanted a little girl at all, and when Mary was born she handed her over to the care of an Ayah, who was made to understand that if she wished to please the Mem Sahib she must keep the child out of sight as much as possible. So when she was a sickly, fretful, ugly little baby she was kept out of the way, and when she became a sickly, fretful, toddling thing she was kept out of the way also. She never remembered seeing familiarly anything but the dark faces of her Ayah and the other native servants, and as they always obeyed her and gave her her own way in everything, because the Mem Sahib would be angry if she was disturbed by her crying, by the time she was six years old she was as tyrannical and selfish a little pig as ever lived. The young English governess who came to teach her to read and write disliked her so much that she gave up her place in three months, and when other governesses came to try to fill it they always went away in a shorter time than the first one. So if Mary had not chosen to really want to know how to read books she would never have learned her letters at all. (Frances Hodgson Burnett, *The Secret Garden*)

3. What word(s) describes the narrator's **tone**? _____

List three phrases you used as clues:

a. _____

b. _____

c. _____

4. What is the **mood** of this selection? _____

Why did you choose this particular word to describe the mood?

_____

_____

Writing Workshop
Avoiding Clichés

What Is a Cliché?

We are all familiar with clichés, or overused expressions, because we hear them constantly. When you hear or see the beginning of a cliché, you already know what the rest of it will be. For example, when you hear "*Last but . . .,*" you can already fill in "*. . . not least.*" If a friend is telling you a story, and says "*Beyond the shadow of . . .,*" you automatically fill in "*. . . a doubt.*"

Let's look at some examples of how clichés can affect the uniqueness of a sentence. Here is Charles Dickens's way of describing what the girl looked like:

> Though much altered by age, I fancied I could recognize in his spare and slender form something of that delicate mould which I had noticed in the child.

A clichéd way to say the same thing would be: "The little girl was *the spitting image* of the old man."

Jack London wrote:

> The land itself was a desolation, lifeless, without movement, so lone and cold that the spirit of it was not even that of sadness.

He could have written, "This place was enough to scare you out of your wits and make you so lonesome you could cry." We may be able to understand those clichés, but we've lost London's own voice.

Clichés were original when someone first thought them up, but they have been used so much that they have almost lost their meaning, and certainly their impact. According to the Oxford English Dictionary, Samuel Taylor Coleridge first used the term "Achilles' heel" as a metaphor for a person's weak point. That was in 1810. Today, it is considered a cliché to use the phrase "Achilles' heel." The writer George Orwell maintained that clichés were used "because they save people the trouble of inventing phrases for themselves." But part of the fun of writing is that you can be creative and experiment with language.

Like lack of variety in sentence structure, writing that is filled with clichés is not likely to interest your reader for long. They are so expected that you don't really hear them when you are listening or reading. Using vivid, unexpected phrases when you write makes your ideas seem fresh and keeps your reader involved with what you are trying to communicate.

Recognizing Clichés

To replace clichés, you must first recognize them. While there are thousands of clichés, here is a list to help you identify some of the most common ones.

hard as nails	nutty as a fruitcake	raining cats and dogs
on the road to recovery	off the beaten track	time and time again
time to kill	needless to say	hook, line, and sinker
the bottom line	at the drop of a hat	I'd give my right arm
fame and fortune	the ladder of success	at the crack of dawn
have a nice day	no problem	been there, done that

Exercise 11.8 Practice Recognizing Clichés

See how many of these clichés you can fill in automatically.

1. competition is _____

2. by a _____ margin

3. in the _____ future

4. waiting with _____ breath

5. a win-_____ situation

6. same old, _____

7. cut to the _____

8. my _____ feeling is that

9. learned his lesson _____ way

10. as quiet as a _____

Replacing Clichés

Looking back at Exercise 11.8, what other phrases could you use to replace the worn-out ones? That's where your imagination and creativity come in.

Instead of:

> She crept through the dark woods *as quietly as a mouse, with bated breath, with a gut feeling* that she was going to *learn her lesson the hard way.*

You might write:

> Tree branches seemed to close like gates behind her as she moved silently down the path. The air was as dank and clammy as her skin, and she wondered again if there was a reason why she had been drawn to this monstrous swamp.

Exercise 11.9 Practice Replacing Clichés

Rewrite each sentence, eliminating the cliché.

1. The coach had us out at *the crack of dawn* practicing our throwing, catching, and batting.

   _____

2. He said he was *fed up with* our losing record.

   _____

3. "It's *high time* we won a game," he growled.

   _____

4. "So let's *get the show on the road!*"

   _____

5. I ran out on the field, determined to *put my best foot forward.*

   _____

6. Once again, our team *went down to defeat.*

   _____

7. Even so, the other team won only *by the skin of its teeth.*

   _____

8. Their best batter was also *sly as a fox* and stole bases all through the game.

   _____

9. He'd start for second, and *quick as a wink* he'd be there.

   _____

10. Needless to say, our coach was *roaring like a lion* in the locker room.

    _____

Grammar Mini-Lesson
Commonly Misused Verbs

Here are five pairs of verbs frequently misused.

1. *Learn* and *teach*

To *learn* means "to receive knowledge."
From their teacher, the students *learned* about space.

To *teach* means "to show" or "instruct."
He *taught* them some theories of star formation.

2. *Borrow* and *lend*

To *borrow* means "to take something with the understanding that it will be returned."
May I *borrow* your eraser? (Not: May I *lend* your eraser?)

To *lend* means "to let someone use something with the understanding that it will be returned."
I shall be glad to *lend* you the money.

3. *Bring* and *take*

To *bring* means "to carry toward" the speaker.
Please *bring* the photographs the next time you come.

To *take* means "to carry away from" the speaker.
Take these letters to the mailbox. (Not: *Bring* these . . .)

Note that the speaker uses *take*, not *bring*, in this example from *The Old Curiosity Shop*: "Come," said I, "I'll take you there." (Not: "I'll bring you there." He's leading the little girl *away*.)

4. *Leave* and *let*

To *leave* means "to depart" or "to let remain."
When you *leave*, turn off the lights.
Leave the door open.

To *let* means "to permit" or "allow."
Let (not *Leave*) her have a chance to speak.

5. *Can* and *may*

Can is a helping verb expressing ability.
Can you (Are you able to) skate?

May is a helping verb expressing permission or possibility.
May (not *Can*) I borrow your notes?
It *may* snow tonight.

Exercise 11.10 Practice Choosing the Right Verb

Fill in the blank with the correct choice of the two verbs in parentheses.

1. I _____ a quarter from Maureen. (borrowed, lent)

2. _____ I please have the sugar? (May, Can)

3. Do not take the milk out; _____ it in the refrigerator. (let, leave)

4. Uncle Ben _____ me to play the guitar. (learned, taught)

5. _____ him solve his own problems. (Let, Leave)

6. Ms. Jones asked me to _____ the attendance report to the office. (bring, take)

7. Did you _____ your dog how to sit? (teach, learn)

8. Tell the neighbor's son that we have just enough sugar for dinner and that we can't _____ any. (borrow, lend)

9. Why not _____ your friend to our next meeting? (bring, take)

10. You _____ have as much time as you need. (may, can)

Polish Your Spelling
Learning Common Homonyms

Homonyms are words that sound alike but have different meanings, and may also be spelled differently. Here are some examples. Read them out loud so you can see the differences in pronunciation as well as meaning.

- The farm's main business was to *produce produce*.

- He could *lead* if he could get the *lead* out.

- The insurance for the *invalid* was *invalid*.

- They were too *close* to the door to *close* it.

- They had to *subject* the *subject* to a number of tests.

All of the words in the examples above are spelled the same way, but many homonyms are spelled differently even though they sound alike:

- The wind *blew* the *blue* dress off the clothesline.

- *Some* of the people can *sum* up what happened.

- I can *accept* anything *except* your criticism.

- The winner *ate eight* pies.
- You're not *allowed* to speak *aloud* during the test.

One way to decide which word to use when you are confused by homonyms is to look at the words within the words. For example, the word *allow* (permit) is in *allowed* and the word *loud* (noisy) is in the word *aloud*.

Sometimes you can tell which one to use by knowing which one you *don't* want to use. Let's say you are trying to decide between *horse* and *hoarse* in the sentence, "His voice was very _____." If you know that the word spelled *horse* is an animal, then you can be sure you want the other word, *hoarse*.

The best way to learn homonyms is to notice when you are reading which word is used. Below is a list of commonly confused homonyms. Study the list and then complete the practice exercise.

billed	requested to pay
build	to construct
brake	stopping device
break	fracture
its	belonging to it
it's	it is
pane	sheet of glass
pain	physical discomfort
past	time gone by
past	beyond
passed	went, gone
sight	vision
site	space of ground
straight	not curvy
strait	narrow waterway
there	in that place
their	belonging to them
they're	they are

to	in the direction of
too	also
too	excessive
two	1 + 1

weight	heaviness
wait	delay
your	belonging to you
you're	you are

Exercise 11.11 Practice Choosing the Correct Homonym

Insert the correct choice on the line provided.

1. I went _____ home. (strait, straight)

2. Has your cat gained any _____? (wait, weight)

3. My teacher thought my essay was effective, except for _____ ending. (its, it's)

4. Months have _____ since I last saw him. (past, passed)

5. How much will it cost to replace the broken _____? (pain, pane)

6. My mom thinks there is a _____ on the passenger side. (break, brake)

7. Do you realize what _____ saying? (you're, your)

8. I'm going to make some lunch. Are you hungry _____? (to, too, two)

9. The repairman _____ us too much. (build, billed)

10. Remind them to bring _____ gloves. (they're, their, there)

Chapter Twelve

Prereading Guide
Words to know and ideas to consider before you jump into the reading.

A. Essential Vocabulary

Word	Meaning	Typical Use
adroit (*adj*) a-DROIT	1. skillful in the use of the hands; dexterous 2. showing mental skill; clever	Brad is an *adroit* carpenter. Charles Dickens was *adroit* in contriving interesting plots and characters.
blithesome (*adj*) BLYTHE-sum	carefree and cheerful; light-hearted	I never see Mom more *blithesome* than when we are vacationing at the lake.
dearth (*n*) DURTH	short supply; lack; insufficiency	There seems to be a *dearth* of reliable information on my research topic.
entreat (*v*) en-TREET	to urgently or repeatedly request; to implore	The speaker planned to *entreat* the business owners to oppose the construction of the giant discount store.
guileless (*adj*) GUYLE-less	free of deceit or cleverness; sincere	People often take advantage of young, *guileless* teens who want to believe that their dreams can be achieved without much effort.
hoax (*n*) HOXE	1. something meant to deceive or swindle people; a trick 2. (*v*) to deceive or defraud someone or a group of people	Don't believe everything you read in your e-mail; *hoaxes* circulate constantly. They had been *hoaxed*, their money was gone, and there was nothing they could do about it.
incessant (*adj*) in-CESS-unt	constant and unceasing	The *incessant* noise of the city got on my parents' nerves, so we moved to the suburbs.
onslaught (*n*) ON-slawt	1. a sudden, violent attack; an assault 2. an overwhelming quantity of something	The *onslaught* of hunters on the American bison nearly exterminated the species. When I finally charged my cell phone, I was greeted by an *onslaught* of messages from friends.

Word	Meaning	Typical Use
panoply (*n*) PAN-uh-plee	a wide-ranging selection; an array	We have a *panoply* of restaurants in our town—what kind of food are you craving?
presage (*v*) PRESS-ij	1. to indicate a future event; to foreshadow 2. (*n*) a premonition of a future event; an omen	The increasing wind and rain *presaged* the arrival of the hurricane. Layoffs at Ford may be a *presage* of layoffs at other auto companies.

B. Vocabulary Practice

Exercise 12.1 Sentence Completion

Using your new vocabulary knowledge, choose the best way to complete the following sentences. Circle the letter of your answer.

1. She appeared so guileless that it was _____ to believe she was an accessory to the crime.
   A. easy
   B. difficult

2. The incessant mosquitoes made it _____ to be blithesome.
   A. difficult
   B. easy

3. We were _____ to find an onslaught of junk mail crowded into the mailbox.
   A. delighted
   B. annoyed

4. The hot, _____ is characterized by a dearth of water.
   A. humid South
   B. dry desert

5. A panoply of _____ was heard at the poetry reading.
   A. styles
   B. rain

6. The dealership said it had lots of cars for only _____, but that was a hoax.
   A. $99.99
   B. $9,999

7. He was adroit at convincing his parents that he needed his own car, so he's _____.
   A. still walking
   B. driving

8. Most advertising entreats us to _____.
   A. hit the "mute" button
   B. buy their products

9. The Fourth of July in our town is a blithesome day of
   _____.
   A. old-fashioned fun
   B. boring speeches and no fireworks

10. Scientists believe that a(an) _____ in small earth-
   quakes may presage a big one.
   A. decrease
   B. increase

Exercise 12.2 Using Fewer Words

Replace the italicized words with a single word from the following list.

blithesome	dearth	adroit	entreat	guileless
hoax	onslaught	panoply	presaged	incessant

1. We *urgently request* you to write to your   1._____
   congressmen today.

2. Kathryn was so *free of deceit or cleverness*   2._____
   that everyone trusted her.

3. My dad can build anything; he is extremely   3._____
   skillful in the use of his hands.

4. Students who voted in a mock election on   4._____
   Monday *indicated the future event of* the
   senator's victory.

5. A(an) *wide-ranging selection* of candy can   5._____
   be found at even the smallest shops.

6. The *sudden, violent attack* of the rainstorm   6._____
   forced fans from the stadium to their cars.

7. I have a(an) *short supply* of friends who   7._____
   want to get up at five A.M. and run with me.

8. E-mails that assure you that you will receive   8._____
   a free airline ticket just for answering a few
   questions are undoubtedly a(an) *deceitful
   trick.*

9. The *constant and unremitting* glare of   9._____
   computer monitors can cause headaches.

10. On the first warm day of spring, we felt   10._____
   carefree and cheerful and ran outdoors
   without our jackets.

Exercise 12.3 Synonyms and Antonyms

Fill in the blanks in column A with the required synonyms or antonyms, selecting them from column B. (Remember: A *synonym* is a word similar in meaning to another word. An *antonym* is a word opposite in meaning to another word.)

A	B
_____	1. synonym for *unceasing*	adroit
_____	2. synonym for *urge*	blithesome
_____	3. antonym for *cheerless*	dearth
_____	4. synonym for *predict*	entreat
_____	5. antonym for *plenty*	guileless
_____	6. synonym for *sincere*	hoax
_____	7. synonym for *array*	onslaught
_____	8. antonym for *clumsy*	panoply
_____	9. synonym for *trick*	presage
_____	10. synonym for *attack*	incessant

C. Journal Freewrite

Before you begin the reading on the next page, take out a journal or sheet of paper and spend some time responding to the following prompt.

TIP: Don't worry about grammar and spelling; just write what comes to mind. The purpose of freewriting is to explore ideas, not to produce a polished work.

If you were with a group of people in a dangerous or tragic situation, how do you think you would interact with them? Do you think everyone would try to help each other survive, or do you think people would just look out for themselves? Why?

from Every Man for Himself

by Beryl Bainbridge

About the Author
**Beryl Bainbridge
(1934–)** has won
numerous prizes for her
writing and is consid-
ered one of England's
finest contemporary
authors. She often
depicts lower- or mid-
dle-class characters
who become involved in
dangerous or violent
situations. In *Every Man
for Himself*, a fictional
novel based on a real
event, her characters
interact on the doomed
Titanic. In this excerpt,
the narrator describes
the behavior of several
of his shipmates and
gives the reader a feel-
ing of what it must have
been like to be on the
ship shortly before it
sank.

There was a fearful crush in the gymnasium, spilling out on
deck and flowing in again as the cold stabbed to the bone.
Hopper was nowhere to be seen. Mrs. Brown jogged my
sleeve and asked if it would be a good idea to start community singing, but before I could answer the far door was
thrust open and ship's band struck up something jolly. Kitty
Webb sat astride one of the mechanical bicycles. She wore
silk pyjamas under a man's leather automobile coat and was
accompanied by Guggenheim's valet. I went out in search of
Hopper. Save for a solitary man gripping the rail there was
no one about under that glorious <u>panoply</u> of stars. I imagined the crew must be all assembled at the stern; before quit-
ting the wheelhouse I had heard Captain Smith's call for all
hands on deck.

I was walking towards the port side when suddenly the
night was rendered hideous by a tremendous blast of steam
escaping from the safety valves of the pipes fore and aft of
the funnels. I clapped my palms over my ears under the
<u>onslaught</u> and turned giddy, for the noise was like a thousand
locomotives thundering through a culvert. Even the stars
seemed to shake. Recovering, I spied Hopper watching an
officer attempting to parley with the bridge above. The officer was pointing at the life-boats and soundlessly roaring for
instructions. Hopper and I, bent double under the din, ran
back inside.

The crowd in the gymnasium had mostly retreated to the
landing of the Grand Staircase and the foyer beneath. The
band was now playing rag-time. Kitty Webb, head lolling like
a doll, danced with Mrs. Brown. Mrs. Carter asked if Captain
Smith was on the boat deck and whether I knew the where-
abouts of Mr. Ismay. I said I expected they were both on the
bridge seeing to things. There was such a <u>dearth</u> of information, of confirmation or denial of rumours—the racquets court
was under water but not the Turkish baths; a spur of the iceberg had ripped the ship from one end to the other but the crew
was fully equipped to make good the damage and were even
now putting it to rights—and such an absence of persons in
authority to whom one might turn that it was possible to imag-

ine the man in the golfing jacket had spoken no more than the truth when presupposing we were victims of a <u>hoax</u>. In part, this lack of communication was due to the awesome size of the wounded ship. It was simply not possible to keep everyone abreast of events. An accident at the summit of a mountain is hardly observable from the slopes. For the rest, what was Smith expected to do? Should he appear on the landing of the Grand Staircase beneath that rococo clock whose hands now stood at twenty-five to one in the morning and announce that in spite of the watertight compartments, the indestructible bulkheads, the unimaginable technology, the unthinkable was in process and his unsinkable vessel, now doomed, unfortunately carried insufficient life-boats to accommodate all on board?

Ginsberg was still in his armchair opposite the elevator, still clutching a handkerchief to his nose. An unknown girl was chatting to him; he introduced her but the loudness of the band blotted out her name. She had an enormous expanse of brow, beneath which her features sat truncated like those of an infant's; it was possibly on account of her hair being dragged back in a fearsome bun. She said, without preamble, that she had known for several years past, from dreams and such like, that it was her destiny to drown. She spoke of it quite calmly and without resorting to melodrama. Her doctor had dismissed her condition as no more than nerves; her mother had enrolled her in the local tennis club, in the hopes that strenuous exercise in the fresh air would banish such fancies. She had become quite exceptionally <u>adroit</u> on the courts, but the dreams persisted.

'There is nothing to worry about,' I said. 'I myself have been plagued by nightmares. I'm convinced they consist of memories of the past rather than portents of the future.'

Ginsberg was leaning back in his chair, breathing like a man recovering from a record-breaking run round the tracks. Hopper asked what was wrong and he explained he was afflicted with asthma. It came on sometimes without reason. His handkerchief was smeared with a concoction of honey obtained from a bee-keeper in a Shaker community in Massachusetts and would do the trick shortly. I thought it was an inspired excuse and fancied he was in a blue funk.

It was then that I realized I hadn't seen Charlie Melchett since the interruption to our game of bridge. In Hopper's opinion it was probable he'd galloped off to play knight errant to the Ellery sisters and Molly Dodge. I made my excuses to the girl with the forehead and went looking for him. Lady Melchett, but six weeks before, had drawn me to one side and <u>entreated</u> me to keep an eye on her boy. 'He is so very fond of you,' she'd said. 'He looks up to you.' 'You may rely on me,' I'd told her, fighting off those damn dogs threatening to lick my face away.

I ran him to earth quite quickly, standing in the deserted gymnasium gazing out at the shadowy deck. The funnels continued intermittently to release those deafening blasts of steam and though the sound was muted by the glass I had to shout to draw his attention. He didn't turn round. 'Why does it keep on with that ghastly noise?' he asked.

'It's a bit like a train,' I said.

'I thought I saw a ship out there a few minutes ago.'

'I expect it's coming to assist us.'

'No,' he said. 'It's stopped moving. Perhaps it's just starlight.'

'You ought to fetch your life-preserver,' I said. 'I've got mine on.'

'I will . . . soon. I needed to mull things over. I should have liked—' The gush of steam started up again; when it had died away he was still rabbiting on and I reckoned he was speaking of his father—'. . . I know he's fond of me but it worries him how I'll face up to things when he's gone. I'm not brainy and I don't often think of anything downright important. My mother dotes on me, and that's rather held me back. I've never had to go it alone, not like some chaps. Not that I'd want to. I'm no good on my own . . . I lack common-sense.'

'Charlie,' I protested, 'you have more common-sense than any man I know . . . and kindness and a generous heart—'

'I would have so liked to make him proud.'

'Hopper and I are in the foyer,' I told him. 'We rather wanted you with us.'

'I'll come and join you in a bit,' he said. I hesitated, but felt it my duty to ask, 'You're not frightened are you, Charlie? There's no need to be.'

'There's nothing on this earth that frightens me,' he said. 'It's what comes after that concerns one. I've not always behaved decently.' His voice wobbled. I couldn't help smiling. If the worst happens, I thought, God will surely send all his angels to bring Charlie to heaven. 'You'll have plenty of time to atone,' I said, 'a lifetime, in fact,' and at that he faced me and, sheepishly grinning, followed me down the stairs.

Understanding the Reading

Complete the next three exercises and see how well you understood the excerpt from *Every Man for Himself*.

Exercise 12.4 Multiple-Choice Questions

Answer the following questions about the reading. Circle the letter of your answer.

TIP: Don't try to answer the questions from memory; go back to the text as often as necessary.

1. One reason the narrator seems to be more aware than other passengers of the possible danger to come is that he
   A. heard the horrible noise of the steam escaping from the valves.
   B. went out on deck and saw the iceberg the ship had hit.
   C. saw an officer pointing at the lifeboats and shouting.
   D. never believed in hoaxes.

2. From context, you can infer that Lady Melchett
   A. is an overprotective mother.
   B. had a premonition that something would go wrong on the ship.
   C. was concerned about Charlie because of his asthma.
   D. is the narrator's employer.

3. Which statement is *false*?
   A. Some of the passengers are confused.
   B. All of the passengers are wearing life preservers.
   C. Some of the passengers are unconcerned.
   D. Some of the passengers are afraid.

4. Bainbridge's purpose for writing *Every Man for Himself* was most likely to
   A. expose the negligence of those who built the *Titanic*.
   B. give an eyewitness account of the night the ship sank.
   C. satirize the movie made about the ship.
   D. entertain readers with fiction based on fact.

Exercise 12.5 Short-Answer Questions

Respond to the following questions in one to two complete sentences. Go back to the text, as you did on the multiple choice.

5. From what point of view is this story told? How would it be different if it were told from another point of view? Explain.

   _____

   _____

   _____

6. Why were many passengers not particularly alarmed when the ship struck the iceberg?

   _____

   _____

   _____

7. How does the sentence, "An accident at the summit of the mountain is hardly observable from the slopes" apply to the situation depicted in this excerpt?

   _____

   _____

   _____

Exercise 12.6 Extending Your Thinking

Respond to the following question in three to four complete sentences. Use details from the text in your answer.

8. The theme of this unit is "Acts of Love and Kindness." Does the narrator's conversation with Charlie Melchett qualify as an "act of kindness"—or would it be better to tell him that he might indeed drown? Explain.

_____

_____

_____

_____

_____

_____

To Anna

by Sarah Kilham Biller

About the Author
Sarah Kilham Biller (flourished around 1837) is one of many unrecognized English female poets who wrote during the Romantic Period. Little is known about her life. Her volume of poetry, *Holkham, the Scenes of My Childhood: and Other Poems*, written in 1837, was recently discovered by students at the University of California at Davis.

Thou hast asked me, dear Anna, to greet with a song
    The day when we hail thee of age;
'Tis the season by nature when <u>blithesome</u> and young
    We little save pleasure <u>presage</u>.
And, oh! may that bosom so <u>guileless</u> and meek
    Never brook disappointment severe,
Nor blighted affection e'er wither thy cheek,
    Or thy breast be the seat of despair.
May all that is lovely encircle thy brow,
    May thy heart be the throne of content,
May the bonds of true friendship <u>incessantly</u> grow,
    And virtue that friendship cement.
And mayst thou reflect when with age growing grey
    On the past without cause for regret,
And the last ray of life as it fadeth away
    In glory eternal be set.

Understanding the Reading

Complete the next three exercises and see how well you understood "To Anna."

Exercise 12.7 Multiple-Choice Questions

Answer the following questions about the reading. Circle the letter of your answer.

TIP: Don't try to answer the questions from memory; go back to the text as often as necessary.

1. Sarah Kilham Biller wrote this poem
   A. as a surprise for Anna.
   B. because Anna's mother asked her to.
   C. because Anna asked her to write a poem for her birthday.
   D. because Anna is her little sister.

2. An accurate paraphrasing of the third and fourth lines is
   A. During this season of the year, everything seems wonderful.
   B. When we are young and happy, we see nothing but good in the future.
   C. Being close to nature helps you to have a positive attitude.
   D. Anna should not assume her life will be perfect.

3. "May thy heart be the throne of content" is another way of wishing that
   A. Anna will have much happiness in her life.
   B. Anna will be lucky in love.
   C. Anna will not suffer from heart trouble.
   D. Anna's heart will never be broken.

Exercise 12.8 Short-Answer Questions

Respond to the following questions in one to two complete sentences. Go back to the text, as you did on the multiple choice.

4. Do you think the author's wishes for Anna are realistic? Why or why not?

   _____

   _____

   _____

5. Describe the setting in which you imagine this poem would be read or given to Anna. (Remember that setting includes time and place.)

   _____

   _____

   _____

6. Describe the mood and tone of the poem.

_____

_____

_____

Exercise 12.9 Extending Your Thinking

Respond to the following question in three to four complete sentences. Use details from the text in your answer.

7. How does the message of this poem, and the reason it was written, connect with the theme of this unit, "Acts of Love and Kindness"?

_____

_____

_____

_____

_____

_____

Reading Strategy Lesson
How to Read Poetry

Reading poetry can seem intimidating if you don't have much practice. Here are eight techniques to help you read and interpret poems with more confidence.

1. Read the title. Then, before you go any further, think about what the poem *may* be about. In "To Anna," the title tells you that the poem is written for someone named Anna.

2. Read aloud if possible. The first time you read through a poem, it helps if you can read it aloud or listen to someone else reading it. This is similar to skimming or scanning a story or nonfiction text, but since poems are shorter you should read the entire piece. Read slowly and thoughtfully. This will give you a basic idea of what the poem is about.

3. Read according to the poem's punctuation. This is one of the most important rules for understanding a poem's meaning, and one of the easiest rules to follow.

Example:
> Thou hast asked me, dear Anna, to greet with a song
> The day when we hail thee of age;
> 'Tis the season by nature when blithesome and young
> We little save pleasure presage.

These lines of the poem should be read like two sentences:

> Thou hast asked me, dear Anna, to greet with a song the day
> when we hail thee of age. 'Tis the season by nature when
> blithesome and young we little save pleasure presage.

The main thing to remember is to pause or stop at the end of a line *only* if there is punctuation that says you should. If there is a comma, pause as you would when reading a sentence. A semicolon or colon indicates a longer pause. No punctuation at the end of a line means you go right on to the next line. If there is a period, a question mark or an exclamation point, then of course you should come to a complete stop.

Reading a poem this way should help to greatly clarify its meaning. You should be able to identify the poem's basic subject (What is the poem about?) and situation (Who is talking? Under what circumstances? To whom? Why?).

4. Think about the speaker. Poets often take on the "voice" of someone or something else. In this poem, the speaker is the poet, but this is not always the case, even when the speaker uses *I*.

> I am a little spider and I'm creeping very near—
> I know that you are frightened, but I wouldn't hurt you,
> dear.

Spiders can't write poetry, but the poet can put herself in the spider's place and write as if she were the spider. Always ask, "Is this the poet talking, or is he or she taking on the voice of something or someone else?"

5. Look back at the poem. See which parts you understand and which parts are still fuzzy. Does the poet use figurative language? (Are there metaphors? Similes? Personification?) Are there symbols—that is, does one thing stand for something else? Do these give you clues to understanding? Let yourself "see" the mental pictures the poet paints for you. These mental pictures are called poetic **imagery** and can involve not only sight but all of your other senses. Getting involved with a poem will enhance your enjoyment of it.

The box on the next page reviews three kinds of figurative language you can look for when you read poetry.

6. Paraphrase the poem. A good poet doesn't waste words. Every word serves a purpose. Therefore, paraphrasing can help you find meaning in the poem. Go over it line by line and put it in your own words. Look up any words you can't define. Read the poem over again several times.

"To Anna" was written more than 150 years ago, and the words and their placement are different from modern poetry. To paraphrase this type of poetry, you often need to rearrange the words in the lines so they make more sense to you.

Following is a paragraph paraphrasing the poem. Refer back to the original poem as you read it.

Paraphrase:

> Dear Anna, you have asked me to write a poem for your birthday. It's natural for us, young as we are, to see only pleasure in the future. You are so honest and sweet, I hope you are never severely disappointed. I hope you never love someone who breaks your heart and leaves you in despair. I wish you love and contentment and true friendship. I hope that when you are old you will be able to look at the past and not regret anything that has happened in your life, and that you will be heading straight for heaven when you do pass on.

7. Check for meter and rhyme. If the poem is written in a specific form, what does the form have to do with the subject? In "To Anna," notice how the "beat" of lines 1, 3, 5, 7, 9, 11, 13, and 15 is the same (four stressed syllables), just as the even-numbered lines have the same beat (three stressed syllables). The rhyme scheme for this poem is ABABCDCDEFEFGHGH. That is, lines 1 and 3 rhyme (A—*song*/*young*). Lines 2 and 4 rhyme (B—*age*/*presage*). Lines 5 and 7 rhyme (C—*meek*/*cheek*), and so forth. The form of this poem would lend itself nicely to a song, and in fact the poet says that her poem is a "song" for Anna.

8. Look for sound effects. The poet may use **alliteration**, consecutive words that begin with the same sound: *My love is like a red, red rose*. In this poem, the poet has used alliteration several times:

> We little save **pleasure presage**
> . . . when with age **growing grey** . . .

Another sound-effect technique is **onomatopoeia**—words that sound like what they do, such as *cut, buzz, swish, whisper, hiss*. Poets use these techniques for two main reasons: to make a poem sound more pleasing and to emphasize certain words.

Exercise 12.10 Practice the Reading Strategy

Take turns with a partner reading "To Anna" out loud. Then read a new poem that follows, "The Lake Isle of Innisfree." Remember to read according to the punctuation. When you're done reading, answer the questions on the lines provided.

The Lake Isle of Innisfree
By William Butler Yeats

I will arise and go now, and go to Innisfree,
And a small cabin build there, of clay and wattles made;
Nine bean rows will I have there, a hive for the honey bee,
  And live alone in the bee-loud glade.

And I shall have some peace there, for peace comes dropping slow,
Dropping from the veils of the morning to where the cricket sings;
There midnight's all a-glimmer, and noon a purple glow,
  And evening full of the linnet's wings.

I will arise and go now, for always night and day
I hear lake water lapping with low sounds by the shore;
While I stand on the roadway, or on the pavements gray,
  I hear it in the deep heart's core.

Discussion Questions

1. What does the title indicate this poem is about?

_____

_____

_____

2. What can you see, hear, smell, and feel as you read this poem?

_____

_____

_____

3. Who is speaking? Where is the speaker?

_____

_____

_____

4. Are there any words that you need to look up? What do they mean?

_____

_____

_____

5. Did Yeats use any figurative language? What are some examples?

_____

_____

_____

Exercise 12.11 Apply the Reading Strategy

On a separate sheet of paper, paraphrase "The Lake Isle of Innisfree." Use the discussion questions and answers from Exercise 12.10 as a guide. (You can use the paraphrase of "To Anna" as an example.)

Writing Workshop
Using Poetic Language

There is often a fine line between poetry and prose. Even though _Every Man for Himself_ is written in prose, Beryl Bainbridge's writing is very poetic. Some of the language she uses could be rearranged and read as a poem. For example:

If the worst happens, I thought,
God will surely send all his angels
to bring Charlie to heaven.
"You'll have plenty of time to atone," I said,
"a lifetime, in fact."

"Found poems" are pieces of prose that can be rearranged to make interesting and moving poems. You can even find poems in newspapers and magazines. Here is a poem that could have been found in the lifestyle section of a British newspaper.

German Shepherd Good for the Heart
Each morning Honey goes round
to Mr. Tralee's door
where she has a bit of roast beef.
Then it's walking on the moor.
They both have a heart condition, you see,
and walking has been recommended for Tralee.
One must wonder, though,
if Honey knows the merits of walking
or only the merits of roast beef
and Mr. Tralee's company.

Exercise 12.12 Apply the Lesson to Find a Poem

Look through the readings in this book and in textbooks, newspapers, and magazines. Choose some sentences that you feel will make a good poem when broken into lines and rearranged as in the examples. Write your found poem on a separate sheet of paper. Aim for at least ten lines.

Exercise 12.13 Apply the Lesson to Your Own Writing

In this chapter, you read a poem written for a young woman named Anna and another about a place in nature about which the poet dreams. Now that you are more familiar with poems, it's time to write your own. You may choose your own idea, or one of the following.

1. Using the thoughts in "To Anna" as a model, write a poem for the younger person you wrote about in your journal. Meter and rhyme are not required, but you may wish to experiment with them. To do this, you might think of a song you know well and substitute your poem's words.

2. Using "The Lake Isle of Innisfree" as a model, write about a favorite place where you would like to be.

Include some figurative language and imagery in your poem. Expect to go over it several times until you get it the way you want it. Read it to your class if you choose, or hand it in to your teacher and ask that your poem be read without identifying you as the poet.

Grammar Mini-Lesson
Correcting Run-on Sentences

What Is a Run-on Sentence?

A run-on sentence occurs when you have two or more sentences strung together without proper punctuation.

Examples:

> We never saw Vanessa after she moved she said she'd visit.
> Mosquitoes are found everywhere in Alaska they are called the "state bird."
> Briana and Sarah went to the game we won it.

Run-on sentences don't allow the reader to pause and can thus be very hard to follow.

How Can You Fix Run-on Sentences?

When you have two sentences (independent clauses) strung together, inserting a comma is not enough. Here are the right ways to correct run-ons.

- Break the sentence into two complete sentences:

  > We never saw Vanessa after she moved. She said she would visit.

  > Mosquitoes are found everywhere. In Alaska they are called the "state bird."

  > Briana and Sarah went to the game. We won it.

- Use a semicolon to separate the two independent clauses:

  > We never saw Vanessa after she moved; she said she would visit.

  > Mosquitoes are found everywhere; in Alaska they are called the "state bird."

  > Briana and Sarah went to the game; we won it.

- Separate the independent clauses with a comma and a coordinating conjunction (*and, but, or, yet*):

  > We never saw Vanessa after she moved, **yet** she said she would visit.

  > Mosquitoes are found everywhere, **but** in Alaska they are called the "state bird."

  > Briana and Sarah went to the game, **and** we won.

- Make one of the independent clauses dependent by using a subordinating conjunction (*although, while, which, because, if*):

  > **Although** Vanessa said she would visit, we never saw her after she moved.

  > **While** mosquitoes are found everywhere, in Alaska they are called the "state bird."

  > Briana and Sarah went to the game, **which** we won.

You may also find it useful when rewriting sentences to use **correlating conjunctions** (*neither . . . nor, not only . . . but also, whether . . . or*). They are always used in pairs. You would use correlating conjunctions with the examples above only if you wanted to change the meaning of the sentences somewhat. Sometimes that may be exactly what you want to do to make your meaning clear. The correlating conjunctions used below add meaning and interest to the sentences.

Vanessa **neither** wrote **nor** called, although she said she would keep in touch.

Mosquitoes are found **not only** in the tropics **but also** in Alaska.

Briana and Sarah said they would enjoy the game **whether** we won **or** not.

When you correct run-on sentences in your own writing, you will need to use your own judgment about which type of correction you want to make. Study the table of conjunctions below and then proceed to Exercise 12.14, where you will practice correcting run-ons.

Conjunctions

A conjunction connects single words or groups of words. There are three kinds of conjunctions. The following table lists the three kinds and their uses.

CONJUNCTIONS		
Coordinating	**Correlating**	**Subordinating**
A coordinating conjunction connects words, phrases, or clauses that are equally important or of the same type. They are also used to join two independent clauses.	Correlating conjunctions are used in pairs—in other words, they correlate.	Subordinating conjunctions introduce a dependent clause in a sentence.
and, but, for, nor, or, so, yet	*either, or; neither, nor; not only, but also; both, and; whether, or; just, as; just, so; as, so*	*after, although, as, as if, as long as, as though, because, before, if, in order that, provided that, since, so, so that, that, though, till, unless, until, when, where, whereas, while, which*
I might as well get in the car *and* drive to the mall. (two actions of equal weight) There is nothing I need, *but* it's always fun to look. (two independent clauses)	It is *neither* rainy *nor* sunny today. You have to go *whether* you want to *or* not.	*Although* it was below zero, the skiers were eager to get to the slopes. *Unless* it starts early, we won't be able to go to the movie.

REMEMBER: A comma is not strong enough to correct a run-on. A comma has to be paired with a conjunction. If you don't want to use a comma-conjunction pair, you can just use a semicolon, which is strong enough to be by itself. (Think of it this way: Semicolons are larger than commas—they have the extra dot on top—so they're stronger!) Both of the following are correct:

He likes the Mets, *but* I like the Yankees.
(comma and conjunction)

He likes the Mets; I like the Yankees.
(just a semicolon)

Exercise 12.14 Practice Correcting Run-ons

Rewrite each run-on sentence using one of the methods outlined above. (More than one answer may be correct, but the sentence must make sense and be grammatically correct.)

1. Many students put off writing research papers they wish they hadn't when the due date gets close.

   _____

   _____

2. No one is sure why it happened there are many theories about why the dinosaurs became extinct.

   _____

   _____

3. We loved the movie we laughed about it all the way home.

   _____

   _____

4. I hate getting recorded messages when I call a business none of the numbers ever match what I want.

   _____

   _____

5. There is a tunnel under the English Channel they call it the Chunnel.

   _____

   _____

Use conjunctions to correctly complete these sentences.

6. _____ walk faster _____ get out of the way.

7. Crocodiles, _____ have been around for many thousands of years, are one of the oldest species living today.

8. _____ you perform well in a recital or play, you feel like a star.

9. We tried to reserve the picnic pavilion for our family reunion, _____ it was already booked.

10. We're having the reunion anyway _____ it rains _____ shines.

Polish Your Spelling
Frequently Misspelled Words

As you know, words are not always spelled the way they sound. To make matters more difficult, some words sound the same but are spelled differently. This section helps you review and practice words that are often misspelled. It is set up differently from the other spelling sections in this book.

First, review the following list. Underline the words that you find the most difficult to spell. If you're not sure if you have difficulty with a particular word, look at it, cover it up, and try to spell it without peeking. If you cannot spell it correctly, underline it. Then write all the underlined words in your notebook under the heading "My Personal Spelling List." You should list at least 20 words. If you have fewer, think of other words you sometimes spell wrong in order to complete the list.

ache	acquaint	across	agreeable
all right	almost	always	among
another	asked	athletic	beautiful
before	believe	benefit	boundary
break	built	captain	certain
character	coming	committee	cough
course	disappear	disappoint	doctor
doesn't	dropped	enough	every
exception	excitement	experience	friend
grammar	having	hear	hospital
immediately	instead	knew	knowledge
library	meant	minute	necessary

occasion	occurred	often	once
piece	pleasant	principal	privilege
probably	realize	really	says
scene	since	speech	straight
studying	success	surely	surprise
though	thought	threw	together
toward	until	which	women

Exercise 12.15 Practice Using a Personal Spelling List

Study your personal spelling list for a few minutes. A good way to learn a word you aren't sure of is to look at it, spell it out loud, cover it up, and see if you can write it without looking. Then have a partner test you by reading you your word list while you write the words on a separate sheet of paper. Check to see if you made any mistakes. Then test your partner the same way.

Unit Four Review

Vocabulary Review

A. Match each word with its definition.

DEFINITION		WORD
_____	1. deliberate trick or swindle	a. presage
_____	2. to have space for	b. confidence
_____	3. sudden violent attack	c. entreat
_____	4. feeling of trust	d. interminable
_____	5. indicate a future event	e. tether
_____	6. seemingly endless	f. accommodate
_____	7. free of deceit or cleverness	g. precaution
_____	8. action taken ahead of time	h. guileless
_____	9. tie or rope	i. onslaught
_____	10. urgently or repeatedly request	j. hoax

B. Match each word with its synonym.

SYNONYM		WORD
_____	11. unceasing	a. curiosity
_____	12. array	b. delicate
_____	13. plea	c. appeal
_____	14. clothing	d. frankness
_____	15. inquisitiveness	e. incessant
_____	16. frail	f. methodical
_____	17. outspokenness	g. throes
_____	18. systematic	h. panoply
_____	19. convulsive	i. attire
_____	20. struggle	j. spasmodic

C. Match each word with its antonym.

ANTONYM	WORD
_____ 21. anxious	a. timidly
_____ 22. disagreeable	b. blithesome
_____ 23. awareness	c. involuntary
_____ 24. huge	d. oblivion
_____ 25. courageously	e. diminutive
_____ 26. intentional	f. unperturbed
_____ 27. honesty	g. dearth
_____ 28. cheerless	h. genial
_____ 29. plenty	i. adroit
_____ 30. clumsy	j. deceit

Grammar Review

The underlined portions of the paragraph may or may not contain errors. If there is an error, circle the letter of the correction in the answer choices. If there is no error, choose D.

The United Kingdom is made up of England, Scotland, Wales, and Northern (1) Ireland is part of the European Union. (1)

Great Britain is the largest island in the British Aisles. Followed by Northern (2) Ireland and the Irish Republic. Their are (3) also island chains. Such as the Hebrides, (3) Orkney, and Shetland. Before large (4) passenger plains. People took ocean liners (4) to America. Now most people fly their in (5) ate ours or less. We have lent a lot of (5) (6)

1. A. Northern Ireland. Its part
   B. Northern Ireland, and is part
   C. Northern Ireland, is part
   D. no change
2. A. British Isles, followed by
   B. British Aisles; followed by
   C. British Isles. Followed by
   D. no change
3. A. There are also island chains, such as the
   B. There are also island chains. Such as the
   C. They're are also island chains, such as the
   D. no change
4. A. large passenger plains, people
   B. large passenger planes, people
   C. large passenger planes. People
   D. no change
5. A. fly their in eight hours or less.
   B. fly there in eight hours or less.
   C. fly they're in eight hours or less.
   D. no change

things from Britain <u>our language for</u>
      (6)   (7)

<u>instants</u>. Our monetary system <u>is different</u>
  (7)   (8)

<u>though we use dollars and sense</u> and they
              (8)

use pounds and pence. <u>Although it's a</u>
                         (9)

<u>different system</u>, most <u>people don't have</u>
    (9)   (10)

<u>no problems with it</u> when they visit
    (10)

England.

6. A. We have lent a lot of things to
   B. We have borrowed a lot of things from
   C. We have borrowed a lot of things to
   D. no change

7. A. our language, for instants
   B. our language, for instance
   C. are language, for instance
   D. no change

8. A. is different. Though we use dollars and sense
   B. is different, though. We use dollars and cents
   C. is different, we use dollars and cents
   D. no change

9. A. All though it's a different system
   B. Although its a different system
   C. Although it's different, the system
   D. no change

10. A. people do not have problems with it
   B. people don't have problems with them
   C. people do not have problems with the system
   D. no change

Spelling Review

A. Change each word below by adding *-or*, *-er*, or *-ar*. Write the new word on the line.

1. contribut____   _____

2. defend____   _____

3. li____   _____

4. supervis____   _____

B. Choose the correct word and write it on the line.

5. He stepped on the (break, brake) _____ just in time.

6. I can't give my speech today because I am too (hoarse, horse) _____.

7. The bus driver didn't see us; he (past, passed) _____ us without stopping.

C. One word on each line is spelled incorrectly. Circle the misspelled word.

8. aquaint   committee   hospital   knowledge

9. necessary   exception   boundry   athletic

10. enough   privelege   probably   success

Writing Review

Choose one of the following topics. On a separate sheet of paper, plan your essay and write your first draft. Then revise and edit your draft, and write your final essay. Don't forget to identify your audience, purpose, and task before you begin planning.

Choose two of the selections in this chapter. Write an essay comparing and contrasting the tone and mood of each piece. Be sure to make specific references to the selections in your writing.

OR

The theme of this unit is "Acts of Love and Kindness." Write an essay comparing and contrasting at least three of these acts as represented in the selections in the unit.

Unit Four Extension Activities

SPEAK/LISTEN
From Prose to Play

In a group of three or four, choose one of the readings from this unit and rewrite a short scene (two to three minutes long) in drama form. Assign parts—in addition to the main roles, you may want to have someone introduce the scene and give background information. For example: "This scene takes place on the *Titanic* and follows the movements of the narrator of *Every Man for Himself* from the port side of the deck, where he hears the sound of steam escaping from the valves . . ." Present your scene to the class.

EXPLORE
Uncover the Lost Poets

Like Sarah Kilham Biller, a number of British women wrote poetry during the Romantic Period but were discovered only recently. Use the Internet to learn about another woman who wrote during this time. Share one of that person's poems with the class. Also present any biographical information you find.

WRITE
Mysterious Encounters

Charles Dickens describes a rather strange encounter with a little girl and an old man. Write a one- to two-page story about a mysterious occurrence in your own life—or one you imagine.

OR

Going Deeper into the Text

Read another story from *West With the Night*, another chapter of *Every Man for Himself*, or a short story by Charles Dickens. Write a three- to four-paragraph analysis of the theme and/or the characters in the piece you read.

CONNECT

Literature and History

Working in a group of four, research the *Titanic*. Assign group members to these areas of research: the ship, the passengers, the crew, the disaster. After you have gathered information, create a large page or poster for each category. Include pictures you print out from the Internet, clip from magazines, copy from books, or sketch yourselves. Imagine that these pages are posted in a museum exhibit about the *Titanic*. They should give visitors basic information and statistics about each of the categories. Display your finished pages and select a group spokesperson to summarize the information you gathered.

Acknowledgments

Grateful acknowledgment is made to the following sources for having granted permission to reprint copyrighted materials. Every effort has been made to obtain permission to use previously published materials. Any errors or omissions are unintentional.

"The Clever One" from THE SPRINGS OF AFFECTION: Stories of Dublin by Maeve Brennan. Copyright © 1997 by The Estate of Maeve Brennan. Reprinted by permission of Houghton Mifflin Company. All rights reserved. Page 7.

From A HOUSE UNLOCKED by Penelope Lively. Copyright © 2001 by Penelope Lively. Used by permission of Grove/Atlantic, Inc. Page 31.

"Chasing the Evanescent Glow" by Nuala O'Faolain. Copyright © 2005 Time Inc. Reprinted by permission of Time Inc. Page 79.

From THE BAY OF ANGELS by Anita Brookner, copyright © 2001 by Anita Brookner. Used by permission of Random House, Inc. Page 83.

From THE REMAINS OF THE DAY by Kazuo Ishiguro, copyright © 1989 by Kazuo Ishiguro. Used by permission of Alfred A. Knopf, a division of Random House, Inc. Page 103.

From AUGUST IS A WICKED MONTH. Reprinted by permission of International Creative Management, Inc. Copyright © 1965 by Edna O'Brien. Page 123.

Excerpt from "Was There a Horse with Wings?" from WEST WITH THE NIGHT by Beryl Markham. Copyright © 1942, 1983 by Beryl Markham. Reprinted by permission of North Point Press, a division of Farrar, Straus and Giroux, LLC. Page 217.

From the book *Every Man for Himself* by Beryl Bainbridge. Copyright © 1996 by Beryl Bainbridge. Appears by permission of the publisher, Carroll & Graf Publishers, a division of Avalon Publishing Group. Page 255.

"To Anna." Reprinted with the permission of the British Women Romantic Poets Digital Project, General Library, University of California, Davis. Page 260.

Photo Credits

Penelope Lively © David Levenson/Getty Images. Page 31.

William Wordsworth © Hulton Archive/Getty Images. Page 55.

Kazuo Ishiguro © David Levenson/Getty Images. Page 103.

Daniel Defoe © Hulton Archive/Getty Images. Page 193.

Beryl Bainbridge © Dave M. Benett/Getty Images. Page 255.

Vocabulary Index

Subject Index

Examples, 36
  clarifying ideas with, 111–113
Expository writing, 18

F
Facts
  distinguishing from opinion, 151–154
  identifying, 154
  using, 157–158
Figurative language, 264, 267
First draft, 19–20
First person point of view, 15
Freewriting, 6, 30, 50, 78, 102, 122, 146, 168, 192, 216, 234, 254

G
Gerund phrases, 63
Gerunds, 63–64, 65
Good/well, 227
Graphic organizers
  character maps, 128–129
  essay map, 201
Gulliver's Travels (Swift), 169–170

H
Historical novels, 12
Homonyms, 247–249
A House Unlocked (Lively), 31–33

I
Ideas, clarifying, with examples, 111–113
Imagery, 263, 267
Independent clauses, 93
  in complex sentences, 94
  in fixing run-on sentences, 268
Inferences, making, 108–109
Infinitives, 65
Informative writing, 12
Instructive writing, 13
Internet, 152–153
Introduction, 21
Ishiguro, Kazuo, 103

J
Joyce, James, 51

L
Language
  figurative, 264, 267
  poetic, 266–267
Limited third person, 15
Lively, Penelope, 31

M
Main ideas, determining, 87
Markham, Beryl, 217–220
Metaphors, 264
Meter, 264–265
Mood, 240–241
  identifying, 241
Mysteries, 12

N
Negatives, double, 201
Nonfiction, 12
  points of view in, 15–16
Nouns
  gerund or gerund phrase as, 63, 65
  infinitives as, 65
  possessive, 187
  predicate, 64
  turning verbs into, with suffixes, 133
  using suffixes to change adjectives into, 116–117

O
O'Brien, Edna, 123
O'Faolain, Nuala, 79
Old Curiosity Shop, The (Dickens), 235–238
Omniscient third person point of view, 15
Onomatopoeia, 265
Opinions
  distinguishing from fact, 151–154
  giving in writing, 12–13
  identifying, 153
  using, 157–158
Outlines, 89–90

P
Paragraphs
  body, 21
  unity in, 130
Paraphrasing, 57–58, 264
Participial phrases, 43

  in beginning sentences, 180
  placement of, 43
  punctuating, 44
  replacement of, with gerund phrase, 64
Participles, 41, 65
  dangling, 43
  past, 41–42
  present, 41
Passive verbs, 131–132
Past participles, 41–42
  common irregular, 42
Personal narratives, 18, 20
  prewriting, 21
Personification, 264
Persuasive writing, 12, 18
Phrases
  gerund, 63
  participial, 43, 44, 64, 180
  prepositional, 180
  transitional, 62
Plagiarism, 57
Plot, 198
Plural subject, 22
Plural verb, 22
Poetic language, 266–267
Poetry, reading, 262–265
Point by point, in developing compare/contrast essay, 61
Point of view
  author's, 14–15
  first person, 15
  nonfiction, 15–16
  third person
    limited, 15
    omniscient, 15
Portrait of the Artist as a Young Man, A (Joyce), 51–52
Possessive nouns, 187
Possessive pronouns, 186–187
Predicate nouns, gerund or gerund phrase as, 64
Prepositional phrase, in beginning sentences, 180
Present participles, 41
Prewriting, 19
Pronouns
  possessive, 186–187
  relative, 184
Protagonist, 128
Publish, 20
Purpose, 18

Q

Quotations
  citing as details, 92–93
  supporting statements
    with, 90–93

R

Reading strategy
  author's purpose in, 12–14
  cause-and-effect relation-
    ships in, 198
  characters in, 128–129
  conflict in, 129
  context clues in, 35–37
  cultural context in, 222–223
  distinguishing fact from
    opinion, 151–154
  drawing conclusions in,
    108–109
  main idea and details in,
    87
  making inferences in,
    108–109
  mood in, 240–241
  paraphrasing in, 57–58
  reading poetry, 262–265
  setting in, 176–177
  tone in, 240, 241
Relative pronouns, 184
Remains of the Day, The
    (Ishiguro), 103–106
Restatements, 36
Revising and editing, 20
Rhyme, 264–265
Robinson Crusoe (Defoe),
    193–195
Run-on sentences, 267–269
  fixing, 268

S

Semicolons, 270
  in fixing run-on sentences,
    268
Sentences
  combining shorter, 179
  complex, 93–96
  placement of participial
    phrases in, 43
  run-on, 267–269
  topic, 87, 88
  varying beginnings of, 180
Sentence structures, variety
    of, 178–179
Settings, 176–177
Short stories, 18

Similes, 264
Singular subject, 22
Singular verb, 22
"Solitary Reaper, The"
    (Wordsworth), 55
Sound effects, 265
Spelling, 185
  adding -*ly* to change adjec-
    tives into adverbs,
    97–98
  adding suffixes to form
    new words, 23–24,
    228–229
  base words in, 45
  contractions, 185–186
  frequently misspelled
    words, 271–272
  homonyms in, 247–249
  possessive pronouns,
    186–187
  troublesome consonants
    in, 66
  turning verbs into nouns
    using -*ion*, -*ation*, and
    -*ure*, 133
  using -*able* or -*ible* and -*abil-
    ity* or -*ibility*, 162
  using suffixes to change
    adjectives into nouns,
    116–117
  words ending in -*ance* and
    -*ence*, 203
Stream of consciousness, 72
Subjects
  plural, 22
  singular, 22
Subject-verb agreement,
    22–23
Subordinate clauses. *See*
    Dependent clauses
Subordinating conjunctions,
    269
  in fixing run-on sentences,
    268
Suffixes
  adding, in creating new
    words, 23–24, 228–229
  common, 24
  defined, 23
  in turning adjectives into
    nouns, 116–117
  in turning verbs into
    nouns, 133
  words ending in -*ance* and
    -*ence*, 203
Supporting details, 90

Swift, Jonathan, 169
Synge, J. M., 147
Synonyms, 5, 30, 36, 49, 77,
    101, 122, 146, 167, 192,
    215, 233, 254

T

Talk to the author technique,
    57
Tasks, 18
Third person point of view
  limited, 15
  omniscient, 15
Time Machine, The (Wells),
    173–174
Title, 87, 88
"To Anna" (Biller), 260
Tone, 240, 241
  identifying, 241
Topic sentences, 87, 88
Transitional words and
    phrases
  for comparing, 62
  for contrasting, 62
Troublesome consonants, 66

U

Unity, in paragraphs, 130
URL extension, 152

V

Verbals, 65
  gerunds, 65
  infinitives, 65
  participles, 65
Verbs
  active, 131
  commonly confused, 246
  passive, 131
  plural, 22
  singular, 22
  turning into nouns with
    suffixes, 133
Voice
  active, 131–132
  passive, 131–132

W

Well/good, 227
Wells, H. G., 173
West With the Night
    (Markham), 217–220
Who, use of, as subject, 160
Whom, use of, as object, 160

Whose/who's, 160
Wordsworth, William, 55
Word-within-a-word clues, 36
Writing, purposes of, 12–13, 18
Writing process, 19
  first draft, 19–20
  prewriting, 19
  publish, 20
  revising and editing, 20

Writing workshop, 38
  American cultural context in, 224–226
  audience in, 17
  avoiding clichés in, 243–245
  cause-and-effect essays in, 199–201
  clarifying ideas with examples in, 111–113
  compare/contrast essay in, 59–62

descriptive words in, 38–40
fact and opinion in, 157–158
poetic language in, 266–267
purpose in, 18
sentence structures in, 178–179
supporting statements with quotations, 90–93
task in, 18
unity in, 130